Risking The Rogues

Tegan O'Ryan

ISBN: 1495926524
ISBN 13: 9781495926525
Library of Congress Control Number: 2014911593
CreateSpace Independent Publishing Platform
North Charleston, South Carolina

Special thanks goes out to my Mom and Glenn, for all their help, encouragement, and support. Love you guys!

One

Watch your back, they told her. He may be handsome, he may be charming, but he's a pirate—and beneath that? He was apparently one cold bastard.

She knew it was true too; it was a bit dark in the tavern, so at first, the most she could make out as he walked in was that he was tall and, going by his swagger, confident. He could have been anyone really, but something about how he carried himself told her this was her prospective client.

Clara took a long drag of her paper smoke in a shady corner of the tavern, hood up to obscure her face as she waited. She saw every woman almost swoon when each of them noticed him, so he was obviously attractive. *Dangerous,* Clara thought instantly, taking a long drink from her tankard.

It was a strange comparison to make at a first, somewhat obscured glance, but there was something about the stranger that reminded her of her home, the Dark Forest. The more beautiful anything was there, the more likely it was to kill you.

The closer he came and the more of his features she could make out, the more apt she felt the comparison was. Yet every female and even a few male eyes trailed after him as he walked in like he'd magnetized their gazes. He certainly carried an undeniable air of charm about him. She had no doubt that all Lucas "Suave" Sinclair had to do was pick which woman he wanted, and with a smile, she'd be his. Clara listened to the bar wenches giggling as he flashed them what she now saw were enticing smiles over the high collar of his long black coat with its bright silver buttons. Those smiles alone confirmed what she felt almost under her skin, a self-serving bastard with what she was willing to bet was way too pretty a face. She could imagine cunning and heartless sat well on this pirate.

Clara rolled her eyes; it eluded her how they all missed or dismissed the fact that he was trouble—it was written all over the way he moved, with that graceful ease she'd seen in predators on the prowl, hunting.

She'd grown up in a place where if your eyes weren't on the lookout for predators, you'd be dead before the day was out; perhaps the upbringing was the advantage. This captain had rather insistently sought out "the Guide," and his perseverance had lead him here—he wanted to offer her a job, badly apparently. His unusual persistence had admittedly intrigued her; so here they were.

Clara looked away as the captain with jet-black hair continued to make his way in her general direction. He swept past her without noticing her, instead heading to the booth behind her, sliding onto the far bench across from her good friend, Fitz.

Her friend always helped her conduct business in this manner, though few ever knew it; Clara liked her anonymity. She leaned ever so slightly to her left to peer at the small, unobtrusive mirror running down the wooden pillar to a few feet ahead of her, allowing her to sit, comfortably drinking ale, and watch the transaction taking place behind her while appearing completely uninvolved in the dealing herself.

With the mirrors assistance, she was given a spectacularly clear view of what all the swooning was about. The well-groomed dark scruff on his face framed full lips and high cheekbones. A compelling confidence in how he held himself, obvious from afar, now saturated the very air around him. He had a muscular build that that was deceptively slim, one that belied how strong he really was according to rumour, a simple grace in his every movement. His hair had that wind tossed look about it, framing a strong jaw and highlighting the devil-may-care spark behind his eyes.

Those eyes, gods they actually startled her they were so blue, cerulean almost. The colour struck her as one you might see at the heart of a glacier and without a doubt his most compelling feature, a focal point in a tan face and attire as black as his hair. He was like a shadow that encapsulated a stunning ice cave. His wanted poster didn't do him justice. *Very dangerous,* she thought again, taking another swig of ale. Clara pretended to survey the tavern, as if looking for someone she was supposed to meet as she listened in on Fitz and Gage.

"You must be the famous Captain Black-Gage," Fitz said by way of greeting, addressing him by his infamous moniker. "You've been making quite the commotion."

"The price of notoriety, I'm afraid, is often being unable to go about your business quietly; are you the Guide?" he asked, eyes sizing up the man he figured to be her.

"The contact," Fitz corrected.

No one ever liked this part; they always wanted her in person and didn't take it well when they didn't get that. The pirate actually laughed at the revelation, though Clara could tell like the many before him he was not pleased.

"I'm not looking to chat with a messenger boy," he told Fitz, voice abruptly cool. Arrogant as well it seemed, not many people had the gall to call a man like Fitz a "messenger boy." With his neatly trimmed, short blond hair, and the big earthy-brown eyes of a kindly neighbour, at just over six foot seven, Fitz was built like a stone house. Though admittedly his clean shaven face often had others mistaken him for being younger than he was, calling Fitz a "boy" was like calling a feral wolf a "puppy."

"Tough," Fitz replied tersely, "you talk to me or you never meet the Guide. See how far you can paddle out of shit creek on your own."

Clara smiled. She never had to worry about anyone pushing him around. Fitz held his ground well—a quality she highly valued in both a friend and an associate. This was all standard procedure of course; everyone wanted to see if they could push a contact around to get what they wanted.

She watched as Gage put the reason for his moniker on the table, that black-gloved hand with the silver emblem that resembled some kind of gauge she'd never seen before, strange symbols and mysterious words in the place of any common measurements. Some said he wore it because he'd shaken hands with the devil to get his ship—*The Grey Ghost*—rumoured to be the fastest sailing any ocean. Like most rumours, Clara put little stock in any of it.

"I've a crew to paddle for me, and we're good at finding what we're looking for."

The subtlety of the threat was not lost on anyone. The air he held about him became determined and focused; add *driven* to his list of attributes.

"Oh, the Guide's heard." Fitz laughed, careful as always to keep gender indications from the conversation. "There's a reason you're coming up empty."

Clara watched Gage quickly reassess Fitz, saw him come to the conclusion that he was more or less dealing with someone who wouldn't be easily bullied or even goaded.

"Very well, how can I persuade him to speak with me?"

"By speaking to me. What do you want?" Fitz asked, prompting Clara to listen even more carefully now.

"What does anyone who seeks the Guide want? I require his services to get through the Dark Forest," Gage said, as if the question were not only pointless but stupid.

To be fair, Clara's reputation was less renowned and more often relegated to myth, so who knew what it was he could have heard she could do for him? It was understandable of course, being chalked up as a myth. She didn't just survive the trials of a forest that had claimed all others before her with a promise to take anymore who entered, but she'd made the place her home. Those who tempted such trails did so in desperation and nothing less; seeking her out for generally one reason. This meant only the desperate knew she was, in fact, very real—and who would ever believe them? So her legend grew. In short Clara could understand the masses being mostly skeptical, her existence did seem incredibly convenient.

The Dark Forest was the shortcut to end all shortcuts between two kingdoms—the divide between Ethona rulers King James and Queen Helen, and Athium, the domain of Queen Airalyn, the Scarlet Queen. It ran between the mountains, three different outs to three different cities on both sides with a three-day trek on each trail.

That "nine bind" as Fitz liked to call it, was what kept the kingdoms of Ethona and Athium from the tide of an all-out war. Queen Airalyn was a Wielder, a manipulator of the magics, and a particularly nasty, power-hungry royal. She was a firm believer in "might makes right," so all relations with her were... strained at best. She'd attempted to invade Ethona through the forest once to gain control over the massive ore deposit that made the domain one of the richest of the twelve kingdoms.

Clara heard she'd failed quite outstandingly, and she didn't doubt that failure had been beyond messy for Queen Airalyn's troops. Now there was no trade between the two kingdoms, which meant good business for Clara. A tentative peace was held only because an attack from the safer but longer routes would be far too direct and therefore suicidal; both had astoundingly vigilant fortifications on the front and back of their kingdoms. The rest was covered by the Dark Forest's many beautiful horrors, all truly wonderful deterrents to war.

"The Guide doesn't take everyone who waves some flashy coins through the forest, Captain," Fitz told the pirate, bringing Clara back to the current conversation.

"Rich enough to turn work down, is he?" Gage returned cheekily. He didn't give Fitz a chance to come back with anything, seeing fit to merely continue speaking. "I need to get to Torin; my ship is docked there. It's not the friendliest of waters, but that's not my rush; I've the law on my tail."

Clara watched his face in the mirror while grinding the end of her paper smoke on the wooden table and frowned. She prided herself on her rather uncanny ability to see the truth, or a lack thereof, in people's words and faces. Though she saw no lies on his face, she didn't see much truth either and that bothered her.

"So if you'll forgive my being rude, I don't have the time to pander to him. I have gold, he has the set of skills I require," Gage said, looking as severe as he sounded. "Now can we deal?"

Fitz was silent, waiting for Clara to give him the yay or nay signal. She put her tankard down loud enough for him to hear, interested but unsure.

"Is it just you?" Fitz asked, getting her more information to help her make her decision.

"Me and some of my crew."

"How many?"

"Five including me."

Clara sighed quietly, that was a lot of people—scratch that—a lot of pirates. She could tell Fitz was thinking the same thing by how Gage was reacting to his expression. She watched him slide his gaze away from the table like he was thinking of a lure to draw Fitz back in.

"Fifty gold pieces a man," he offered.

Clara nearly swallowed her tongue; that was an *obscene* amount of gold. Judging by his expression, he was thinking much the same, almost smugly. He must think for sure that would lock her services down. It almost was; unfortunately there were other issues Clara had to consider. It would be difficult to get five people through the forest alive and to Torin no less, the capital of Athium. Clara *hated* Athium; The Scarlet Queen was a paranoid tyrant who seemed to relish in filling her capitals with armed guards, and the last thing Clara wanted was to get stiffed because a random patrol collected her criminal client upon arrival, or worse, be apprehended herself for any reason. Her determination to stay a legend and avoid the attention of the more... unsavory in her unique brand of smuggling forced her to choose her clients carefully, which made work at times scarce—rock and a hard place really.

Fitz had continued on with the questions, leaving her to listen closely once more.

"And when you say the law is on your tail...?" Fitz trailed off.

"I mean other routes out of this town are, at the very least, highly inadvisable at the moment; my presence here is pushing it as it is."

Again Clara felt at a bit of a loss as she watched his face in the mirror: no lies but no definitive truth either. She didn't like the obscurity of Captain Black-Gage. Sure, Clara liked what she saw of him in the sense that she found it hard to resist a bastard—their company was simple, to the point, a great deal of fun, and the whole "no strings attached" thing never hurt. But this was business, and for business, bastard pirates were a spin of the wheel—it could go very well or very badly. It was a lot of gold, yes, but also more work and higher risk. Top it all off with the captain of *The Grey Ghost* handsome but enigmatic face and Clara found herself feeling very much *not* in the mood for gambling. She was out. Clara gave Fitz the "turn job down" signal by standing and preparing to leave. She put some coin on the table that Fitz would use to pay for their drinks after he stalled the conversation long enough for her to get scarce, a little extra there for his pocket as was their arrangement. She only got a few steps away when Gage's voice called out and stopped her cold.

"Leaving so soon? Here I was hoping you'd pull your hand out of your puppet's arse, and we could discuss business like gentlemen."

Clara should have kept walking, but she'd already paused a moment too long, and she could feel those eyes boring into her back now. Smart, observant—more traits to add to the list, the ones that made her the wariest thus far. She didn't move, turning her head very slightly to better hear his next words.

"Or does the Guide have trouble speaking for himself?" Gage challenged.

"Keep walking," Fitz told her. She could feel the tension in his voice; no one had ever made her before.

"Oh, I wouldn't suggest it," Gage countered, voice tinged with amusement, she could practically feel his smirk. "I may be moved to make a scene," he told them both amiably.

"With the law on you?" Fitz snorted. "Not likely."

"Well, not a great many people really know if the smuggling guide is man or myth."

Clara could almost hear him shrug.

"With all the secrecy you two walk in, I assume you prefer it this way?"

Clara supposed she'd practically been screaming that with all the cloak and dagger thus far; notoriety would make her work and life harder. Clara remained motionless, looking at the door that led out of the tavern.

"I thought so. If you don't hear me out, I have no problem outing us all; without you, I'm very likely caught anyways," he said airily.

"We're not the ones on the run from the law," Fitz countered.

"Running, no—but I'm sure the law would be *very* interested in such an elusive and elite couple of smugglers like yourselves."

"Who would believe you?" Fitz asked

"Do you *really* want to risk being scrutinized should I happen to sway someone into looking more closely at the pair of you?" Clara turned her head just a bit more to see the smile he wore was sharp enough to cut.

"I can be terribly convincing when I need to be."

For some reason Clara could not explain, she felt her lips quirking as if to smile; it appeared they were all in check. She could already feel Fitz reaching for the short blade he kept secured to his thigh and held a hand up to signal him to wait. She didn't much mind a fight, relished it at times even, but Clara despised killing and preferred not to unless absolutely necessary. She felt confident that they were very far from that point, and strangely he had her interest now.

Gage didn't fail to notice the full extent of the exchange.

"Good call," he remarked lightly. "Bad business picking fights with pirates."

Fitz and Clara both heard the sound of a flintlock pistol hammer clicking back.

"We're rarely averse to fighting dirty."

Fitz eyes flickered down to the table as if he could see the gun hiding under it before glaring up coldly. "That's because they'd never win a fair fight," he replied cheekily, keeping all emotion from his voice.

Gage laughed as though amused by Fitz before Clara heard the sound of him ease the hammer back and return said pistol to its holster at his side. Clara turned on her heel and walked back to the table.

Gage watched her as she kept her face angled away from him to look into Fitz's big brown eyes.

"You should go," she said softly.

Fitz eyed her, as if questioning whether that was wise.

She felt confident that she could handle the captain; he'd already made her—the worst he could do now was attack her or try to shoot her, and she was rarely unprepared for such violence.

She nodded her assurance, and Fitz gave Gage one last untrustworthy glare.

"Bye," Gage said dismissively, wearing a wide insolent smile.

Fitz looked like he wanted to throttle Gage, but he slid out of the booth as Clara had directed, muttering something cautionary under his breath as he left and she took up his vacated spot.

She could almost feel the pirate's gaze, trying to peer through the shadows cast by the hood which made her features indistinct at best, a little charm she'd had a Wielder cast on the hood. However she saw the exact moment he realized that said indistinct features were *distinctly* feminine. His eyes darted to her chest before rebounding back to what he could see of her face.

"You're a woman," he said at last, sounding stunned.

Clara looked down at her chest much like he had, as if she herself had never noticed this.

"Would you look at that?" she said with exaggerated shock, "It appears I am."

To the captain's credit, he regained his composure quickly.

"Forgive me. One does not expect beautiful women when seeking the Guide of the Dark Forest," he apologized, a smooth, charming smile instantly gracing his face like it was the most natural expression he wore.

Clara actually didn't doubt that as she smirked back. She was tempted to call him out on the beautiful part when he could barely *see* her face, but she figured he'd just have another smooth answer ready. Same game, different plays—could she be pushed around? Or in this case, she thought, watching him begin to utilize his considerable charms, *led* around.

"Wow, that took you all of five seconds. Don't waste your smiles on me, Lucas Sinclair; they won't work." She'd pushed back, denying him the recognition of his hard-earned alias by using his real name, something not easily found unless you had at least a few good contacts—his move.

That smile of his took on a sharper quality, not missing the slight.

"Not many people take leave to use my name, lass," he told her.

"I'm not a fan of monikers," she replied sweetly.

"Coming from 'the Guide,' I find that rather rich." He leaned in closer and speared her with those ice-blue eyes of his, black-gloved hand sliding across the wood in a somewhat curiously stiff manner... interesting. A sly invasion of space, nice tactic; too bad it wouldn't work.

Clara leaned in to meet him, their faces close enough to appear intimate to any casual observer.

Their nearness allowed him a better look at her eyes. For a moment he found himself at a bit of a loss, she had the kind of eyes that didn't capture the light so much as defy it—they almost seemed to radiate a shade of green that reminded him of the storm churned waters of distant exotic shores, only darker. All else of this woman might be ugly, but the eyes at least were beautiful, he thought briefly.

"Price of notoriety, I'm afraid," she said, somehow angling her head in such a way that the casting of shadows over her face rendered it still too obscure to make out, even as her eyes locked with his. "Even as a myth," she added. Either some spell was at work here or this one played with shadows like an artist played with the colours on his palette.

"Indeed," he agreed smoothly. They stayed like that for a moment; she could practically feel him weighing her out, trying to figure out how she ticked, how to best manipulate her.

"Well, you have me at something of a disadvantage, love, as I don't know your name. May I have the pleasure?" he purred, pulling back a little to offer his bare hand.

She looked down at said hand, flicking a quick look at the other before refocusing on his face. Clara knew if she accepted and politely gave her name it was as good as telling a pirate she'd be taking him through the Dark Forest; names were a closer on a deal in her books, and she wasn't sold just yet.

"Pleasure comes after business, Sinclair," she told him, ignoring the offered pleasantry. She caught the frown in his brow a split second before it disappeared with a shrug and he retracted his hand.

"As you wish. Can you get me through the forest?" he asked, leaning back from her. Round One went to her it seemed.

"The issue isn't *can* I; the issue is *will* I," Clara told him, lacing her fingers together on the table.

"Fifty gold pieces a man is more than fair," Gage said coolly.

"No, it's downright generous," she conceded to his surprise, "and, see, that's where I get nervous."

He raised an eyebrow at her in a silent query.

"Don't get me wrong," she clarified. "You need to be desperate to want to go into the Dark Forest, and your story along with your offer certainly suggests desperation." She leaned back as well, pulling another paper-wrapped smoke from a pouch at her side and playing with it as if to amuse herself, giving off an air like just maybe he and his job offer were a waste of her time.

"But I've seen desperate men; you don't strike me as one of them," she observed, putting the rolled paper between her lips.

He moved so fast, with such natural grace, she didn't even get the chance to flinch. He struck a match he'd pulled from the gods know where, holding the flame just before the end of the rolled tobacco before she could object. Clara's eyes widened as he held himself perfectly still, watching her serenely. Clara narrowed her eyes at him and the gentlemanly gesture, seeing it for the veiled threat it was. He could have easily struck her before she could have thought to dodge, a showcase of his speed and precision as a fighter. It was a reminder to not write him off more than once, or to make a show of it as she just had. Slowly Clara leaned forward to close that short distance and light the end of her smoke. He waited until she gave a slight nod before pulling the match back, the acceding the fault of her arrogance towards him in guise of a polite thanks.

"Darling, pirates never let desperation show," he told her conversationally. "We don't wear it very well." He didn't blow the match out, holding it up as the flame burned, letting it inch closer and closer to his fingertips.

"No matter how hot the fire, one must know how to keep one's cool," he told her, holding her gaze.

Clara could see the flame in her peripheral as she too refused to break eye contact, noting he showed no sign the flame was practically licking his fingertips. A theatrical man with an iron-cast face of lies—she didn't like him. At the same time, there was something she found...

Clara didn't trust him as far as she could throw him of course, but she was definitely fascinated by him. Gage played the game well, and the occasional times she was forced to play it, few managed to intrigue her the way he was doing—difficult to not respect that. *Dangerous,* Clara thought once more with a smirk, licking her thumb and forefinger; dangerous because he made her *want* to gamble.

"You should treat your hand with more care," she said, reached over to him and snuffing the flame out between her fingers. "You only have the full use of one after all."

Gage froze for a brief moment. Yes, she'd noticed the lack of life in the hand and the odd way he manoeuvred it—either it was damaged or paralysed.

"Heard rumours, have we?" he asked, as if unconcerned by how she'd known.

"No," she said simply, explaining no further.

"Couldn't be blessed with it all, lass; it'd be unfair to the rest," he said, giving her a devilishly heart-stopping smirk. *The prettier they are Clara...*

"I'm sure you're still a regular gift to the world," she said with just a trace of sarcasm, visibly irking him. "If you were straight with me, I'd take this job."

"I have been straight with you."

That one had been easy to see through. "Lie."

"I assure you, lass, I've told you every—"

"Lie," Clara cut him off, narrowing her eyes.

His expression steeled a bit, masking the wariness he felt creeping into him, all but in his eyes.

"I'm very good at picking up on people's bullshit, Captain," she explained flatly. "Care to try again?" Clara got the impression he was trying very hard not to glare.

"The details I keep to myself are strictly *my* business; I have confidentiality of clients to protect," he told her somewhat coolly.

"Hmm, truth. I'm fine with that as long as it's not anything that will get me killed, or interfere with my job."

"It's not." Truth.

"Dangerous cargo?"

"Not to you, no," he replied. Obscurity. How the hell did he do that?

He watched her face, and he must have sussed out some of her confusion from the shadows of her hood because he almost smiled when he asked, "Am I lying?"

That put her in a bit of a spot, because he wasn't as far as she could tell. That was off-putting because she could almost *always* tell. Clara couldn't say yes, and she couldn't say no.

"Are you?" she asked instead.

"Can't tell?" he tried again, watching her carefully.

"Think I've proved in spades that I can, Captain Black-Gage," she replied, putting a mocking emphasis on his moniker. He surprised her with another of his laughs, a strangely engaging and attractive sound.

"You're an interesting mix of blunt and coy, love, I'll give you that."

Clara nodded her head, accepting a compliment before moving on; she still needed more information if she was to agree.

"Any—let's say—unwilling passengers on this journey?" she asked.

Gage raised an eyebrow. "If we go, we all go willingly," he assured her.

"Any children?" she asked out of habit.

Gage laughed. "I hope not. Curious to see if I'm attached?" he inquired in a husky voice.

"Curious to know if you're bringing children," she told him coolly, "because I don't guide anyone with children."

"Not very fond of little ones?" he asked, feigning shock.

"Not very fond of seeing them die." It was a sobering statement as she took a long drag on her smoke.

"No, no children," he answered solemnly, shaking his head.

Clara thought about it, letting smoke curl from her nostrils as she breathed out. She'd taken all kinds through the forest; Sinclair wouldn't even be the first pirate, so she already knew you couldn't trust any of them. She'd been set on passing this deal a mere few minutes ago, his face could turn on a copper piece to a canvas of grey she had trouble reading and that unnerved her. Yet now that he was presenting his case directly to her, engaging her in this dance of a conversation, she felt somewhat obligated to play the challenge till she conquered it; she loved a challenge.

All in all, as long as he kept her out of his business and let her do her job, she'd get him through the forest and make a lot of money. When it came down to it she'd just have to be careful, but when was she not? If she just assumed he was always lying she wouldn't be surprised when he proved her right anyways

Clara examined him once more with a sweep of her eyes; he remained still under her gaze, face impassive and currently unreadable. Finally she reached up and pulled her hood back, exposing her face to him at last.

He seemed surprised by the move for a moment, then those sharp eyes swept over her to take her in. Her long red-blond hair fell past her shoulders like gold and fire had become one flowing element, her skin spinning tales of the many days she'd spent under the sun. The planes of her face were all angles and sharp edges, like some god had fashioned an exquisite blade into flesh.

The only soft feature his gaze found was her pale pink lips, where he found his eyes pausing a moment longer than they had the rest of her, pert and full—very far from ugly. She watched him look his fill (which, though appreciative of what he saw, was surprisingly not all that lecherous) before offering her hand.

"Clara Fox," she said.

He smiled as he took her hand and laid an unexpected kiss on the back of it. "What a lovely name," Gage said. His eyes didn't leave her face; he knew he had her.

Clara took comfort knowing it was on her terms.

"I take half up front and the other half when we reach Torin," she told him, withdrawing her hand as she outlined how this transaction would work.

"Done."

"When are you looking to leave?" she asked.

"Yesterday."

"Forest's edge at first light, then."

He nodded as he made to slide out of the booth, their business all but concluded. Clara reached out across the table and snagged him by the cuff of his coat before he could get up and walk away. He pointedly stared at the offending hand before leveling her with a cautionary glower.

"Try to cross me and you will regret it," she warned him softly, wishing for them to be crystal clear about this.

His smirk darkened as he placed his gloved hand on the back of her wrist. Only his thumb and first two fingers curled to grasp at her, the last two digits remaining dead and unmoving.

She suddenly felt the sensation of bugs crawling over her skin and had to fight not to shiver or jerk back.

Is he a fucking Wielder? Her eyes bounced between his face and the glove sporting that strange gauge on his hand. The gauge was glowing ever so slightly, the needle that shouldn't have moved at all flickering. That gloved hand had a damned spell on it, and though Clara had little experience with magic, even she knew it was a nasty one.

"Likewise," he said, pulling her hand off his sleeve. He let her jerk her hand back from his grip, calmly finishing getting to his feet while Clara flexed her fingers and gave her hand a shake under the table, like that would rid her of the disconcerting sensation. She realized she may have to keep a much closer eye on this pirate than she first thought she would.

"It was a pleasure, Clara." He gave her a courteous, pointed nod of farewell and turned to face the door. He seemed to catch sight of something and froze.

Clara looked too, curious as to what had stopped him. When she saw four royal soldiers walking into the tavern she was suddenly less disconcerted by his display of magic and more cautiously amused. She heard Gage curse under his breath, a bad turn of this wanted man's luck from what she saw. Thank the gods it wasn't her luck.

She chuckled. "Well, that's just unfortunate."

Two

Clara snubbed out her smoke as she stood. "Good luck," she said with a crooked smile, stepping past him to leave.

Gage grabbed her arm and pulled her back, turning them both so his back was to the soldiers while she was pinned between the back of the booth and his chest. She had the dagger on her wrist unsheathed and the point pressed under his chin almost instantly. The move itself looked playful, flirty on his part, to any watching eyes, his body shielding the fact she was threatening to slit his throat.

"This part of the courtship is more look and no touch, Sinclair," she growled. His eyes flitted down to note the knife and then back to hold her gaze.

"I get caught, you don't get paid," he said, ignoring the sharpness of her blade.

"You need me more than I need the money," Clara told him bluntly.

"And you require far more anonymity than I," he countered.

"I wouldn't think the great Captain Black-Gage would need my help to get out of a roadside tavern."

"Need? No," he acknowledged. "However I'd prefer not to make a scene; it complicates our arrangement you understand. Let us not *press* the fates, shall we?" he reasoned, his gloved hand squeezing her hip in warning.

She pressed the point of the dagger a little more firmly into his skin in reply.

"Threaten me with that hand again and I will open your throat," she hissed.

"Now, now; not threatening you, love," he said, voice strained yet strangely at ease. "Let's both play nice, *Clara*." He whispered her name and made it sound far more intimate than any name should. She didn't reply, her expression hard and unyielding; If Gage was trying to work her, he'd have to do *a lot* better than that. As if he'd read her mind he very slowly began to move, lowering his face to hers as if going in for a kiss.

"Lady's choice, of course," he breathed.

He wielded his charm and good looks like a weapon, as very handsome men often did—though, unlike most, he seemed to have mastered the art. He kept leaning in, leaving the decision to her on whether or not to hold the blade steady and let him cut his throat.

Clara was not the only one who liked to gamble apparently. On any other day she just might have let him, but here? Now? She grit her teeth; here was not the best place to drop a pirate, especially when Ethona royal guards were *literally* ten feet away.

Round Two went to him it seemed. She lowered the blade and unobtrusively resheathed it again at her wrist. He grinned until she used her freed hand to press her thumb into his throat and stop him from leaning in any closer. He made a slight choking sound as he stopped.

"Firm grip," he almost wheezed.

"Firm boundary," she retorted in a whisper. No one was the wiser to the tension and power struggle going on in their corner of the tavern; they'd been the epitome of discretion.

Clara released his throat and reached down to grab his gloved hand on her hip while cupping the back of his neck and pulling him down to her. It put them cheek to cheek, giving the appearance of a necking couple while in truth she was looking over his shoulder to watch the four royal guards looking for a table. Off duty, probably tired, that would make leaving mildly easier: table near the door and very sober, scratch previous advantage.

"Willing to part with this a moment for convenience's sake?" she whispered against his ear, working the glove off his hand; she didn't want anyone to recognize it, and she preferred him parted from whatever magic it held. He pulled his head back to look her in the eye.

"Why not?" he whispered back, lips almost brushing hers and sending little shockwaves through her. Still flirting and doing it well even now—she suspected just to be a bold prick.

"Wanna keep those lips, pretty boy?" she asked as she quickly peeled the glove from his hand and slipped it into her back pocket.

"Very much so. Clear?" he asked, putting his face back into the crook of her neck to give her a clearer view over his shoulder. The royal guards shared a laugh just then, taking a table by the door and ordering a round.

"As clear as it's going to get," she confirmed. "Shall we?"

"If the lady insists," he whispered against her throat, making the hair stand up on the back of her neck. Goddamn him.

He wrapped his arm around her waist inside her cloak, winking at her when she glanced at him. Finding pleasure in necessity, he was a pirate through and through.

Clara ran a hand across his chest, playing the part of a besotted girl with giggles and sharing playfully intimate looks with him. They were almost out when she noticed one particular guard was watching them with a little more scrutiny than was called for, like maybe he recognized one of them. It certainly wasn't her. The tension she felt in Gage's body said he didn't fail to notice either as they walked closer to the door and therefore closer to the guards' table.

"He's going to recognize you," Clara sang past a simpering smile.

"No, he's not," Gage replied through his deceivingly charming grin, tone tense, trying to shield his face by turning it to give her a smouldering look.

But with every step, she could feel it: there was something about Sinclair that was ringing a bell for the man. They were so damn close...

Well, desperate times—not that she minded if she was being honest. Clara swung around on Gage so she was in front of him, walking backwards towards the door.

"Don't read too much into this," she told him, then she kissed him.

He was shocked for about a second and a half, then he was returning the kiss full force. The arm around her tightened as the other swept under her knees and lifted her bridal style off the floor.

Clara caught a glimpse of the soldier losing interest in them both at the display, his drink conveniently arriving. It was an impressively brief glimpse, as Gage somehow never missed a step while kissing her.

He carried her the last few steps out of the tavern and through the door. Her feet hit the ground, and she expected the kiss to break, now that they were home free. And it did—for about four seconds and by about an inch.

It seemed Gage had different ideas as he pressed his lips back to hers. She made a sound of surprise as he kissed her again; then Clara found herself kissing him back, caught up in the sheer fever-inducing draw of his considerable attentions. Though she'd never tell him, gods, his skill in this was *marvellous*. Then she felt his hand taking a liberty too far.

Clara pushed Gage off her and slapped him. His wide-eyed expression made it clear he had certainly not expected that, hand on his cheek.

"Not that lucky, Sinclair," she told him, managing to hide how breathless she was.

"You kissed me, love," he reminded her with a smug look.

"I don't recall grabbing your ass."

"Well, if we're playing tit for tat..." He smiled.

Clara roughly pushed past him with her head turned to keep him in her line of sight. "Hope you enjoyed it," she said. "It'll never happen again."

"Don't be hasty, love," Gage said as he backed away from her into the night, watching her with a grin, even while she gave him her back and started to leave. "Never is an awful long time."

Clara scoffed as she turned on the spot at his words. "Not long enough actually; don't want your glove back?" she asked smugly, reaching into her pocket for his namesake...

The smile dropped off her face when her hand touched nothing but empty pocket. When she looked back she saw him holding it up before he blew her a final kiss, turning and continuing on his way.

"Got it, lass, my thanks," he said over his shoulder. He hadn't been coping a feel; he'd been lifting the damn thing from her, she thought as she glared after him. Then the weirdest thing happened—Clara actually almost smiled in spite of herself. *What a devious prick.*

One thing was for sure: she was one tough lass. He manoeuvred his damaged hand back into the glove as he walked through the shadows to where he and the few members of the crew were hunkered down, reflecting back on the lovely Guide—Clara Fox.

Yes, he certainly had been expecting anything but her—sharp witted, pretty, obviously smart, and ready for a fight at the drop of a hat. The most worrisome skill was her uncanny ability to call him out on lies, showcasing a highly intuitive nature. However, she seemed to have a bit more trouble spotting half-truths; he'd have the upper hand if he could utilize that. He always tried to keep the upper hand on everyone he did business with.

He didn't expect the lithe, little woman with red-gold hair and her hard, green eyes to be eating out of his hand right away of course, but it offended him in a way that she didn't seem at least tempted, like most of the women he tried to seduce into doing what he wanted.

She hadn't immediately pulled back from the kiss though, so give him time; he'd get her around his finger eventually. It was more fun when he had to work for it; he loved a challenge, and it would make victory more satisfying. She certainly knew how to play the game—he'd give her that.

Daring little thing, he thought with a grin as he entered the little hovel; he genuinely liked that about her.

He heard the sound of metal scraping against its sheath as a dagger was drawn and held up a hand to placate the tall, lanky, young man whose dirty blond hair stuck out from under his trademark blue cap in tufts, just stepping into his line of sight.

"Easy, William, it's me," he said to his first mate.

William's hazel eyes glinted with recognition just before he spoke, already putting the dagger away. "Captain, forgive me. Bit tense in this town," he apologized.

"Been a hell of a week," Gage said, patting his shoulder as he passed him. "The others?" he asked as he walked deeper into the hovel with William right behind him.

"Sleeping, Captain."

"We meet the Guide at first light outside the forest; make sure we're ready to leave before then," he ordered.

"You convinced him, then?" William asked.

"Her," Gage corrected.

"The Guide's a woman?" William asked, appearing a touch shocked.

"And what a woman," Gage said with a nod and a smirk. "I like her."

"You like most women sir," William replied as Gage took a sharp turn to enter a small room with a mirror that had been jammed in it. William did not follow him in, ducking his tall frame a bit to keep him in sight.

"I *enjoy* most women, as most enjoy me," Gage corrected. He looked away from William and faced the mirror.

"See to our arrangements before dawn," Gage ordered dismissively.

"Yes, Captain," William said, hurriedly leaving his presence.

Gage stood in front of the mirror and knocked three times against its glassy surface. At first, nothing happened, and all he saw was his own reflection. Then the surface distorted like clear water that had been disturbed by a pebble. Suddenly he was looking at Airalyn, the Scarlet Queen herself.

She had a beautiful, oval face, with skin so parchment white and fair it almost didn't look real, and albino red eyes—the only colour anyone ever saw on her—framed with powder-white lashes.

"Lucas," she greeted, giving him that unsettling smile of hers that always came off as if she had a particularly unpleasant fate in mind for any she graced with it. She wore her black dress with the high, stiff collar, her white hair done up in complicated buns weaved with diamonds and other finery.

Gage bowed in front of the mirror with flirtatious eye contact, ignoring her casual use of his name.

"Your Majesty."

"Did you find what I was looking for?" she asked, arching a delicately shaped eyebrow.

Always start with good news.

"Did you ever doubt I would?" he asked with feigned hurt.

Her smile widened. "I'm so glad to hear it. When can I expect you back?"

Now for the bad news.

"Unfortunately there have been a few complications."

The smile fell from her face, that renowned cruelty began to show behind her eyes with her obvious displeasure.

"What sort of *complications*?" the Scarlet Queen hissed at him.

"I'm afraid my arrival was anticipated; my presence in Ethona has been one vigilantly marked by the law. It has... somewhat restricted my movements. In hiding at the moment but I can't hide forever," Gage informed her. "I was forced to send message to my ship to head for Torin without me."

"Can your crew be trusted to follow that order?" she asked.

"They know they'd be fools to do much else," he answered darkly before smiling at her.

Her frown turned for the worse in response. "For someone in dire straits, you appear to be in good cheer," Airalyn observed coolly. "Care to explain?"

"I've hired the Guide to take me through the Dark Forest," he said, letting that bit of news sink in.

At first, he saw genuine surprise on her face, and then she laughed. Lovely as it was even that managed to somehow sound off-putting.

"The Guide? You've *hired* the Guide?" She laughed again. "Oh, Lucas, that is simply devious in the most wonderful way."

"Thank you," Gage said, accepting the compliment with a nod of his head.

"You'll be arriving ahead of schedule, then?" Airalyn asked, sounding pleased.

"My ship has a four-day head start. I understand it's a three-day trek, so they should arrive in Torin the day before we do," he confirmed.

"And I shall arrive the day after you," she told him, "when we shall then conclude our business. I'm glad to see the pirate for hire's ability to procure anything for the right price was not... exaggerated." The Scarlet Queen infused the words with the subtlest of threats behind the veil that was her dark saccharine-sweet smile.

"As I'm glad rumours of the queen's benevolence were not exaggerated," he returned thinly.

It was considered suicidal to come that close to insulting the Scarlet Queen, but she needed him and they both knew it. She chose to merely reply to his words with a sneer before the mirror went dark.

He let out a sigh after her departure. In his opinion, she was terribly lucky she had what he desperately needed or he wouldn't be dealing with her at all. The next three days would be... interesting to say the least. If only Gage had known how interesting.

Three

Clara sat on a bolder just beyond the trees of the forest, the wide buffer between town and the savagery of the Dark Forest. She waited patiently for Gage and his men to arrive as the first rays of light began to climb over the edge of the earth.

It was always quiet and peaceful at this time, Clara liked that, the stillness before the world woke up and began. She needed the quiet as she mulled over the conversation she'd had with Fitz before she'd left...

"I don't like this, Clara; you didn't even like this before he made you," he said, sounding agitated as she handed him his usual cut.

"I'm not allowed to change my mind?"

"Depends on why you're changing your mind," he answered. "I know how you are when someone goads you right." Of course he did—as her oldest friend almost no one else knew her better than Fitz.

"I don't like him, I don't trust him, I'm going to be very careful," she said calmly. "I'm just guiding him through, and he has no reason I can see to try to cross me."

"I'm sure he'll find one—he's a pirate," he argued.

"I'm not dumb; I can handle this."

"Clara—"

"Fitz," she'd returned pointedly. She'd agreed; it was too late to back out now, and she knew that he saw that on her face. He sighed again, getting up from the table in his little cottage to grab something out of a cabinet drawer.

"If there is one predictable thing about pirates, it's that they feel the most at home on the sea," he said, approaching her with his closed fist outstretched to offer her something. Clara held out her hand, and Fitz dropped a small round violet pearl attached to a black cord into her palm.

"If something should happen and you need help, use this," he said, watching her examine it.

"What is it?"

"It's a siren's pearl," Fitz told her as he closed her hand around it.

Clara laughed. "I'm probably not going to get that close to the ocean."

"In the forest, no one could hold their own better than you; this is for if you're on unfamiliar turf," he explained.

"Thank you," she said after a moment, a soft, grateful smile spreading onto her face.

He quickly told her how it worked before continuing to mother-hen her. "You still carrying your homing?" he asked.

Clara smiled, shaking her head as she pulled out the white, kidney-bean-shaped stone, the "homing" that Fina, Fitz's messenger bird, was trained to find in order to ferry letters between them; his lover had one as well.

"You mean this thing I always carry everywhere?" Clara shook her head. "Nope."

Fitz rolled his eyes as she put it back in the pouch on her bag. "Smart-ass." His good humour slowly vanished as he took to looking into her eyes, searching for something in them.

"You sure about this?"

"You need to stop worrying, Fitz," Clara deflected. "I'm a big girl now."

She turned the violet pearl over in her hand, admiring how the light brought out all the complex, deep shades that ribboned through it before she slipped the cord around her neck for safekeeping.

She heard the sound of multiple footsteps long before she saw the band of pirates making for her position. Gage was wearing the black, chemise shirt that looked far too good on him and matching pants with high boots. He was going to regret the choice of footwear later.

"I do hope you don't intend to trample that loudly through the forest," Clara said as Gage's eyes land on her at last.

"Afraid we'll bring down the wrath of the trees?" he asked like a true-blue smart-ass.

"No, it's just annoying," she retorted, sliding off the rock and landing soundlessly at its base.

"This everybody?" she asked, eying the other four men with swords, flintlock pistols, and canteens on their hips. The tall one with the knit blue hat on his head gave a bit of a wave while the others openly gawked at her. Why did men always do this when they met her?

"It is," Gage confirmed, coming to stand by her side. He admired the worn, green cloak and the soft, leather boots she wore; stiff, black fingerless gloves on her hands (looked to be dragon hide actually), long, fire-blond hair flowing down her back. She truly was a fine sight.

"Prepared to lead us into the unknown?" he asked, taking a step closer into her personal space than was strictly necessary; almost intruding but not quite, wearing his "make them melt" smile she'd seen him flashing around in the tavern.

He certainly liked to push his luck. She wasn't sure if he knew that she saw how calculated the move was—how she saw him using it to test what kind of person he was dealing with. Would she be uncomfortable? Receptive? Confrontational? Hostile? Meek?

Clara kept her expression unimpressed, holding her ground in a way that dared him to test her.

"Prepared to follow?" Clara challenged, not stepping back. His smirk widened, a devil-may-care look swimming through the crystal blue waters of his eyes.

"I'd follow you anywhere, lass; it's not a bad view," he told her with a wink.

"Just keep to the 'look but don't touch' rule and we won't have a problem. Also, you know my name; try using it." She turned away from him as if he bored her and examined his band of fellow pirates; she practically felt his annoyance.

"As you wish, *love*," he said stepping back to look with her.

Asshole, she thought, her eyes stopping on one particular crew member almost immediately—short, messy, brown hair, tall with soft, brown eyes, olive coloured skin and a sharp chin, very handsome. Very young.

"You said no children," she almost snapped, turning her head sharply to Gage. He returned her angry scrutiny with some confusion, glancing at his men before looking back at her.

"There aren't."

Her eyes narrowed before she turned her gaze on the boy, stalking up to him while he watched her approach somewhat warily. Clara stopped two feet in front of him

"How old are you? Don't lie."

The boy blinked at her before he looked past her to his captain, who prodded him to answer with a curt nod of his head.

"Twenty-three, ma'am."

"How old are you *really*?" Clara demanded, rolling her eyes.

"Nineteen," he told her after a minute, clearly surprised at being called on it. It was almost believable with his build. Almost.

"Right. What part of 'don't lie' was unclear?" she asked with contrived confusion. He shifted uncomfortably after being called out twice; she could see Gage crossing his arms in her peripheral, looking interested in the scene unfolding before him.

"Time's a wasting, kid," she noted a bit coolly when he'd been quiet for another long minute. He said something too softly to hear.

"Sorry, *what?*" Clara seethed, eyes widening.

"Sixteen," he admitted a bit louder, not making eye contact.

Her glare remained fixed on the kid squirming in front of her in silence for a beat before she calmly addressed Gage, voice belying her anger. "Sinclair—what the *hell?*"

"I'm as surprised as you are," he told her. He'd known the lad had lied about his age but not so drastically. "But sixteen was manhood last I checked, love." He shrugged.

Clara gritted her teeth together as she continued to let her stare bored into the teenager before her. She should have walked away right there; she knew Gage knew that was what she was thinking. He tried to look unconcerned, but she could practically feel him holding his breath behind her. If she said no, he was screwed. Unless he was superstitious, she thought, then he could try summoning the only other legend that might be able to help him—the Mage.

No one, however, sent summons to him unless they had no other choices left. He was the Wielder who had practically coined the phrase "deal with the devil."

Those that did had to pay rather... unusual prices for services rendered. Clara had heard he wanted souls; sometimes people said he wanted things intricate to who you were, like a talent, your voice, or, even more strangely, a temperament. She'd even heard people close to you were not off the table as payment. Her price was a pittance compared to whatever his would be if one believed the talk.

Honestly though, she wasn't even sure if he was real; townspeople loved to tell stories, and everywhere she'd went she heard more lavish, dramatic details. He was immortal; he communed with gods and devils; he preyed on the royal houses and owned most of their souls already; he was omnipotent and feasted on the blood of children and old women.

And no one had seen him in years.

Sure thing. A myth disbelieving of another myth, oh the irony. Even if he was real, she was still the only one who guaranteed she could get people through. She knew little of magic, admittedly, and those who used it. Her forest, on the other hand, had secrets it used against Wielders.

"What's your name, kid?" she asked, still deciding.

"Peter," he answered, holding his head higher and giving her his best stare of defiance. Sixteen was not a child she knew, but dammit, it was still young. She pointed a finger at him, not saying anything for a few moments as she made her decision.

"Walk near the front," she ordered coldly, turning to return to where Gage stood, just barely hiding his relief as she held out her hand. "You have it, I trust?"

Gage looped his thumb through a drawstring at his side and dropped a heavy pouch in her outstretched palm. She in turn walked back to the rock and dropped it in a pack that was at its base.

"Not going to count it?" he asked.

"I count at the end of the day. If you're short, I go home, and you walk yourself out." Clara looked over her shoulder and smiled sweetly. "Sorry, *if* you can walk yourself out," she corrected.

That threat had made a great deal of people fess up to cheating. Clara hadn't had to leave a single person in the forest, and she'd prefer to keep that streak going; it was after all a bit cold even for her. If they believed she'd leave them, she had to worry less about being cheated. Clara watched him process that before his grin turned decidedly a little less pleasant.

"Of course I could." Vindictive, strongly at that; she filed that under the many qualities of Lucas Sinclair that were good to know and addressed the ragtag group.

"OK, the rules are simple: do as I say and you'll survive this venture. If it's pretty, stay the hell away from it, because it will try to kill you. If anything nicks you, let me know no matter how small; depending on what it is, it could be either serious or very serious."

She reached into her pack and pulled out two similar-looking dead snakes, holding them both up so everyone could see them. "These babies are dangerous, in their mating season, and particularly aggressive right now—"

"So if attacked, fake orgasm?" a pirate with a scruffy beard and a squint eye interrupted, earning him a chuckle from his peers.

"Squint," Gage said, his name a warning.

Squint? How original, Clara thought briefly, replying without missing a beat. "Go for it, I'm sure you've heard enough faked ones to do the imitation justice."

This earned her a sour look from him and a louder laugh at his expense from his crewmates. Gage looked surprised before joining with the laughter—quick as a whip, this girl.

Clara continued on, as unmoved as she had been before. "They look similar but only one of them will outright kill you."

She held the right one out, its scales luminescent in an eerily beautiful way. "Both are blue, green, white, and black, so remember this—black touches green, thank the queen; the venom causes some terrible pain, but you'll live."

She dropped the snake and held out the left snake. "Black touches blue... you have three minutes before you go into shock and die." A beat of silence passed.

"That doesn't rhyme," the tall pirate with the knit blue cap observed dryly. So dryly it actually took Clara a moment to realize he was making a joke and not an idiot.

"Very much hope you remember it anyway, Mr....?"

"Just William," he offered with a smile, making his hazel eyes shine a little. Hmm, friendly for a pirate.

"Just William," she repeated, returning a tiny smile of her own. She dropped the dead snake as she went on. "There are a thousand other critters and plants that will try to kill you in there, but I won't go through them all; we'll deal with them when and if they come at us." Clara pulled an empty sack from her bag and threw it on the ground.

"I need all your firearms. You can't take them into the forest." The response to that was instantly and overwhelmingly negative, but she'd expected that.

"Get stuffed!" was among the few responses she received.

"You must be joking," Gage said, looking most unamused.

"The only thing a gun will do for you in there," Clara said seriously, pointing to the forest cut line, "is get you killed. The smell of gun powder and oil attracts some rather unsavoury creatures I'd rather not encounter."

Her explanation was met with more verbal protest from all except Gage and William. Gage chose merely to scrutinize her with those blue eyes of his, William watched his Captain and awaited his verdict. Clara didn't have that much patience.

"Fine," Clara shrugged, turning away from them all, "I don't need your money."

"Wait."

Clara stopped and turned back to Gage with an expectant look. After a moment Gage took the pistol from his hip and tossed it on the sack, followed closely by William's.

"Give 'em up boys," William said.

"Captain, you can't be serious!" the pirate with the tricorn hat exclaimed.

"Can't I Jared?" Gage asked, his voice soft but dangerous, almost daring the man to challenge him. "Give up your pistols."

"Jared" looked to the others, like maybe they would support him as he exclaimed "There are monsters in there!"

"I don't travel without my pistol," Squint followed up tersely. William stepped closer to both men, that friendly air about him disappearing as he towered above them.

"Your captain gave you an order." Jared and Squint suddenly looked less outraged and more nervous.

"I have survived without guns my whole life. If you want to live, my word is law." Clara picked up both pistols and stuffed them in the bag, holding it out to Jared.

"Up to you," she said to them. Peter and Squint exchanged a look, then Peter reluctantly drew his pistol and threw it in the bag as well, followed slowly by Squints piece.

Jared looked about him like the men had gone mad, and seeing he was the only one still holding out, he let out an angry huff before ripping the entire holster from his waist and throwing it in the bag.

"We are all going to regret this," he predicted bitterly.

"I'll admit if you had the gun you'd have none—the dead have no regrets," Clara countered tartly, quickly disposing of the bag in a thorn bush a few steps to her left.

"Last rule, keep up," she said, hefting her pack onto her shoulders. "Any questions?" Gage watched her surveying his men. When no one asked anything, she nodded. "We have a long day ahead of us, so let's get started."

Clara moved towards the trees, men already falling in line to follow, about to leave when she seemed to come up short. Everyone followed her line of sight to see what had stopped her. Standing ahead of them, toeing the border of the forest, was a *very* large white wolf.

It was easily the biggest wolf Gage had ever seen, its sleek fur coat as pure white as fresh snow, a striking silhouette against the green, shifting from paw to paw. What stood out the most, even from this distance, was the eyes—one amber eye and one such a dark blue it could almost be called black, keenly watching them all.

Gage tensed, his good hand immediately gripped the hilt of his sword, preparing to draw it. Clara reached over and gently touched his arm

"Easy," she said, smiling a little at the wolf.

"She's a friend," she said, then Clara called out to the white beast, "It's all right, Nahleese! They're with me!"

At first the wolf didn't move, unblinking gaze fixed upon them all almost calculatingly. Then she trotted out to them, moving quite gracefully for a creature so big. The pirates warily moved back a big step or two from Clara and the approaching wolf by proxy, its head coming up just under Clara's breasts as it nuzzled its massive head against her hands.

"Fitz send you?" Gage heard her ask, scratching under the beast's chin. The wolf made a chuffing noise in response, panting happily up at her.

"Care to join us?" Clara asked the wolf affectionately, making Gage roll his eyes at the absurdity of how she addressed the animal, as if it were an actual person.

"Bringing your pets, excellent," Gage sighed impatiently. "We've appointments to keep, love; the hour wanes."

Clara glared at him, but more impressively was the wolf turning that big white head to glare with her. It unnerved him a bit though he concealed it well, how it was just like the beast understood him. Clara patted the wolf's side, sending it off silently into the bush ahead of her.

"She's not a pet," Clara sneered at him before continuing after Nahleese.

"... Of course not," Gage replied, falling in step behind her.

For a place called the Dark Forest, Gage couldn't help but notice it wasn't very dark. In fact, it was rather bright and beautiful. There was no path really, merely places with less underbrush than others that Clara carefully navigated with five pairs of stomping boots following her every step.

The wolf was always either ahead of them or following from a distance to either side, never too close and never too far. Despite the whiteness of the beast's fur Gage was impressed by how often he lost track of where Nahleese was.

The trees towered above them so the sunlight streamed through their leaves and pooled all over the place, like spotlights. Every now and then, something would stir, but by the time he looked, whatever had caused the disturbance was gone. Vines hung from the long branches of the trees so they dangled down like curtains, some adorned with exquisitely beautiful yellow flowers.

His gaze fell on Clara's back as she trekked ahead of him and Gage smiled to himself a little, their colour reminded him a bit of the gold sheen to her hair. He was about to tell her as much, restart the game they were playing if you will, when Clara stopped abruptly—forcing him and everyone behind him to come to a halt as well.

"Problem, Fox?" Gage inquired, looking ahead to see why she'd stopped.

"Spitters," she said, as if that were explanation enough, taking off her pack.

Gage tried to spot exactly what this "spitter" was, but all he saw was a curtain of vines, all sporting a host of the yellow flowers like a curtain of gold. He saw no animals or apparent danger.

"Spitters?" he repeated, still looking as Clara pulled out a tin of matches and a round little ball of what looked like tightly packed cotton.

"The nasty little blooms hanging about head height," she explained. He realized she was talking about the beautiful little flowers. In fact, now that he looked at them more closely, he noticed there was something a bit off about them, mainly that all the blooms seemed to move when Clara moved.

She struck the match, and the flowers seemed to focus more on her, a sweet scent filling the air as their petals quivered. The men were watching curiously now, along with Gage, a tad unnerved by the flowers but not overly worried by them. Clara lit the little cotton ball and tossed it in the air towards them, causing all the blooms to turn their petals in its direction.

From the heart of each flower shot tiny black spurs, nailing the flaming cotton ball in midair. It hit the ground, smoking, looking like a ball of black spikes.

"Whoa," Peter said.

"They react to heat," she told Gage over her shoulder. "Their poison will make you hallucinate for about six hours, if you live that long stumbling around in here. Then you die of toxic shock," she said, heaving her pack back onto her shoulders. "Not a pretty way to go. Takes a few minutes for them to spit again. Let's go."

Clara noticed how Gage reevaluated the tiny flowers, now seeing the beautiful blooms in a new, harsher light.

"The more beautiful, the more deadly," she reminded him.

"Then you must be the most dangerous thing in this forest," he told her smoothly. He found himself surprised by how she responded.

"Don't cut yourself short, Sinclair," she returned with a smirk. "I'm sure you're all kinds of dangerous as you're certainly all kinds of pretty."

Translation—*I'm onto you, and it's not going to work*. Gage stepped in front of her before she could take the lead, pulling the vines from the path and making an elegant gesture with his hand for her to precede him.

"Ladies first." He was sure to note her reaction carefully.

"For a pirate, you sure love the gentleman's act," she observed just as carefully, walking through the opening while Gage followed on her heel. He leaned in close behind her.

"I'm always a gentleman, love." The words were said just close enough to her ear that for some reason all the hair stood up at her nape. He was bound and determined to get under her skin it seemed.

It was working to some extent unfortunately. She thrust her elbow back and hit him in the chest just hard enough to draw a startled noise from him as he fell back a few steps.

"Name's not 'love,' Sinclair," she told him, trying to sound as if she'd been utterly unaffected.

"Yes, you do so like using names," he remarked pointedly, referring to her use of his.

"Would you prefer your moniker?" she asked with a shrug, like it didn't matter to her either way.

"No, I like the way you say my name," he said, waving the offer away. "If you're amiable to the idea, I'd love to hear you scream it."

She narrowed her eyes at him over her shoulder, but he only turned his charming smile into a more seductive suggestive one. Like he could make her scream *his* name, her partners screamed hers. That thought startled her a bit, almost flustering her actually. They were so *not* going to find out who screamed who's name, good gods.

"I'll make you walk at the back of the line, *Gage*. Don't push me." She continued forwards at a faster pace, leaving him to walk behind her. His laughter at her retreat irked her to no end; *fucking pirates*.

Four

She marched them hard, she'd admit, harder than she marched others. Mostly because she'd decided to put *Gage* in his place. High noon they arrived at the halfway clearing, and she told them they were taking a half-hour break. Most of the pirates almost collapsed on the spot with sheer relief. They seemed to all collect together when they sat, as if being grouped together made them feel more secure about being in the Dark Forest. Clara couldn't really say she understood it, but whatever helped she supposed. Either way, she could tell by their huffing and puffing they were virtually guaranteed not to move from their spot till they had to.

Gage, interestingly enough, seemed to not need the illusion of safety that his group provided, sitting on a log a bit farther from the others, sweat beading his face as he tried to hide how much he needed the break. It gave her a small sense of satisfaction, seeing him out of breath and out of his element while she was only mildly winded by the increased pace. Running for her life in here for nineteen years had been great conditioning. She saw Peter taking a long swig from his canteen and figured she'd check on him first.

"Holding up, kid?" she asked, coming to stand next to him. He swiveled his body to address her, posturing a little bit as if ruffled by the question.

"Not a kid," he shot back testily.

She held up a hand, a wordless concession. "No offense intended."

"I'm holding up fine," he lied. Clara knew better than to call him on it now; she would make him look bad if she did. Perhaps she already had before they'd begun by calling him out on his real age. They were all watching her talk to him, so she supposed the posturing was necessary—being pirates and all. Unknown to her, Gage was watching her even more closely as she interacted with Peter.

"Of course," she said, "but your canteen is almost empty."

"How do you know?" Peter asked her, frowning.

"Saw you pour some on your head a while back; your canteen isn't that big." Clara shrugged, holding her hand out for it. Hesitantly he handed it to her as she walked to the edge of the small clearing. She wandered at the edge before she found a long, thick-looking purple plant shoot, pulling out her knife and cutting deeply into it, holding the mouth of the canteen under it.

Clara kicked the plant's base, and a few glugs of water spilt from the cut into the bottle. A few more kicks had it completely filled. She strode back to Peter and returned the canteen to him.

"Water's precious; don't waste it to cool off." Peter reluctantly nodded.

"Thank you... Miss Fox," he said, his address more respectful now. For some reason that prompted Clara to pat his shoulder. She frowned at herself almost immediately for the overly familiar and friendly gesture, drawing her hand back.

"If anyone else needs more water, get it now; this is our only stop point till nightfall," she said hastily, voice harder as she pointed at the plant she'd just used. "Just kick the base like I did."

Everyone got up slowly and staggered a bit to do as instructed, grumbling about their feet. Gage stayed where he was, patting his front pocket as if to assure himself something was still there. Clara noted the action curiously before approaching him.

"Your precious cargo?" she asked. Gage looked up and let his hand fall back to his side casually.

"Perhaps."

"Playing coy doesn't suit you, Sinclair." Lie—it suited him very well. "Must be valuable to keep so close."

"I recall a conversation where we agreed 'need to know' was part of our arrangement," he reminded her, smile sharp. Clara grinned back with a veneer of false civility, definitely precious cargo.

"You should get water now," she advised him.

"I've been a sailor a long time, love," he stated, pulling out a flask and unscrewing it. "I know how to conserve fresh water." He took a swig, and she caught a whiff of what smelt like—

"Is that *rum?*" she asked incredulously, feeling a sudden urge to slap him.

"Course it's rum," he answered. "I'm also a pirate, am I not?"

"You do know if you drink nothing but rum you'll be dehydrated and cramping before the day is out?"

"Relax, love, I've water, and it's not my first trek," he told her with a measure of sarcasm.

Clara shook her head, she silently reserved the right to mock him as soon as he got his first cramp or headache before she sat beside him. "How are your feet?" she asked. Clara had noticed a few clicks ago that he'd begun to take his steps more gingerly. She knew he'd regret wearing those boots.

"They're fine, sweetheart," he assured her, waving her off. "Love" she could take, if he switched to "sweetheart," she might throttle him. Since that wasn't very professional, she called him out just a little louder than necessary hoping to be overheard by his men.

"Lie."

He glared at her. "I doubt you've any idea how annoying that is."

She shrugged. "I think I have a pretty good idea actually. Boots off."

His eyes turned to slits; he didn't respond well to orders. He gave them; he didn't take them. Clara returned the look with a calm stare, removing her fingerless gloves and stuffing them into a pouch at her side.

"I can help, you know," she told him when he didn't move to do as she'd asked.

"Fox, are you concerned for my well-being?" he asked, mood suddenly amused.

"You are sort of paying me to," she reminded him sweetly.

"Ah, lass," he said, taking one boot off, "excuses, excuses."

She examined his foot without touching it and frowned at the red chaffing that would soon bleed. "Yes, clearly they're just fine," she said sarcastically after a moment, reaching into her pack for something. She pulled a few things out as she looked, putting them aside before finally finding what she was looking for.

"Here." She offered Gage a sack of powder and a clean wrap.

"What's this?" he asked, looking at the extended pouch as she opened it to reveal a yellowish powder.

"It's glice powder," she told him "I make it from the pulp of... well, a plant you've probably never heard of. It'll dry your feet and numb the pain a little; wrap your ankle a bit, and you should be fine the rest of the way. Just make sure not to get any in your eyes; it hurts like a bastard, and it'll temporarily blind you."

Gage took the pouch, letting his fingers linger a little longer against hers than was strictly necessary.

"Thank you, milady."

"Do you ever stop?"

"Try me, and find out," he dared playfully. Did he honestly expect her to blush or something?

"Please," Clara said, rolling her eyes before spearing him with a look that was challenging, mocking, and suggestive all at once. "Much like this hike, you'd never be able to keep up." She smirked.

He almost let his surprise show. "Well, look at you, love, returning flirtations—with me no less?" he inquired, pretending to be utterly shocked.

"Is that what you're doing?" Clara asked, tilting her head with amusement. "Funny, feels more like power playing."

Gage merely answered with a wider grin; in truth, he felt a bit cross—she'd seen through him. She was by far the most challenging woman he'd ever attempted to lure in with charm, a fact that intrigued him and needled him all at once.

It also brought out his more competitive nature. He'd use a more romantic approach if he'd thought it would work, but he could tell Clara wouldn't bite. He fully intended to figure out what would work eventually and utilize it mercilessly when he did. Right then, it was like she saw that very thought cross his face.

"Sinclair," she began, looking down to unscrew the lid of her canteen, "start this game with me at your own peril. It will not end well for you," she warned him, taking a swig.

Neither noticed William, who had been last to the plant, was kicking it without getting the same result of water like the others had, finding it was now a dry tap.

He looked around, seeing if he could spot any other purple shoots like Clara had...

It took Clara a moment to realize Gage was simply staring at her, so she stared back waiting for him to say something as a few long moments passed under the study of those unwavering blue eyes.

"Yes?" she asked, breaking first.

"Just reading that pretty face of yours," he said nonchalantly.

She scoffed at that; however his eyes didn't leave her as she put her things back in her pack, and he explained no further. He was trying to make her ask; guess he was going to ignore her warning, then.

"Sure you are," she said instead, refusing to show how his eyes on her made her... uncomfortable?

"You're not quite as inscrutable as you may believe, Fox," he told her.

She finished closing up her bag before returning his gaze, looking for the lie in it, feeling just a little unnerved when she didn't see one. He could just think he knew...

"How does the story read?" she asked finally, challenging him.

"Tragically."

"The depth of your insight is truly worthy of awe," she answered sarcastically, clearly unimpressed as she started to stand.

"Well, those abandoned usually have a tragic element I'll admit, but those who've lost someone hold a bit more."

She froze in place, her face steeling instantly; Gage knew he'd hit the proverbial nail on the head.

"Judging by how you treat Peter and your refusal to guide with children, I'd put gold on someone young, perhaps someone you couldn't protect through these very trees, maybe you were even close to them."

A flicker of pain shot across her face as she refused to look at him; he was onto something here...

"Who?" he asked.

"So curious," she deflected somewhat airily. "I'll tell you who if you tell me her name."

"Who's name?" Gage asked, suddenly confused. When she locked eyes with him, there was anything but flippancy in her expression, her green eyes fierce and on fire with the undercurrents of her anger.

"The woman you loved who burned you."

Gage continued to smile, but it turned almost arctic in temperature in the space of a heartbeat, laced with *his* pain now.

"Oh, not burned you—*died* on you," Clara corrected herself. "Going by the look in *your* eyes I'd say... murdered." Clara leaned forwards so she could say her next words with the razor sharpness of a blade. "Takes one to know one." Her voice was as cold as his smile; he answered her with silence.

There it was, the line where she didn't just push back but shoved violently with her own uncanny insights. In that moment, he wasn't the charming flirt, and she wasn't the walking barb of wit; they were two people who'd found old open wounds in one another. Because of that, an unspoken truce was understood between them then. Treading on those injuries would not be seen as a game but an act of war; those wounds were to be ignored.

"It was rude of me to pry; forgive me," he said in a strained voice, inclining his head with a stiff nod of apology.

"Of course," Clara replied just as rigidly. She looked away first, point clearly made and honestly needing something else to focus on. That was when she saw William leaning into the bush towards what she instantly realized he thought was another water shoot.

It wasn't. It was a lure.

"WAIT!" she screamed, dropping her canteen and getting to her feet before Gage could so much as look to the reason for her panic. However she didn't move fast enough to prevent what she knew was coming.

All heads turned in her direction, even William's as he continued to reach for the plant, fingers brushing it lightly. The plant was suddenly a flurry of movement, leaves that camouflaged a massive, shimmering, green eggplant-like body twice the size of a large man. It seemed to split itself open with a screeching yowl that froze the blood and revealed the shadowy maw of a beast with no end.

A barbed, vine-like tongue lashed out like a whip and wrapped around William's middle, pulling him into that dark hungry void and closing with him inside before he could scream. Then it was slithering back, deeper into the brush and out of sight.

If Gage had blinked, he'd have missed the terrifying sight of his first mate being swallowed by a monster plant before being drawn back into the bush. However nothing could erase the sound of that ungodly screech from his mind. He was on his feet, falling into a dead run behind Clara, who was only a few feet ahead of him.

"William!" he yelled as Clara dove into the bushes after the man with no hesitation. Gage stopped briefly to give orders to the men who were still standing there, frozen.

"Jared, with me! You two stay here!" he ordered.

Gage didn't bother to see if Jared was coming, just ran into the bush, following after the mere glimpses of fiery hair that shot through the trees.

Five

Fucking pirates, Clara thought as she frantically swatted braches and greenery from her path, pulling the dagger at her wrist as her eyes scoured the ground for tracks. She heard Gage following behind her; good, she was probably going to need his help. She caught sight of the shimmering green leaves as the plant creature settled to try and digest. Clara nearly launched herself to the monsters side undaunted, one hand boldly reaching out to feel the rubbery expanse of its body as she heard the muffled screams of the pirate inside.

"Get him out!" Gage ordered. Oh good, he'd caught up. The rubbery flesh jiggled and contracted under her hand, smooth and unblemished as she searched for it...

"Damn you, where is it?" she muttered.

"Cut him out already!" Gage snapped, drawing his blade and moving to stab it into the creature.

Clara instantly stopped what she was doing and caught him by his wrist. "Stop! Hurt it, and it fills up with digestive acids faster so it can fight; you have to hit this thing right the first time," she snapped.

He yanked his arm from her hand as the brash one named Jared finally stumbled upon them.

"Get my man out, Fox," Gage growled.

"I know what I'm doing, Sinclair, trust me," she sang impatiently, returning to her work of saving Gage's blue-capped crew member.

His lips thinned as he realized he didn't really have much of a choice in the matter.

"What do we do?" Gage spat past clenched teeth, sheathing his sword.

"We've got to split this thing," Clara told him, hand going back to the creature's side, sliding over plant-and-animal-hybrid flesh searching...

Her hand slid over an irregular patch, a small, almost invisible raised line that ran from top to bottom of the creature. *There you are.*

"Let's peel this bitch open, boys," Clara yelled, readying her knife.

"Jared, to her left," Gage ordered.

"Aye, Captain," Jared answered roughly, moving to stand on the other side of Clara opposite him, both waiting at the ready.

Clara drove her dagger right into the creatures fissure of flesh and a horrid shrieking began, monster shuddering violently as she pulled the blade down towards her and prised into it. A loud snap was heard before that line split open, a foul-smelling, yellowish fluid pouring out and soaking her boots.

"Now!" Clara yelled. Both men grabbed the edge of the wound Clara had inflicted and pulled at it, struggling to open it wider. The monster wiggled and contracted under their hands, trying to pull itself closed again.

Clara reached into the dark belly of the beast open before her while it shrieked and shuddered, seeing the shape of a man and grabbing at the silhouette. She felt William's hand wrap around her wrist as she pulled, holding on for dear life as first his arm came out and then his shoulder. His pale, screaming face met the light of day, covered in the yellow fluid, eyes wide with fear, and she didn't blame him. Clara braced her foot against the creature and pulled with everything she had while Gage and Jared fought to keep the slit open.

Clara realized this tug-of-war would only get them so far; this thing apparently needed more convincing that they were not prey. She flipped her blade one-handed to hold it in a reverse grip and plunged it into the side of the creature again, tearing another god-awful howl from it.

Something seemed to snap, and William came tumbling out, hitting the dirt hard and nearly taking Clara down with him.

"Pick him up! Go!" she yelled, jerking her blade back out as Jared pulled William to his feet and started to run back to the clearing. Gage released the creature and ran after them with Clara on his heels. The plant creature, however, wasn't quite done with them yet.

The only reason William was out was because the vine-like tongue had let him go and was targeting the bigger threat—her.

She made it all of two steps before the prodded vine shot out of the wound she'd given it and wrapped around her arm so tightly she cried out. The knife dropped from her hand as the beast yanked, trying to draw her in to the sulphurous black hole that was its mouth. Gage had already disappeared into the bush in front of her, leaving her to face this thing alone.

The plant tugged violently again with the green ropy tongue, its sharp barbs biting into her skin, ripping another cry from her as she dug her heels into the ground and tried to pull loose. It had a firm grip on her now, and it wasn't letting go as inch by inch it dragged her closer to its shapeless maw.

Clara tried to grab something, anything, to stop from going into that stinking belly of death, but this thing was quick, strong, and worst of all it was still hungry...

Gage only stopped when he heard her voice cry out, glancing over his shoulder and realizing she wasn't behind him. Gage skidded to a stop, turning to look back for her, eyes casting through the brush for any sign of his Guide.

"Clara!" he yelled. He heard another cry of pain and cursed under his breath before running back the way he'd came.

Clara's hand scraped the ground as she leaned back, trying to wriggle free, gritting her teeth.

"Sonuvabitch!" she barked. *This will NOT be the trip that kills me,* she thought, hand grasping a rock. She smashed it fruitlessly into the vine to get it to at least loosen, but this thing was determined to have its meal. The pirates may have fled without her, but she still had someone who had her back.

"Nahleese!" she screamed. "NAHLEESE!"

She was almost in now, feet barely keeping purchase on the ground as her arm disappeared inside—

She felt the nearness of teeth on her back, the white wolf just a flash of fur in her peripherals as her jaws locked into her cloak, pulling backwards, joining in the effort to pull her free.

One step back, two steps. Clara kept smashing the rock into the vine as the wolf worried its head from side to side in an effort to gain more ground.

"Come on, girl, pull!" she yelled, digging in her heels as Nahleese growled, bearing down, and digging her heels in. They gained more ground, three steps back, four!

For a second, it looked as if the wolf might be able to pull her free. Until the plant shuddered, and the vine pulled so hard Clara almost felt her shoulder pull out of its socket. The clasp on her cloak snapped open, falling away and sending Nahleese rolling into the bush, yipping with the sudden lack of resistance.

This can't be it, Clara thought, going forwards as the mouth of the plant opened more to take her in.

Fingers curled tightly under her free arm above her elbow like a vise, holding her back from the very literal jaws of death.

"Sorry!"

The black-gloved hand with its silver gauge pressed to the vine. Clara was shocked as she watched the silver gauge burn, its image coming to life as the needle swung violently.

The vine blackened like it was being burnt, the creature shrieking for all it was worth as the vine turned brittle and withered before it snapped, bits of it crumbling away like ash.

"This one's mine!" Gage hollered, wrapping his arm around her waist and pulling her with him into a run. He shoved her in front of him.

"Go, go, go!" he yelled.

Clara only stumbled a few steps, one hand scooping her blade up from the forest floor before finding her footing and taking off as fast as she could, Nahleese covering their retreat from behind. They both broke into the clearing out of breath and looking harried.

Nahleese entered after them, trotting up to Clara with her green cloak still in her teeth.

Clara let her knees hit the ground gasping for air while Nahleese dropped the cloak beside her. "Good girl," she huffed, patting the wolf. Nahleese nipped at her fingers, as if chastising her carelessness before resting her big head on her shoulder.

Gage braced one hand on his knee to catch his breath, gloved forefinger pulling at his collar.

"What the hell kind of magic do you have on that thing?" Clara demanded, gulping for air.

"One that allows only very sparse usage. You're welcome," he answered in such a blasé manner that for a moment Clara didn't even know how to respond. He straightened himself, and she didn't miss him patting that front pocket once more before relaxing a little, his package obviously secure.

"Well, that was certainly exciting," Gage said to them all with a grin.

"Oh yeah, a regular good fucking time," Clara spat.

"Are you all right, Miss Fox?" Peter asked, showing concern as she unwrapped the severed vine from her arm, flexing her fingers and finding nothing broken.

"Fine, Peter," she answered as the white wolf whined and licking her face.

"Sound off," Gage puffed.

"Alive," Jared said, taking off his hat.

"Me too," Squint all but grumbled.

"Still here," Peter said, kneeling by William and offering him his canteen. William retched violently instead.

"Mr. William, you all right?" Gage asked.

"Alive, Captain," he rasped after a moment.

"What in the ungodly hells was that?" Squint asked, his one eye staring warily into the bushes.

"Haven't named it yet." Clara shrugged, stroking the white wolf's head to placate her, still out of breath.

"I'm all right, girl," she said into the soft white fur.

"But it's the third one that's tried to eat me this month, so I think I'm obligated to now," she said to everyone else, rolling her eyes as if the idea itself was a chore.

Gage just stared at her for a moment before he started to laugh, hands on his knees while his shoulders shook with it. Slowly everyone else joined in until the clearing was filled with the sound of their laughter.

Clara looked about her at the laughing pirates, confused as to what they found so funny.

"What did I say?" she asked, making them laugh harder. *Must be a hysterical thing,* she thought, sharing a look with Nahleese, who merely panted happily in response as she rubbed her head.

Six

The crew hadn't seemed to wish to stay in the clearing after that. Clara wasn't sure why to be honest: the clearing was perfectly safe if they didn't stray from it. Despite that assurance, they still insisted on leaving. Nevertheless, she'd made them wait until she'd tended to William. Clara helped him clean some of the digestive juices out of his eyes with a bandage cloth and water from her canteen.

Gage had stayed at her side and watched her work, looking out for his first mate. It garnered him some more of her respect.

"You're going to stink for a bit," she told William, reaching into another pouch and pulling out a handful of fine bluish powder, "but this will see to it that none of its stomach acid rashes your skin out."

She tried a reassuring smile as she'd rubbed it over his arms. William was still looking like he was in some kind of shock.

"Oh, he's used to stinking, aren't you, William?" Gage joked. William nodded somewhat absently. Gage looked to her as if asking if he was going to be okay, and she'd nodded in reply to the unasked question.

"Just shock," she said, waving his unvoiced concern away. "The first time I brushed up with one of those things it got my arm in its mouth right up to my shoulder," she told him, remembering the event vividly.

"Luckily it was smaller than the one that got you, and I had a blade. I got free, but I had a rash all the way down my arm for two weeks. Hurt like hell." She chuckled to William, rubbing the powder on his skin, trying to draw him out of his stupor.

"Thank you," he whispered at last. William actually looked at her when he said it, gratefulness shining in his hazel eyes.

"I thought I was going to die, thank you," he repeated. Clara never knew how to handle people's sincere gratitude, never felt right since she was being paid. So she did what she always did when she was faced with being thanked; she turned flippant.

"Don't mention it. Ever. To anyone," she told him with a wink. When William gave a weak laugh, she knew he was going to be fine.

They'd continued on, the rest of the day wasn't nearly as eventful as their high-noon break but not uneventful either with Clara guiding them through, past dangerous plants and critters.

Gage could see why so few left the forest alive. Nahleese had taken to sticking close to Clara, trotting by her side the rest of the day, which kept the others back. Not far enough to lose sight of her but just far enough where she didn't need to keep up any conversations and of that she was glad, especially with Gage.

How he'd saved her life had somewhat thrown her. One minute prying into her wounds, next minute pulling her from the jaws of death. It chaffed at her pride a bit, having someone *she* was protecting and leading through her forest save *her* life. And that gloved hand of his—she'd never seen magic work like that in the forest. He'd put that hand on her at one point—it gave her shivers to think on it now.

Clara was off balance; the last thing she wanted was for him to catch her in any moment unprepared. He needed her alive to survive himself, true, but now she felt as if he had something over her and she didn't like it.

"Good gods, William. Take a few steps back, will ya?" Jared complained. "You smell like the back end of a horse."

"At least I don't *look* like the back end of the horse," William jeered back.

"Knock it off," Gage snapped, cowing both men to silence.

It was quiet for a moment.

"How much farther?" Peter piped up, breaking the silence from behind his captain.

"Don't start," Squint all but barked.

"Ladies!" Clara called behind her, annoyed. "You're *all* pretty, so quit bickering; we're here." She stopped at last to look around, relieved.

They'd arrived at the stop point just as the sun began to set, like she'd planned; they had made good time. The last thing she wanted was to try walking five pirates through the dark in this forest; she'd never be able keep them alive.

"Is this a campsite?" Jared asked, considering the inhospitable-looking ground about him.

"Yes," Clara answered, dropping her pack and stretching.

"Doesn't look like the best place to stop, love," Gage said, seeing as the ground looked even less safe than the clearing they'd been in, and they all remembered what had happened there.

"Looks perfect to me, Sinclair." Clara shrugged, looking up. Gage followed her gaze to see a surprisingly big round hovel built high up in the tree.

"A tree fort," Gage remarked dryly. "Feels as if I've returned to the Eternity Isle," he muttered to himself.

"It's not a tree fort," Clara argued defensively, not even bothering to ask about whatever island he referred to. "It's a lookout point."

"That you live in," William added as he passed, like this was evidence against her claim.

"It's a fort, Fox, and it's in a tree—tree fort." Gage levelled her with a look that told her he clearly thought she was deluding herself if she thought otherwise on this matter.

"Would you like to sleep on the ground, come nightfall?" Clara asked with an insincere pleasantness, daring him to make another quip.

"My, what a lovely, little lookout point," he said after a beat, sounding overly awed. "However I don't see a ladder—" Gage observed, taking a step towards her. He was pulled up short by growling, looking to the sound and finding the mismatched eyes of the white wolf fixed on him, lip curled back in a warning.

"Your friend is a tad ornery," Gage observed, taking a measured step back.

"Nahleese, relax."

The wolf quit growling, looked back up to her, and whined. In response, Clara reached down and pat her head.

Gage noticed she did it with the arm that hadn't been latched onto by the vine; in fact, she'd been avoiding using that arm much at all.

Clara saw him watching her and assumed it was because of Nahleese.

"She's a bit protective sometimes," she explained. "Also she doesn't like strangers."

Gage grinned at the wolf, who stared back with eerily intense eyes. "Oh, I don't know, I think I could win her over."

"I think if you value your limbs you won't try," Clara said, shaking her head at him.

"How are we getting up there?" Gage asked, taking off his hat to wipe his forehead with the back of his sleeve.

Normally Clara would climb up herself and lower down the pulley rope she had rigged to bring visitors up, but her arm had stopped being numb hours ago and now hurt enough that she was trying to limit its use. She wasn't entirely sure she was up to climbing. Clara wasn't about to admit that any time soon, so she supposed she was going to find out.

"There're a few pulley ropes at the top," she began, flexing her fingers to test the arm as she spoke. Stabs of pain shot up from wrist to shoulder, and she clenched her teeth before continuing.

"I'll climb up and lower it down," she told them, walking to the tree.

"Actually," Gage began smoothly, turning Clara back towards him at the sound of his voice, "if you don't mind, I'd rather send Peter up."

"What? Why me?" Peter asked incredulously.

"Perhaps as punishment for lying to your captain," Gage answered, voice conveying a hard edge of displeasure. "I recommend doing as you're told, *Peter*."

The kid looked suddenly sheepish and nervous.

"Yes, Captain," he relented quietly.

"Well, you're not my captain, and I do mind," Clara interjected brightly.

"Think you can get all the way to the top while carrying your pride, do you, love?" Gage asked, glancing at her arm. She got the sense this was his misguided attempt to help her save face if she wasn't up to the climb, as he'd apparently guessed at her injury.

Clara laughed but managed to sound entirely unamused, pretending she didn't notice the meaningful look. "Sinclair, I could get to the top of this tree carrying your *ego*—a great deal heavier than my pride, I suspect."

Gage raised an eyebrow. "Is that a challenge, Fox?"

It wasn't, more of a taunt actually. But now... well, now she understood Peter's posturing better than she had a few hours ago. Her pride *was* heavy.

"Maybe it is," she decided, attempting to stare him down. She should have known better. Gage stared back a short moment before slinging his canteen off his shoulder and handing it to William.

"Hold this," he ordered, striding towards Clara with that same swagger he'd had in the bar, cocky and confident.

That alone was enough to put a fire in Clara's gut. She patted the wolf's head and pointed at another tree with a nook hollowed out at its base. The wolf trotted away dutifully and disappeared inside the tree as Gage approached her. Those eyes of his locked with hers, playfully goading her. She fell into step beside him, both breaking eye contact to fix their gazes on the tree.

"If I get to the top before you, I get your rum," Clara wagered, upping the ante if only to make his defeat cost him something more.

"If I win, I get another kiss," Gage countered before looking to her with a sly smile. He'd be lying if he said he wouldn't love seeing if he couldn't sway her to be less stubborn with more... physical charms, if she allowed him the chance.

"But try not to throw the game on that account," he leaned over and whispered.

Clara saw he expected this to have an effect on her, be it discomfort or to stir some secret wanting in her. It really just made her want to punch him in the face.

"Just climb," she said, grabbing onto one of the roots that circled the tree and pulling herself up. She'd figured that with her hurt arm and the fact that his other hand was partially paralysed they would be fairly even, but she'd been wrong.

Gage was swift and agile, years of learning how to best utilize whatever functionality left in his hand to his advantage, making him efficient and quick. Clara's hurt arm didn't want to obey her as she grit her teeth, fingers clumsy as she demanded the limb do as it was told.

"All right there, love?" she heard him ask.

She looked over to see he had rather cockily stopped climbing and was looking down at her, as if he were trying to give her a chance to catch up, his smile smug and mocking. If it hadn't been on before, it most certainly was now.

Clara smiled back before reaching up with her good arm and punching his foot from its hold, causing him to yelp as he clutched onto a vine to keep from falling. He was still trying to regain his footing when Clara passed him.

"Never better," she quipped, pulling ahead of him.

Bitch, Gage thought, even as he grinned up after her. He caught his foothold quickly after that and double-timed it after her. She'd picked up her pace, masterfully putting to use any advantage she had on him, her lightness and knowledge of a climb she'd made a thousand times before.

Gage wedged his gloved hand into a crack in the tree and grabbed the same vine from below that she was just reaching for and pulled it so she missed, hand clutching at air and very nearly causing her to fall.

She caught herself by grabbing a handful of moss just in time, managing to hold on and scrambling to get a good grip on the tree once more. By the time Clara did, Gage had pulled even with her once more.

"Turnabout's fair play, love," he told her with a wink.

Bastard, she thought, prickly smile widening. His men were cheering for him as both put their all into the last leg of the climb. Clara felt like her fingers were going to stop listening to her any second as pain stabbed into her shoulder right down to her fingertips.

Hearing him panting right next to her was just enough to make her competitive side force her to ignore the pain. She reached up at last and slammed her hand down on the wooden planks, grinning from ear to ear before looking over to Sinclair...

Who had slammed his hand down in victory at the exact same moment she had.

For a second, they just looked at each other as their cocky smiles were replaced by looks of surprise. Then he laughed, a good, almost hearty sound.

"I never admit defeat, Fox," he told her. "But occasionally I'll amend to a tie," he finished, pulling himself up under the railing and onto the platform. He offered her a hand to pull her the rest of the way up. Clara smiled at the offer but ignored it as she pulled herself up, getting to her feet to face him.

"Not bad for a man with virtually one hand," she admitted to him while catching her breath, not realizing she was still smiling.

"Not bad for a girl with an injured arm."

"It's not injured," she lied; it was aching so badly she had to put a great deal of effort to stop her hand from shaking. "It's sore, and who are you calling 'girl,' sea dog?" she asked.

"Sea dog?" Gage repeated as she walked away to go untie a few pulley ropes with stirrups for a person's foot. "That's the best you got?" he asked, coming to stand beside her.

"Of course not, but I don't want to make you cry," Clara returned, throwing the ropes over the edge with her good arm.

Gage watched her, still wearing that half grin of hers; the lass liked a challenge. He could relate, he thought, admiring the flush in her cheeks. "You've a beautiful smile, lass; you should wear it more often." Like he knew it would it vanished from her face and was replaced with something much like begrudging surprise.

"You're so full of crap," Clara replied, rolling her eyes.

"Are you suggesting I'm lying?" he asked. To that she didn't seem to have an answer.

"Next time we make a bet, your rum is mine," she told him instead, kicking the pulley and making the wheels crack, squealing loudly with its usual protest at hauling up the first three of her guests.

"Keep dreaming, sweetheart," Gage said, watching her observe their steady progress a moment. Feeling curious, he turned away from her to go exploring the "lookout point."

The platform was larger than the actual hut, providing a little path that one could walk around the entirety of the building, a simple, sturdy wood railing that provided some measure of protection from losing one's footing and falling to their death. Upon entering, he saw the little hut was quite basic, open netted windows and two doorways, one hung with some kind of fine netting, the other bare and open. It was a big circular open space with a fire pit in the middle, thin, bamboo-like wood knitted together to make the walls, while a straw-like grass provided an arching roof. That was it really. Not all that clean either, with dirt and leaves littering the cabin space.

"Not one to clean for company, I see," Gage called over his shoulder with a smirk, kicking a small collection of leaves from his path. It was actually a quaint little lookout, he thought, watching through the netted window as the sun dropped slowly behind the horizon, reflecting against the vivid green treetops so that they almost glinted. It was almost like an ocean of foliage, the wind rippling through a sea of leaves...

Something was twining around his leg. He looked down, and instantly he felt as if his turned blood had turned to ice. It appeared he'd disturbed a wayward creature when he'd carelessly been kicking leaves about.

A coil of blue, black, white, and green gripped his ankle tightly. Round amber eyes and a thin slit of a pupil glared up at him with an unforgiving glint as the snake climbed up his leg like lightning.

Before he could call out, the lower half of its muscled length was wrapped around his thigh; the more dangerous half pulled back with its mouth wide and fangs bared.

It held itself in a menacing pose, threatening to strike with a sinister hissing.

"Don't. Move."

Seven

She had looked away for ten seconds, and he was off to explore. Clara had heard his voice teasingly commenting on the state of the place and was about to rattle off a comeback when she realized something—she hadn't cleared the platform yet.

It was something she usually did before anyone else was even done coming up on the pulley ropes, but she hadn't gotten the chance yet; she didn't usually race clients to the top. Immediately Clara found herself hurrying to follow him into the hut where she'd heard Gage's voice. She found him in deep trouble—"eye level and sinking fast" trouble.

"Don't. Move," she ordered, voice tense and soft.

"Wouldn't dream of it," Gage answered just as softly, staring at the long, ivory fangs glinting in the fading light.

"Not the best creature to be making friends with, Sinclair" Clara said, trying to keep him calm while easing farther into the room.

"Fox," Gage said quietly, not taking his eyes off the posed creature hugging his thigh, ready to strike, "blue touching black."

He swallowed the lump in his throat as he watched Clara move around him slowly out of the corner of his eye. A bead of sweat ran down his face as she carefully moved further into his line of sight, still a healthy distance away from him.

"What's it doing?" he asked quietly, watching it hold the threatening pose, weaving ever so slightly. He had to squash the urge to make a grab for the creature and throw it away from him as hard as he could; it was far too fast for that to work.

"Looking for a sweet spot," she told him softly while pulling a short blade from a sheath at her waist, a reverse curve on the deadly looking knife.

"Their usual prey is harder to kill than us," she explained, trying to use her words to focus him as she watched the snake's head weave back and forth, the glinting scales mesmerizing in the last fading rays of sun. Truly a beautiful creature.

"What do I do?" Gage asked, daring only to move his eyes to look at her.

"Pick a God and pray."

"Are jokes terribly appropriate right now?" Gage hissed, watching Clara's face. Her hard green eyes were trained unwaveringly on the snake as she pulled one, fingerless, dragon-hide glove onto her other hand with her teeth.

"I wasn't joking. Don't move until I say, then slowly exit the hut," she instructed, crouching down so she was level with the snake wrapped tightly to his thigh, still a good arm's length away.

Clara slapped her gloved hand to the floor. Something sewn into the middle of the glove ignited, a bright light now burning in her palm, saved from being burnt by the protective dragon hide.

The snake's head turned in Clara's direction, violently, hissing loudly as its pupils widened and poison dripped from its ivory fangs.

Gage felt his heart pounding in his throat, hands balled up into a tight fist as he tried not to react to the lightning-fast movement. His senses were on such high alert from all the adrenaline in his veins that he felt the movement in the corner of the room before he saw it, a slithering motion to his left.

Barely daring to turn his head, he spotted another snake, previously undisturbed, now gliding its way slowly towards the light and, by extension, her.

"Clara," Gage warned, voice strained.

"I see her," she assured him, shifting her footing to accommodate the other snake's approach.

"Quite the hero today, aren't you, love?" he asked, his lips twitching in an attempt to grin, beads of sweat trailing down from his brow to his neck.

"You're one to talk, and I can afford to be with what you're paying me," she told him, ends of her lips turning up to match his far-too-tense-to-be-real smile. Clara was trying to appear as confident as possible to keep him calm; his calm equalled his survival.

"Plus, I never pass up a chance to cross off an IOU." She almost shrugged, mimicking the snake's weaving motion with the burning light.

"Is that your extremely belated version of a thank-you for today?" he asked.

She grinned wider in an attempt to keep them both calm. "No."

"Well, there's gratitude for you."

The snake closed its mouth and weaved its way back down his leg until it was back on the floor and slithering towards Clara, drawing even with its mate.

Gage let out a visible sigh of relief, wiping his brow with the back of his sleeve whilst the danger moved steadily away from him and towards Clara.

"Go," she ordered. Gage happily turned to go to the door, trusting that if anyone knew what they doing it would be her.

Then he heard a noise that drew his attention to something above him, and he stopped; what he saw found him suddenly doubting her odds. He glanced back to her and found that doubt deepening when he noticed that her gloved hand (and injured arm) was trembling.

"That's it—follow me, pretty baby," she cooed to the venomous snakes, which approached in something of a daze, mesmerized by the fluid movement of the light.

"Getting a bit crowded in here, love."

Clara glanced up to see what he was referring to, rustling above catching her attention to see two more snakes wriggling loose from the straw roofing and climbing down the walls, drawn by the light.

She cursed under her breath; apparently it was one of *those* days. Her focus couldn't stay on them long; she had to keep her eyes trained on the nearest two threats.

That's when she also noticed that instead of getting to safety Gage was slowly drawing his cutlass.

"I said *go*, Sinclair," she ordered, taking another crouched step back to give her more time to strategize as the snakes closed in.

"Numbers are staggering a bit out of your favour, darling," Gage returned coolly, facing off against the two new poisonous reptiles.

"What kind of gentlemen would I be if I left you in a bind?" he asked, watching the two snakes weaving their way down the wall.

"A smart one?"

"Can't get out of these trees without you," he reminded her. "Also I'm fond of how you lead—fantastic view."

"Regretting saving you already," Clara answered dryly. Seeing he wasn't going to leave, she quickly gave advice, because frankly she didn't have the time to argue with him—he was a big boy.

"They're fast; wait till they rear to strike, and then take their heads."

It was reaching that point of the dance where it was do or die; one of Gage's snakes was already on the floor and fast approaching, the other moving a bit slower as it climbed down the door frame. They had a thread of a plan; it was admittedly shaky. The next five to ten seconds would see who had watched their last sunset today.

"Captain, William's wonderin'—" Peter began as he walked into the hut, oblivious to the danger he was intruding upon.

Clara felt her heart stop in that brief second—so did Gage's. His timing could not have been worse; the snake making its way down the door frame was now level with Peter's head. And he didn't see it.

Peter did the absolute worst thing he possibly could have done—he froze in the doorway. He sensed he'd walked into something but was still unsure of what.

There was a moment where Gage and Clara made the briefest of eye contact, half of a split second where it was perfectly understood and agreed upon exactly what the other was going to do.

It happened so fast it would take Clara playing it through in her mind more than once to get it all straight. It seemed like a blur, like everyone had been waiting on a cue and every creature got it at the same time.

Clara struck out with her blade and sliced the closest snake's head clean off just as the light on her glove burnt out, tucking into a roll, and barely avoiding the fangs that tried to bury themselves in her throat.

At the same time, Gage's first quarry launched itself into a strike so violent it left the ground. His blade flicked down with an expert precision that split the creature flying at him neatly down the middle from tongue to tail.

Clara dropped the curved blade and rolled forwards just as Gage pivoted on his heel, her hand going to her wrist for her straight blade while the snake at her back followed her, mouth open wide so as to plunge its long fangs into her back.

The snake was fast; Gage's blade was faster. His steel cut through the space between them and lofted its head into the air, body hitting the floor and coiling itself into death knots. Peter had turned his head just in time to see the snake rearing back, eyes going as wide as saucers.

Clara flicked her wrist, sending the knife through the air so it was a mere flash of silver before it impaled itself through the creature's eye and speared it to the door frame.

All in the span of five seconds, flat.

For a minute, all was still. Peter stood almost as if he were immobile; his eyes never leaving the creature writhing against the door frame in its death throes, while poison dripped from its fangs onto the floor. Clara was on one knee, hand still out stretched from the follow-through of the throw. Gage was the first to move as he wiped snake blood off his blade on his boot and resheathed his cutlass.

"Excellent form," he complemented Clara, looking at the evidence of her marksmanship with a smile. "You'd take a fair share of coin at darts if you played," he remarked lightly.

Clara stood and strode over to the still-stunned Peter, grabbed him by the front of his shirt, and shoved him so hard he stumbled out of the hut and hit the railing.

This shocked both Squint and William, who were lowering down the pulley rope for Jared.

It didn't fail to take Gage by surprise either, watching as Clara yanked her blade from the wall, letting the dead snake hit the floor while sliding it back into its sheath on her wrist and following Peter out.

"What is wrong with you?!" she snarled, almost yelling.

"I-I-I'm sorry," he stuttered, everything still happening a little fast for him and not entirely sure what exactly he was apologizing for.

"You're just an idiot, is that it? That was a nest of death we were just wading through!" she snarled at him mercilessly. Clara knew deep down he'd done absolutely nothing wrong, but at that moment, she couldn't see that; all she saw was a young boy who'd been looking death in the face.

"Fox—" Gage began, coming up behind her.

"And you just walk in like you own the godsdamn place? *Are you insane?!*" Now she was yelling.

"How was I supposed to know?" he asked, sounding both alarmed and harried. She took an almost involuntary step forwards like she was going to hit Peter. And she might have, had a hand not grabbed her by her arm and held her back.

"Clara," Gage snapped in her ear, giving her one firm shake. It was almost like that shake had snapped her out of some angry trance as she blinked at Gage, watching her with a mixture of shock and sternness, an expression that clearly said he wouldn't allow her to rough up any of *his* crew.

Like that, all of Clara's anger turned into something heavier in her chest—guilt. Ripping her arm out of his grasp, she stomped back into the hut before he could see it on her face.

"Stay the hell out of here until I've cleared it, *everyone,*" she growled, not stopping to hear anyone's answer.

Gage watched her disappear into the hut before turning his attention to a bewildered Peter.

"I didn't know, Captain—" Peter tried, but Gage was already waving him off.

"Wrong place, wrong time, lad," he told him, patting his shoulder roughly. He looked back after Clara as she collected something off the floor, the bodies of the dead snakes he assumed.

"She really doesn't like me," Peter shared, sounding almost puzzled by this.

"I think you make her think of things she'd rather forget," Gage shared, still looking after her.

William approached his captain somewhat hesitantly. "Seems we've missed something exciting?"

"More or less," Gage replied.

"Shame," William commented unenthusiastically, "been incredibly dull for almost five minutes."

No one dared even ask when it would be okay for them to enter while Clara strode through the hut like an angry storm cloud, checking every nook and cranny of the place, dust and leaves flying out of the doorway with a violence that provoked a strange urge to laugh in Gage. He, however, managed to smother the impulse, assuming it wouldn't be very good for his health if Clara were to overhear him. Finally, after a solid fifteen minutes, they heard her voice call out.

"It's safe."

Everyone stumbled in from the dark of the platform's walkways to the hut to see it was now free of debris. Clara had lit a fire and had a few things roasting on a spit.

"Well," Gage started, looking about the place, "aren't you just a little homemaker?"

"It was clean or choke someone; be thankful, Sinclair," she said, throwing another piece of wood on the flames with a bit more force than necessary.

A few looks were directed at Peter and Gage, not sure which one of them she referred to. Everyone took a seat around the fire as the smell of cooking meat filled the air. It took Gage a minute or so to realize she was cooking the headless snakes they'd killed.

"How very practical of you," he said, wrinkling his nose.

She smiled sweetly at him in response. "Sensitive stomach, Captain?" she asked innocently.

"Not at all," he returned with faux pleasantness. But he wasn't going to enjoy it, and she knew it.

Clara took the spit off the fire, using the blade to cut him a generous slab before rolling it in a leaf.

"So glad to hear it," she said, holding it out to him.

Everyone was exhausted, almost too exhausted to talk. Clara gave them all a share of snake meat, though she enjoyed watching Gage hesitantly take his first bite, if only to cheer herself a little with his reluctance to admit he didn't want to eat it. She managed to give Peter his without looking at him, completely ignoring his muttered thanks.

They ate (the meat was tough and a bit rubbery but not unpleasant tasting), and then everyone laid out a roll to bed down on for the night.

Clara pushed herself into a corner not bothering to lay down any bedding. She sat propped up against the wall opposite everyone else before speaking.

"Just in case anyone gets any less than gentlemanly inclinations tonight, know I always sleep armed," she warned them. She looked to Gage who had yet to pick a spot to sleep, to be sure he took her seriously.

He met her gaze and actually surprised her by looking shocked and offended that she would think he would ever have such ungentlemanly "inclinations." His face turned inscrutable as he looked back at her, then he aimed a lethally serious expression at his men.

"And know if she does not succeed in using that weapon to kill you, *I* will see to it your tied to a tree and left for whatever ungodly critters that hanker for human flesh."

No one replied, but it was clear by their expressions everyone was on the same page. Gage nodded when he saw all was understood before meeting her eyes once more, a promise in his gaze to Clara that he would never allow something so vulgar to pass under his watch.

All she found she could do was blink back at him as he situated himself directly across from her, settling in for the night.

"We go at first light," she told him. He nodded, lying down, eyes watching her for a minute in the crackling light of the fire's dying embers.

"Yes?" Clara sighed, sounding tired.

"Nothing," he replied, sounding at ease.

"Good." Clara crossed her arms gingerly, and with a bit of difficulty, she coaxed herself into closing her eyes.

Eight

She sat like that for some time, watching the crew through slit eyelids and pretending to sleep. When she was sure everyone had dropped off, she quietly got to her feet, her soft leather boots making no noise as she tiptoed past Gage. She paused only a moment to look down at him, eyes flickering to that securely latched front pocket of his. A small part of her wanted to peek inside, but a larger part seriously doubted that was a good idea. So Clara made for the door, sweeping the netting from her path and exiting the hut onto the walkway.

She sat down so her feet hung over the edge and carefully rolled up the sleeve on her injured arm and sighed.

Just as she'd thought—all the way up her arm, along the bruise lines from where the creature had latched onto her, were about thirteen or fifteen red stingers with sharp little heads digging into her flesh. Like most things, the plant creature had venom, but it only used it against other predators, and it wasn't lethal to humans; it merely caused immobility and pain.

She hadn't bothered to check for stingers, as most often she was not considered a predator. Clara was actually kind of flattered. She had figured earlier on as the pain in the arm worsened that maybe she'd got stuck with a few. Since she didn't tend her wounds in front of clients, she'd had to wait; she liked to maintain the illusion she was untouchable.

Everyone was asleep now, so once she pulled all the stingers out, most of the pain would go away, she'd regain mobility, and she'd just have to deal with the bruising; no one would be the wiser.

"Those look like some nasty bits of work," a voice commented softly. *For fuck sakes...*

Clara looked back to see Gage standing in the threshold, watching her.

"And you're still here; guess that means I counted the coin out right," he added.

"You're supposed to be asleep," she told him, turning away.

"I was, but I'm a light sleeper," he said, crossing to her side. Clara tried to roll down her sleeve covertly before he could get a better look.

"Ah, ah, ah," he tutted, reaching down to pull the sleeve back up. "That needs to be taken care of, love," he told her. She pushed his hand away with an annoyed glare.

"Let me help."

"Go back to bed, Sinclair; long day ahead of you tomorrow," she said as a way of declining.

He shook his head like he wasn't letting her off that easy, sitting down next to her. "Let's see it," he said, holding his hand out for her arm.

"It's fine," she lied stubbornly, refusing the help and attempting again to roll the sleeve down. However Gage apparently was not letting this go.

"Come now," he said, reaching over and gently swatting her hand away, his attempt at showing his sincere offer of help. "We both know it's not," he finished. He fixed her with a stare that clearly said either way she chose he wasn't leaving, so she would be fool to dismiss his aid.

As tempted as she was to shove him away, the move felt more than a little childish. If he wasn't leaving either way she may as well make use of an extra hand. Slowly, she offered her arm to him.

He gripped her gently around the wrist and pulled it closer to better examine. "Hmm, they're in deep. Might be a touch difficult to free them," he said, his black-gloved hand with that foreign silver gauge shining in the moonlight reaching for the first stinger.

Clara tensed as she flashed back to earlier and instinctively pulled away from him, remembering the destructive power of its touch that she'd witnessed today. She'd made as little a deal about it as possible so far, part because she didn't want to know and the other because she didn't want to admit the display had unnerved her.

He frowned at her sudden withdraw from him, then seemed to realize the reason for it.

"I've no intention of harming you, Fox; I merely wish to help," he assured her. She was relieved to see that as truth, but all the same...

"I've never seen magic work in the forest; that must be some spell."

"It is."

Clara frowned. Why did that ring untrue? "Wait," she said, glance at his gloved hand.

"It's not a spell, is it?" Clara knew very little about magic, but she felt she'd hit the nail on the head here.

"Enchantment?" she guessed, vaguely recalling there was apparently some differences between spells and the like.

His face remained completely impassive at the question. "As I've said, it can only be used sparsely. I must choose my moments wisely; I have full control of it."

He held out his hand for her arm again, but she still held it away from him. If it wasn't an enchantment, then what the hell was it? He sighed and raised the hand to his mouth, grasping the glove with his teeth and pulling it off before dropping it in his lap. "Satisfied?"

Clara nodded, allowing him to gently take her wrist and pull her arm back over to him, noticing as he did that his middle finger appeared to be stiffer and less mobile than it had before. He grasped the end of the first stinger and pulled it out, making Clara gasp.

"Ow!"

"Come, don't be a child."

"Yes, ever the gentleman, I see," she answered sarcastically.

"Always," he replied flirtatiously.

Normally she wouldn't have allowed this at all, but he was surprisingly gentle as he went on plucking each stinger out. The poison had made it a chore to move the arm, true, but despite the fact that she could do most of this herself, for some reason she let him continue, watching his progress with as neutral a face as she could manage. What was he up to?

"So magic isn't supposed to work here?" he asked absently, like he was just making conversation. She doubted Gage ever "just made conversation" with anyone.

"Not the big kinds, really small healing charms at best. I've seen a locator spell fizzle out like someone snuffing out a candle at the cutline," Clara shared.

She saw his eyes start to look at his front pocket, but he seemed to catch himself, quickly refocusing back on her arm. So his cargo was magic in nature? *Interesting.*

"How puzzling," was all the reply Gage gave her.

Clara watched his hand work carefully, still seeing only his thumb and forefinger working efficiently. Yes, whatever it was on that glove did seem to cost him, then again all magic had a cost she'd heard.

"Regardless of what magic is imbued in your glove, Sinclair, the dampening effects on magic only get stronger as we travel in. Fair warning, whatever it is in all likelihood won't work next time."

"Just as well—I have no plans to use it again," Gage said shortly. "Bit of an overreaction with Peter today," he remarked calmly, changing the subject while keeping his eyes on his work.

"He could have gotten himself killed," Clara replied defensively, choosing to stare straight ahead of her.

"Yet you weren't nearly as cross with me," he pointed out. She was too tired to dance these steps with him.

"You know if I'd hurt my other arm? He'd be dead," she said emotionlessly, letting her guard slip a bit.

"True," he admitted. "But it wasn't, and he lived," Gage reminded her. "Try not to take out your anger over... past experiences on him."

Her first impulse was violent, to yank her arm from his grip and use it to break his nose, because he had no idea what he implied. Clara realized however much that was something of an overreaction because he really only had only an inkling of her past, and he'd at least attempted to phrased it delicately. This situation should not be getting under her skin so much; it was dangerous. Clara knew she'd been unfair; every time she looked at Peter she saw what *he* would have been had he...

Yes, that was very dangerous for her indeed. Gage was right; she had to detach herself from her bias. Clara actually forced herself to swallow her pride, not an easy task when it was Captain Black-Gage who made her realize she had to. After another minute of silence, she nodded.

"As it is, we seem to make one hell of a team," he continued on, mercifully changing the subject again.

"When we're not trying to play one another, we do." Her candour and casual tone about their "relationship" if you will put him a bit off balance.

"What makes you think I'm trying to play you?" Gage asked after a moment.

"You must be kidding," she replied dryly.

"Not everything I do is a calculated move, Fox." He appeared sincere, but they both knew appearances could be deceiving.

She chuckled, not buying the line. "Oh, don't bother, I know where I stand with you; it's why you don't bother me."

"Is that so?" he asked, feeling the competitive beast in him stir at the unintentional invite of a challenge from her.

"Quite so," she answered, sounding almost bored.

That irked Gage; that irked him to a maddening degree.

"I think you're just a sore loser," he said casually.

"I'm sorry, sore loser?" she asked incredulously. "Exactly when did I lose *anything*?" she demanded angrily, the uncaring demeanour evaporating.

"Just now, when you lost your cool," Gage told her with a cocky grin.

She blinked, caught off guard by the words, mischievous glint in his eyes all but singing "got you." What was it about this man that he could get under her skin with a snap of his fingers?

"Cute," she said after a moment. He pulled out a stinger that was fairly deep, and she let a breath hiss out between her teeth.

"Ow," Clara spat, glaring at him.

"You come up with a name for that beastie yet?" he asked, ignoring her in favour of examining the stinger he'd just pulled.

"Yeah—a Blue Cap," she told him instantly. Gage gave her a puzzled look.

"The creature had no blue on it," he pointed out.

"I know. Just William has a blue cap, and it tried to eat him." She shrugged with her one shoulder. "The beastie is named in his honour," she explained with a nod to the hut where he and the others slept.

Gage chuckled. "I'm sure he'll be thrilled to have left his mark." There was silence again for a time before he decided he wanted to continue talking. "Is it always this hot at night in the forest?" he asked her out of the blue.

"This isn't hot," Clara assured him, "but yes, it's never much cooler than this."

"And that would be why I prefer the ocean life."

It was then that a question that Clara had always wanted to ask a pirate came to mind, one she never asked because she preferred not to make casual chitchat with most of her clients. However, as she let him take care of her arm, she found herself blurting it out.

"What's the ocean like?"

Gage's expression was one of disbelief. "You've never seen the ocean?"

"I've seen it from afar," Clara said quickly, "but I've never gotten close enough to touch it." Gage watched her face as she said this and saw a little longing.

"Longing for the pirate life, are you, lass?" he asked with a note of teasing in his voice.

"Ha, no," she said, shaking her head, "just curious about it is all."

"Well," he began, tossing another stinger over the rail, "the ocean has a rhythm all her own, nothing like it. You best have your wits about you when you sail her back because she's a temperamental mistress; she's tossed me and beat me against the beach more than once—and that's about as merciful as she gets."

Gage could tell she was trying not to show how his words drew her in, and inwardly he felt like grinning; lass loved a tale apparently.

"One minute you're sailing with the sun on your face, and the next she'll buck and be trying to crush you or swallow you whole. But the prizes for surviving her wrath? It's freedom out there; it's adventure and a challenge. If you live on the sea, it's because you earn it," he said, feeling a sense of pride fill him about the life he led and the continued challenge of trying to master it.

He looked out like he could see it, as if it was the wide expanse of water in front of him instead of the forest. She could almost see the moon reflected in waves swelling and crashing behind those pale blue eyes. There was something powerfully mesmerizing in that expression of his...

"I can relate," Clara said, staring off with him into the trees.

"I've no doubt; it's a daring life you lead, Clara Fox," he said, pulling another stinger from her arm.

"I'm definitely not well acquainted with boredom," she admitted, letting that little half smile he doubted she knew she was wearing climb onto her face once more.

"Are the legends true?" he asked in an overly dramatic whisper. "Did the Guide truly grow up in the dreaded Dark Forest?"

"Wouldn't you love to know?" she asked with that mischievous "I'll never tell" look in her eyes.

"Well, aren't you mysterious?" Gage mocked before adding, "You must have some powerful gods watching over you if it's true."

"Who knows, don't really think about them very much."

"Not a believer of the gods?" he asked.

Clara shrugged. "Like I said, I don't really give gods much thought. They have the heavens and I have my life—just don't really see how they intersect, I suppose."

Gage stared at her a moment. She grew more interesting by the word, and she'd been fascinating to start with.

"A women who tempts death, the fates, and favours no gods, living in her scary forest," he said, his tone a mixture of the melodramatic and a kind of playfulness. "Can't say I understand that last bit."

"Why?"

"Don't get me wrong, I understand guiding others through it; you have a rare profitable skill," he acknowledged. "But why *live* in this place?" he asked, gesturing to their surroundings with a sweep of his arm.

"Perhaps this forest is my ocean," Clara answered with a half shrug.

"Is it now?"

"My forest, your ocean—bit like our versions of lovers, aren't they?" she asked.

He gave her a blank stare and she shook her head before gazing out at the lush forest that was blanketed in the hues reserved only for the night.

"Abstract, Sinclair; they can be cruel but they always let us know when they're about to rise up and unleash all hell. They've taught us to save ourselves, and that's a hell of a gift in this world." At this, she looked away from the trees and back at him, eyes meeting his.

"They're ours, and we're theirs. It's us and them, and we prove we can ride their very worst; from that, we reap strength and see their solitary wonders." The way she'd looked out over those trees was still lingering in her eyes, like she'd found the rarest of treasures in these pits of hell she called home. She seemed to him in that moment as something close to ethereal, moonlight softening all her edges, turning blazing fire gold hair into soft smoldering embers that fell over her shoulders, her skin aglow, green eyes playing with the light so they reflected all the shades of the forest. *Who are you, Clara...?*

"Sounds like a dangerous love life," he observed after a moment.

"Affairs like these always are," Clara answered, almost wistfully.

For some strange reason, it was then that Gage realized she was lonely. She hid it well of course, better than most even, but there it was. The thing about Clara, he'd noticed, was you could tell what she was hiding by how she tried to hide it. Despite her "don't give a rat's ass" attitude, Clara Fox was lonely. Half of him was strangely more intrigued by this revelation into the enigma that was her. His other more pirate half was wondering if this was his opening...

His fingers trailed down her arm to her hand, thumb rubbing slow circles on the back of her hand. Her eyes flickered down to his hold on her and then up to him, looking... curious.

"Not all lovers are so rough or demanding," Gage told her softly, sincerely. "Some offer comfort instead of tests."

Clara remained silent, simply watching his face. He held her eyes for a long moment before he leaned into her, slowly, coming closer inch by inch, bright blue eyes fixing on her lips as he did. His face was only a few inches from hers before he stopped, holding, waiting for her to close that last inch between them, the tension staggeringly high...

But Clara didn't close it—she laughed. Gage actually jumped a little, shocked by the sound and the sudden obvious amusement in her eyes.

"Wow," she said before laughing again. "I'm sorry, did you really think that would work?" she asked tilting her head with amusement still glowing behind her eyes.

Gage let his more natural devilish smile work its way onto his face to cover the fact that he was frustrated, before pulling back with a shrug. Gods, he'd never been outright *laughed* at before.

"Well, figured it was worth a try," he replied roguishly. Seducing her should not be this difficult; strangely he found himself appreciating this annoying fact, enjoying it even.

Little did he know her heart had been in her throat, and Clara was doing her best to slow it down and not let it show. He might have had her, but she saw it for what it was when he'd begun to lean in, calculating.

"Of course you did; bastards always do."

He put his hand on his chest, as if she'd wounded him. "Ouch, love," he pouted with an exaggerated frown, hand releasing hers as he pulled the last stinger from her arm.

"Ow!" she punched his arm. "You're an asshole," she growled when Gage laughed, pulling a flask from his side.

"I think you'd be suspicious if I were anything otherwise."

"So true," she admitted with that hard crooked smile of hers. The stingers gone, no longer pumping their venom into her muscles, left her arm feeling almost light with the lack of pain, she sighed with relief.

"What are you doing?" she asked when she saw him use his teeth to pull the cork from the top and let it drop so it was hanging by a bit of string.

"You have your balms; I have mine." He poured a stream of amber liquid down her arm and washing away a few thin streams of blood.

"Ahhh! What the hell!" she hissed between clench teeth. She tried to pull her arm away, but his hand around her wrist kept it where it was.

"Easy, lass. Don't want these to get infected," he chided.

"You'd waste rum on me?" Clara asked, eyes clenching shut as the alcohol burned. "I'm flattered," she managed to add sarcastically as he released her.

"Don't be; I lifted it off Jared," he confessed to her sardonically. Clara just stared at him silently for a moment before just shaking her head.

"Of course you did. You're a pirate to the bone, Sinclair," she muttered.

"Thank you, milady," he said with a playful cordial nod of his head. Gage used his teeth to recork the flask before using what looked like a handkerchief to dab her arm dry. A silence filled the space between them again, by no means uncomfortable, which is why he was surprised when she decided to break it.

"Can you swim in it, or is it too dangerous for that?" Clara asked suddenly.

"Sorry?" Gage asked, thrown by the abrupt change of topic and mood.

"The ocean," she said slowly, as if hoping he'd catch up.

He answered her after a brief pause, one eyebrow raised. "Of course you can swim in it; most of the time it's safe." Why was she talking about the ocean again?

"Most of the time?" she repeated skeptically.

"Always risks, lass." He shrugged. "You have a desire to swim the great blue?"

"Maybe... I mean, I don't know if I can."

"Can what?" Gage asked, unsure of her meaning.

"Swim," she admitted. "I've never tried."

He realized then that she was trying to keep the conversation going. It seemed Clara disliked comfortable silence between them, of all people, but he could see it wasn't as simple as that either. Whether she realized it or not, Clara was drinking in the human contact he figured she so often denied herself.

"No lakes or lagoons to practice in?" he asked, obliging her.

"Would you swim in one of the Dark Forest's ponds or lagoons?"

Lass had a point. "Not even if you paid me," Gage admitted.

"You are paying me, and even then I wouldn't," she said with an exaggerated shudder before smiling slyly.

"Well, an interesting first try it should make either way," he said, dabbing the last of the rum from her arm.

"I can only imagine," she agreed.

Gage looked at her a bit expectantly as he finished tending her arm. It took her a minute to realize what he was after.

"Awaiting my thanks?" she asked with one brow arched.

"It is customary after someone lends you assistance of some kind, yes," Gage replied innocently.

Ha—that's funny. "I only thank people who help me out of some kind of genuine desire to help—not people who use injury as an opportunity to get under my skin." She gave him a pointed look.

"Didn't start that way," he said. "But I take the only openings you afford me, love, to further divine the woman I'm dealing with," Gage prodded with a smile.

"Then I guess I'll forever remain a mystery," she sighed.

"Don't pretend you don't find it occasionally entertaining to engage in the game."

"You wish." Yet despite that stunt earlier she was still begrudgingly... enjoying his company. *Careful, Clara,* she thought to herself, *don't let him inside your guard.*

Clara looked at Gage's arm as he pulled away and spotted something unusual on the back of his wrist, normally covered by his glove. A smallish tattoo, no bigger than a silver piece. It looked like a dove, a banner draped across its wing with a name...

"Anna?" she read out loud, not thinking anything of doing so.

Gage's muscles stiffened as he froze in the middle of putting his glove back on, drawing Clara's eye to his face. Just in time to see a raw vulnerability fleet through his expression, pain and anger chasing it away so fast she almost thought she'd imagined it.

A stony façade shut the emotions from his face down before she could take her next breath, his eyes now trained directly in front of him in a tense silence. Clara felt her heart in her throat for a moment as she realized she was unwittingly close to crossing the line of that unspoken truce.

She could see he was waiting, possibly with venom on his tongue if she dared toe that line, much like she had earlier. Yet she felt something when she'd caught that brief glimpse of loss and anger, like she'd saw the man behind all the swagger and games. That brief second of his humanity had caught her off guard. Only deep love could turn to that depth of... agony, of rage when it was ripped from you so unceremoniously—especially when there was someone to blame as she surely knew there was.

Unbidden, she felt a swell of genuine empathy for him in her chest, because Clara understood the gut-wrenching pain of loss... she knew it well. What she should have done was change the topic and forget the indiscretion had happened, what she'd seen. Instead she found her arm reaching out and her hand gently grasping his shoulder.

Gage looked at her at last, face a mask of stone, yet a curious glint growing in his eyes—like he was trying to figure out what exactly she was doing.

He'd been waiting to see which move she would make: leave it alone or go for it and try to use this against him somehow; because Gage was ready if she tried, just waiting for the signal to reach viciously for those wounds of hers and dig into them to hurt her back.

So when he felt her gentle touch on his shoulder, he was unsure exactly what she was doing, eyes glancing to her hand and then to her face questioningly.

Clara opened her mouth, but nothing came out. What was she doing? Why did she want to lend some comfort to him of all people? She should not give a damn, not about a bastard pirate's feelings or his loss, she thought, closing her mouth, her eyes meeting his. She found herself searching for something in them she couldn't name, didn't fully understand.

Gage watched her expression shift from an unsure look of compassion to something much like conviction as she opened her mouth to speak once more. Clara uttered seven simple words, but she said them like they were some infallible truth of the world.

"You'll get the one who did it."

His face was openly surprised and shocked. Of all the things he'd expected, empathy and rallying assurance had been the furthest thing from his mind. Both were silent for a second, caught in possibly the most unexpected moment of sincerity either had faced in some time.

Clara pulled her hand back, not sure if she'd overstepped their careful boundary. Whether she had or not, she'd lost her nerve to find out, getting to her feet with a swift ease.

"Good night, Sinclair," she said quickly, hurrying away from him and into the hut, making a retreat as it were.

Gage stayed put, thrown off balance and unsure of how to react to what had just happened, her words ringing in his head. *Careful, Lucas,* he thought to himself as he looked after her, *don't let her inside your guard.*

Nine

Clara was asleep, or some kind of in-between as she usually was when she slept in the forest, when she felt a hand reaching for her. Years of sleeping in the dangers of these trees had trained her to feel the very disturbance of air around her. Her hand shot up and gripped a wrist before the offending hand could touch her shoulder, making the person gasp.

"Peter," Clara said calmly, eyes still closed, "if you wish to wake me, saying my name is more than satisfactory."

"S-sorry," Peter apologized as she opened her eyes. He looked a bit haggard in the scant light of a bluing sky, sun having not yet crawled up over the horizon. She swallowed an instinctive sense of concern, squashing it as best she could. Peter was a pirate, young true, but youth should not make her less wary of that fact.

"Sun's not up quite yet; you've got another twenty minutes to sleep. I'd suggest you take it," she told him, glancing at the sky again to confirm the time.

"I... uh... I can't sleep," he said, looking down at the floor as she released his wrist.

"Nervous?" she asked, rubbing her face. Clara would very much like to be resting still, but if she had to talk to a pirate right now, she would prefer it to be Peter than Sinclair. Peter didn't answer her inquiry; he didn't really have to though—it was plain on his face. "You're safe up here: the snakes don't move much at night; nets pretty much keep everything else out," she explained quietly so as not to wake the others, trying to put him enough at ease to leave her alone.

"Yeah, yeah, of course, right," he said, agreeing quickly in the same hushed voice. He actually looked a little flustered, like he didn't know how to speak to her. Clara looked him up and down curiously; what was with this kid?

"I almost died," he said, like he'd only grasped this fact now and didn't know what else to say. Clara resisted the urge to roll her eyes; cute how he thought that was a big deal in the Dark Forest.

"Join the club," she said, suddenly in no mood to be sensitive. He seemed a little thrown by her lack of tact.

"Have I done something to personally offend you?" he asked a bit testily, that disconcerted air about him disappearing to be replaced by annoyance.

"You've woke me up to talk about feelings; I'd rather be sleeping," she told him in a biting tone, rubbing her face.

"I don't want to talk about feelings; I want you to stop treating me like a kid, Clara."

Her eyes widened by the vehemence he managed to muster into that hushed sentence. He stared hard at her, posturing once more. Ah, so Peter wanted her respect, did he? While not so subtly trying to impress her a little at the same time.

Even now she could see how he was doing his very best to show he was determined and resolved, two things Clara legitimately admired in a person. And it was in that moment she found some clarity.

Clara realized that she hated this kid a little bit. He made her think of things she didn't want to remember; they hurt too damn much. He made her heart ache. However if they were to continue forwards successfully, apparently this had to be resolved. This should prove interesting.

"All right," she said, sitting up and giving him her full attention. "Show me what you got, Peter. Why should I?" She'd give him his shot; everyone deserved one.

"I've been sailing with the captain for a year now. I've faced death and fought for my life just as many times as the rest of these pirates you consider adults. You may not like me or want me here but I am, so... so deal with it and treat me like everyone else."

Clara narrowed her eyes at how very bold he suddenly was and felt her smile sharpen dangerously while he tried to look unfazed by it.

"Look at you, putting on your big boy pants," Clara said derisively, testing him.

To his credit, Peter ignored the taunt, a feat she would not have thought a sixteen-year-old testosterone stress ball capable of. He stared at her, waiting for her reply as she weighed out this new side of him. He'd attempted no heroics as of yet; he hadn't been overly insolent, and he was standing his ground against her.

Begrudgingly she admitted that was worthy of some of her respect; at last, she gave a nod of her head.

"All right. You're tougher than I gave you credit for, Peter."

He almost smiled, then he tried to cover it with a cough.

"Now as I would everyone else here, you get fresh with me again and I will kick your ass. Clear?"

He actually did smile this time. "Crystal." Well, that hadn't been... *so* terrible, had it?

"Okay, good, right. Now that that's, uh, solved I just wanted to... apologize for... upsetting you," Peter said, suddenly almost shy, looking up at her through his lashes as that uncertain air about him returned.

His yo-yo from confident to unsure was almost jarring, but his sentiment was what caught her off guard. Gratitude, she was good at reasoning away and deflecting because she was being paid for her services. Apologies were new territory. It made Clara feel bad, because he hadn't done anything terribly wrong except for being young really. Dammit, there were those biases again.

"Don't... don't worry about it," she sighed, patting his arm, trying to put aside that animosity and make a connection with the kid that wasn't hostile. Then something occurred to her. "Is there a reason you didn't want to come through the forest?" she asked, reflecting upon his earlier remark. *If we go, we all go willingly...* had Gage been talking about Peter?

His eyes flickered to the side for just a moment before going back to her. The hesitancy was carefully noted by Clara.

"The fact that everything in here wants to kill us all isn't enough?" he asked. That actually made her laugh a little.

"I suppose it is."

He smiled back, and he looked so young again it hurt. *Adult, Clara, one year as a pirate.*

"I'll get you all through," she assured him, looking into his eyes and smiling softly with her hand still on his shoulder. Why did he look flustered again? His face was getting kind of red—oh crap. Sixteen and crushing. This was awkward.

She found herself glancing at Gage, who had come in from the walkway much later than her, hoping he was really asleep and not lying there listening to everything.

When she glanced back, Peter was leaning in, eyes closed as if to kiss her. Sixteen, crushing, and going for it—suicidal consequences be damned. Clara would admit her reaction was just a bit overzealous. She palmed his face before he could come closer and shoved.

Peter went tumbling ass over teakettle backwards and crashed into the burnt-out logs in the middle of the room causing a loud commotion.

Everyone was suddenly in a flurry of movement, startled by the crash and flailing awake. Gage was sitting straight up, his cutlass drawn and ready to impale the first threat he saw.

Only to see there was no threat, just Peter covered in ash scrambling to get to his feet while Clara stood and stared at the boy incredulously.

"The hell!" Jared grunted, trying to untangle himself from his bedding.

"Up and at 'em, boys," Clara said loudly, like this was exactly how she intended to wake them all. Gage's eyes went to Peter, whose face was so red he looked like a tomato that wanted to go crawl under a rock, then back at Clara who was looking a tad bewildered and a bit angry.

"Everything all right?" he asked carefully.

"Yeah," Clara said, off balance and not knowing what to think, had that been harsh? He did say he wanted to be treated like everyone else, she'd have given anyone else hell for that. That thought made Clara smirk a touch, careful what you wish for. "Everything's fine. I'm gonna go gather breakfast. We leave in fifteen." She disappeared out the door before he could ask her anything else.

Peter brushed the ash off him, tried to grab his stuff, and slip away to pack it far from everyone else much like Clara had. Unfortunately Gage was on his feet now, grabbing him by the collar of his shirt and yanking him back.

"And just where are you going, lad?" he asked, narrowing his eyes

"I... uh..."

"What did you do?" Gage demanded through clenched teeth. He did not need the boy straining their relations with the woman keeping them all alive, and he'd given a caveat which he fully intended to follow through with should it be necessary. Peter refused to look at him, eyes shooting to the other crew members, who were watching curiously.

Gage didn't fail to notice this either. "I need new boots, and I'm not afraid to skin one of you lot to get them; we move in ten—pack!" he snarled.

Suddenly everyone was very busy, pulling their things together and getting their boots back on.

Gage pulled Peter a little farther from the rest of the crew none to gently and glared at him, awaiting his answer. As softly as possible, Peter slowly told him.

"We were talking and, there was... a second, and I thought what the hell... I thought she liked me."

"Straight answer, lad. Now."

"I... I went in for a kiss, I'm so sorry, Captain. Please don't tie me to a tree and leave me here," Peter begged, sweat breaking on his brow.

At first, Gage was stunned, and then he was pissed. He really didn't like that Peter had tried to kiss Fox for some reason. Then he remembered that Peter was sixteen and had been shoved into the burnt-out fire place for his troubles and he found himself laughing. This served only to embarrass Peter even more.

"Lad," he said, letting his shirt collar go and shaking his shoulder as he chuckled, "that was ballsy, and it seems she's satisfied by how she dealt with you."

Peter gave a half smile, shoulders relaxing as he let out a relived breath. Gage's face sobered in the next instant as he looked at Peter, whose relief turned to alarm once more by his Captain's sudden mood change.

"But Fox is off-limits, Peter. The next indiscretion will be your last."

It was moments like these he remembered why people feared the great Captain Black-Gage. "Yes, Captain," he answered, almost standing at attention.

"Good. Pack your roll," Gage ordered, letting him go with a slight push forwards to get him going.

Gage went looking for her, done packing before the rest of his crew. She wasn't on the walkway in the orange rays of first light, and when he looked down to see if she was on the ground, all he saw was her pack slumped against a tree. He slipped his foot into the stirrup of one of the pulley ropes and stepped off the platform.

His descent was smooth, bending his knees slightly when his boots hit the ground. He gave the rope a tug and watched as it rolled its way back to the top of the tree and found himself wondering how long it had taken her to build this whole setup.

Gage strolled over to the tree where her pack was and looked up to see her, that fascinating fire-gold hair still a bit tussled, green cloak thrown over her shoulder so the hood was open like a bag on her chest, allowing her to drop the brown pieces of fruit she was picking into it, keeping her hands free.

Gage knew she knew he was there even as she refused to look at him. He could feel something different about her attempt to ignore him; usually it was out of exasperation or some sort of disdain, this felt almost... awkward. They both knew why—last night something had changed.

Clara was waiting for him to say something so she would know where they stood. He for one would rather forget anything had happened; he couldn't afford for things to change between them, for it to be anything more than their little game.

"Sun's barely up, and I hear you're already breaking hearts, Fox," he called up to her. "I must admit I've never seen a turn down quite like that," he went on when she looked down at him, surprised by his teasing tone. He put one hand on his heart like she'd dealt him a blow.

"I don't mind it rough either you know," he winked.

She felt all the tension go out of her at his words; they were going to pretend her indiscretion hadn't happen. She was just fine with that.

"Near-death experiences and stress make people reckless, Sinclair. He's just a walking bag of hormones and adrenaline right now, if there had been a nicer girl in this group he'd have tried his luck there," she said, looking back to her work, still testing the waters of this conversation.

"You underestimate your draw, as he underestimated your barbs, love," he replied.

Clara shook her head and tossed him a fruit with her usual sharp smile. Gage caught it one-handed, and she turned to sit a bit more comfortably on the branch she was perched in, looking as natural there as an exotic bird.

"What's this?" he asked, examining the fuzzy, ugly brown fruit that was about as big as his palm.

"Breakfast, I call them sunrise fruit."

He looked curiously at the brown sphere for a moment, wondering how she could have possibly come to that name for such an unappealing-looking thing.

"Why?" he asked slowly.

"Take a bite and find out," Clara encouraged with a wave of her hand. He looked at her suspiciously, and she rolled her eyes at the unspoken implication.

"For the love of the gods, I'm not trying to poison you; just try it."

He examined her for another second before he took a bite out of the fruit. The texture was different than he was used to, but the flesh was so juicy it spilt down his chin, deliciously sweet and tangy with a hint of warmth much like you'd get from drinking a bit of rum.

Gage looked to where he'd bitten into the fruit to see the inside was the most vivid mixture of orange and pink he'd ever seen. Clara smirked, enjoying the surprise on his face.

"Ye of little faith," she tsked with a slight shake of her head.

"Forest of death, forgive me a little hesitancy, Fox," he replied, taking another bite.

"You, hesitant?" she asked sarcastically. "Surely not."

His expression told her he thought she was simply *hilarious*.

"You're packed," she said, noticing his compact little bag on his shoulder. Clara figured he'd just have one of his crew do that for him.

"Your powers of observation serve you well," he responded, wiping the juices from his chin with the back of his sleeve. Clara narrowed her gaze at the casual backhanded insult. He watched as her eyes flicked over his head for a brief moment before fixing back on him, the ends of her lips barely quirking upwards for a smile.

"Yours don't," she countered, pleasant tone of voice putting him instantly on edge. She gave a short high whistle and Gage felt teeth nip into his boot, yanking back hard and sending him face-first into the dirt with a grunt. He scrambled to move back from whatever it was, flipping himself over to see one blue-black eye and one amber eye looking down at him. He tried to move but Nahleese put one giant paw on his chest and pinned him to the ground under her. Gage clenched his teeth, hand moving for the grip of his cutlass when he heard a "whomping" sound, like that of wings beating the air. Confused, his gaze moved past the large head of the wolf restraining him, just as the blur of some great creature swooped over them. Nahleese raised her head to snap at claw like feet that grazed the air above them as she kept him pinned, *protecting* him Gage realized. He didn't get a chance to make out much more than the general shape of their attacker before the creature retreated back into the half-light morning shadows it had come from. Nahleese sniffed the air for a few moments before she made a snorting noise and took her heavy paw off his chest, backing away from him. Gage's heart was pounding in his chest, letting what had just happened fully sink in. That's when he heard Clara laughing.

"Oh gods Sinclair, the look on your face right now is priceless," she laughed, wiping a tear from her eye. She dropped from her tree branch to her feet, putting the cloak with its hood full of fruit on the ground as she moved to stand over him. As he looked up at her he could scarcely think of a fitting rebuke.

"You are bloody insane woman," Gage managed at last.

"Oh please," Clara said, rolling her eyes, "A 'swooper' has never laid a claw on anybody on my watch, they are not that big a deal compared to the other things in here. If you want me to lose my cool after every single attempt on our lives, *then* I'd undoubtedly be insane by now." She smiled even wider. "Besides, seeing you get knocked on your ass might just have been the highlight of my morn—"

Before her she'd finished speaking, Gage reached out with his good hand, grabbed her ankle and jerking her foot from under her. Clara yelped and fell, back hitting the ground next to him.

He laughed as she groaned. "Mine too."

"I just saved your life you dick," she wheezed, punching his arm.

"Strictly speaking that was Nahleese actually." He nodded to Nahleese, who was already standing by Clara protectively, glaring at him.

"And you said it wasn't a big deal anyways."

"Gentleman. My. Ass," Clara said, shaking her head at the ridiculousness of it all.

"I'm only human... an excruciatingly handsome one, but none the less human." They just laid there for a moment saying nothing, which should have been odd and uncomfortable but somehow managed to be neither.

"Do you always so easily shake off all your close calls, love?" he asked. She almost told him that didn't really fit her definition of a "close call" but decided that sounded a lot like bragging.

"What good does freaking out about it do anyone?" Clara countered with a shrug, reaching up to stroke Nahleese's big white head as she panted above her.

"Nothing I suppose—but people are rarely that practical."

Out of all the conversations she'd had with Gage so far this was the one throwing her the most. Every exchange they'd had had been a game on some level, minus their sincere moment last night. This one had an ease and lightheartedness to it the previous exchanges had noticeably lacked, (which considering it was coming directly after a "close call" was actually a little weird.)

When she recognized that, it scared her a little.

"Safe to return to a more vertical position?" he asked, the question something between a joke and a legit concern.

"Should be," Clara said. Gage got to his feet with ease while she chose not to move, trying to glean something about this new development from him with just her eyes. Had something fundamental truly changed between them? The thought alarmed Clara, she could only hope not. Gage turned to see her still lying there, watching him.

He bent low to offer her a hand up. Clara looked at the hand but didn't reach for it; Nahleese looked at the hand, which was by extension a bit close to her muzzle, and growled. Gage watched the wolf carefully for a moment but didn't retract the offered hand, a move that was either truly brave or truly stupid.

"She seems to have coveted a firm dislike of me," he noted, almost like that confused him.

Clara shrugged, still lying flat on her back. "Don't take it personal, Sinclair, she doesn't much like anybody."

"Maybe she should try giving someone a chance," Gage suggested, pale cerulean eyes looking into her, ignoring the large wolf growling and baring her teeth as if she weren't there at all.

"That's not really in her nature anymore." She didn't mean Nahleese, but she was pretty sure they both knew that. Nothing had changed, she thought, looking at that hand offering to help her. *It's just a game,* she told herself.

"Ease up, Nahleese," Clara ordered. The wolf immediately quit growling. She reached over to grab hold of her friend's flank and pull herself up, disregarding his hand entirely.

He stepped back and lowered his arm with a grin like he'd hardly expected less. Like the wolf, Clara never let anyone get too close.

"Captain," a voice called, drawing both of their eyes to the three men descending on the pulley ropes. It was Squint, coming down with Peter and Jared. William watched their descent from the top, waiting for a rope. When they hit the ground, Peter had to reach over to keep Jared steady, hat falling off his head.

"Something's a matter with Jared," Squint said, his bad eye twitching a bit. Gage and Clara shared a brief look before they both strode over to the men trying to support Jared. The pirate was having a hard time staying on his feet; he almost appeared to be drunk.

"Has he been at his rum?" Gage demanded, not looking pleased in the slightest.

"No, Captain; he was fine five minutes ago," Peter offered, helping Jared to sit on a nearby moss-covered rock before his legs gave out, thoughtfully putting his hat back on his head.

"Did he eat anything?" Clara asked as she knelt in front of him, taking his hand and examining his fingers. He didn't pull away from her touch, but she got the feeling it was because he couldn't.

"He's foolish but he's not *that* foolish," William said, just joining the group as he stepped out of the pulley ropes stirrup.

"Jared, can you hear me?" Clara asked, checking his arms for scratches or discoloration. He didn't say anything, which prompted her to look up and examine his face.

All colour had drained from his cheeks, lips pressed into a tight line. It was his eyes that stopped her midexamination—they were cloudy, and not in the drunken poisoned way. It was as if a thin film covered his eyeballs and marred the colour of his irises; behind that film was a crisp look of terror.

"Fox," Gage said, tone tense as he noticed this change as well, "what's wrong with his eyes?"

Despite these frightening physical symptoms, she actually sighed, relieved.

"Nothing," she told Gage, standing.

"That doesn't look like 'nothing' to me, love."

"Squint, Just William—kindly hold Mr. Jared," she said politely.

Both men looked to their Captain, as if asking if it was all right to follow her orders.

"You heard the woman," Gage snapped, kicking both men into gear. Each man took hold of one of Jared's passive shoulders.

"Very firmly please," Clara instructed before she reached into another small pouch at her side, coating her fingers in a clear liquid that smelt like pure grain alcohol.

"What's wrong with him?" Gage asked, though his tone made it seem more like a demand for her answer.

"He's picked up a passenger," Clara answered cryptically, taking a handful of his hair and pulling his head forwards to expose the back of his neck. Peter and Gage took a curious step forwards to look with everyone else.

On the back of Jared's neck was a shiny, black, beetle, about the size of a man's thumb and twice as wide, six, long and fuzzy legs braced against Jared's neck.

"What the hell is that?" Peter asked, sounding a bit horrified as Clara's fingers hovered over it.

"Nightmare beetle," she answered before returning her attention to William and Squint. "Ready?"

Both gave her a nod. Clara grasped the bug firmly between her thumb, index, and middle fingers and pulled. As soon as she touched it, there was a high-pitched whining sound; she gave a sharp tug, pulling the creature off Jared's neck, leaving three, neat, needle-like puncture wounds in a vertical line to well up with blood behind.

At few moments later, Jared came to life, film retreating from his eyes as he screamed and tried to tear himself away from both men in a panic.

"I don't know! I didn't take it! Please stop!" he shouted, voice shrill with pure terror.

"It's all right, man, easy!" William said, tone strained as he tried to hold him from running into the bush. He very nearly knocked Squint to the ground trying. It took a few more seconds of struggling, but Jared stopped trying to run, gasping for air with wide, wild eyes.

"Are you with us, Mr. Jared?" Gage asked, watching his panicked crewman carefully as he seemed to realize once more where he was.

"W-w-what happened?" he stuttered, hands shaking.

"This happened," Clara said, holding the bug out as its legs waved in the air lethargically. Jared pulled back like he was afraid it was going to fly from her fingers and attack him.

"Nightmare beetle," she repeated, holding it up for everyone to see.

"Just one isn't lethal; it feeds off fear or whatever fear puts in the blood," she explained, noticing how everyone had taken the smallest of steps back from her and the bug except for Gage.

"It pumps you full of something that makes you sluggish at first, a mild paralytic. It can look like you've drank too much. Once you're fully incapacitated, that same paralytic induces horrifying hallucinations or nightmares."

She examined the bug wriggling between her thumb and forefinger as it began to make a high pitched whining sound.

"Lovely," William said coolly, a touch of disgust in his droll words.

"When it's full, it flies off, and you go back to normal, physically they're the least harmful thing in these trees." The whining noise it was making got louder as it shuddered in her fingers.

"The strain it puts on the mind however is a different story," she said, glaring at the bug.

There were white lines, almost like veins, branching out from where her fingers touched its shiny black body now, drawing Gage in closer to examine it. Clara watched him fearlessly lean in to look; she'd be lying if she said she hadn't been betting on him to flinch back like the others.

But not him. Never, Captain Black-Gage.

"What's wrong with it?" he asked with a furrowed brow.

"Salt burns leeches; alcohol does the same to these things," she explained. Clara dropped it on the ground and stepped on it, a loud crunch proceeded by silence.

Clara saw Jared watch her do it, some of the tension going out of him with it dead, but he still looked shaken. He was pale, eyes too wide and looking like he'd seen a particularly frightening ghost. She grabbed his shoulder and gave him a bit of a shake to get his attention on her.

"What you need is to stretch your legs, get your balance back before we get moving, yeah?" she said, grabbing his hand and pulling him to his feet, one hand firmly gripping his upper arm as he swayed a little.

"Let's do a lap shall we?" to the rest she said, "one last chance to check your packs, I'd take advantage of that." She nodded to Gage who returned the gesture as she began guiding Jared around the clearing, keeping one hand braced on his arm.

"I'm actually not that dizzy..." Jared said, trying to pull away from her and retain what was left of his dignity. Clara dug her nails in when he tried with a surprisingly strong grip, keeping them both moving.

"I didn't much expect you to be," she admitted, "but funny thing about Nightmare beetles—they don't usually fly alone, or this far from their nests. Not unless they pick up on something particularly attractive. Like maybe a pheromone from another nest."

They had marched as far as they could go in the clearing without trudging into the bush as she pulled him to a stop, facing him with a hard accusing look.

"Or mistake something else for a pheromone, like the scent of gun powder or gun oil."

Jared went a bit rigid, his eyes only able to hold hers for a moment or two before casting away for something else to look at.

"Anything you want to tell me, Jared?" Clara asked, voice deadly calm. Jared glanced back to the rest of the group, then he reached under his shirt, turning his body to shield the small snub-nosed flintlock pistol he drew from hiding.

Clara's hand darted forward and ripped it out of his hand, green eyes on fire, which only served to make the calm of her words more chilling.

"Do you have any idea what could have happened if we walked closer to a whole nest of those with you carrying this?"

Jared utilized some good sense and did not answer her.

"Enough of those things latch onto you and they can literally scare you to death. People could have died, in a very, very awful way, Jared. When I say to ditch something, you best fucking listen," Clara snapped under her breath, shoving the gun into a pocket of her cloak.

"The next time you decide you know best, *know* that *I* will leave you in here where your stupidity will kill only you—and I'll sleep like a baby the same night."

He tried to hide it from her, but his hands shook even as he tried to meet her gaze as though her threat didn't shake him, his face still quite pale. His gaze broke only to look back where his captain stood, eyeing them both a bit suspiciously from across the clearing.

Oh, he feared Clara all right, but she knew he feared Gage more, and he was afraid of how his Captain would chastise him next. Clara sighed, releasing his arm as she took a deep breath, rubbing her eyes. Clara was almost less inclined to deal with that drama than Jared was, the damage had been minimal to her mind anyways, thankfully.

"As it is, I think your acquaintance with Nightmare beetles was punishment enough." She saw a great tension go out of him, the simple implication she would keep this to herself a source of obvious relief.

"The gods know those visions are as close as the living get to the hells," she muttered to herself.

He flinched at her words, experience still too fresh. When he did Clara's voice softened ever so slightly.

"Sometimes the paralytic... unearths horrors of the past." He swallowed as if past a lump of ice in his throat and she knew she was right again.

"It's in the past for good, Jared." It was a small comfort to offer him, but a comfort offered where she was not obligated to do so after what he'd just pulled.

"I know," he answered, a touch bitterly. Clara decided to let his tone slide before shoving all the sunrise fruit she collected into his arms.

"Good, go hand out breakfast while I dispose of the evidence of your idiocy."

That seemed to smarten him up a bit as he walked away, juggling the fruit. Clara didn't walk far from the group to retrieve the small gun from her cloak. The metal and polished wood handle gleamed in the morning sun as it flew through the air and lost itself in the foliage.

Clara frowned at her hands, feeling some residue of the oil on her fingertips. She used an ugly-looking, little grey plant to dry it from her hands and eliminate the smell of it before rejoining the others.

"Where did you go?" Gage asked, eyeing her suspiciously as she walked past him.

"To make cookies," she answered with a big fake smile.

He frowned back as Nahleese took off ahead of Clara who gestured for the group to follow.

"Shall we?"

Ten

It was hot, the pools of sunlight that streamed through the bright green leaves of the tall trees intensifying, somehow exaggerating the smells of the mosses and undergrowth on the ground until you could practically taste it. Now in the very heart of the Dark Forest, it seemed louder, the chirping of unfamiliar birds and the sounds of unseen creatures going about their business crowded the forest, their marching and occasional chatting only adding to the little symphony. Once again, Nahleese stayed close to her, keeping the others at a bit of a distance.

But unnoticed to Clara, every now and then she'd drop back from her side and wander by Gage, examining him for a few moments with mismatched eyes before snorting and then trotting back up to Clara.

"Fox," Gage called finally after about the fifth time the wolf came to eye him up. She stopped walking and turned to address him.

"Sinclair?"

"Is there something wrong with her?" he asked, indicating Nahleese with a nod of his head.

Clara frowned, looking at Nahleese, who panted happily up at her. "She looks fine, why?"

"Nothing I suppose," Gage said slowly, watching the wolf as its tongue lolled from its mouth, eyes only for Clara.

Clara gave him a queer look before she shrugged and continued forwards.

Nahleese quit panting as soon as Clara looked away, and Gage *swore* the beast glared at him. Gage tilt his head, staring back cautiously; it unnerved him how human the wolf seemed at times. Peter made to walk past Gage, unaware of the strange standoff, the other crew members lagging behind him a little. Nahleese made that strange snorting sound at Gage as he did, startling the gangly teen to a stop, the wolf showing her teeth this time before turning to go.

"What was that?" Peter asked, watching Nahleese slink off after Clara.

"Call me crazy," he replied, "but I think that wolf is trying to pick a fight with me," Gage finished.

"Captain?"

"Keep moving, lad," he said, trekking forwards.

Clara kept a tab on Nahleese after Sinclair's odd question, wondering if perhaps Nahleese was showing some signs of injury she had failed to see; so this time she noticed when the wolf slowly peeled off from her side, turning her head ever so slightly to see exactly what she was doing. The wolf fell back slowly, foot by foot until she was trotting next to Gage, who seemed to be expecting her.

"Yes, I'm well aware you don't like me," she just barely heard Gage sneer. "For the record, I'm not terribly fond of you either." She heard the wolf make a strange half-growl, half-bark sound. Clara knew that sound; she made it when she wanted to fight something drawing too near to the group.

Or when she was testing someone she was jealous of. She'd made that noise with Clara when they first met for three months before they'd made peace and become friends. Clara turned on her heel, shocked by the behaviour towards Gage of all people.

"Nahleese!" she scolded. Instantly the wolf's head dipped down low to the ground, as if ashamed she'd been caught.

"Get up here," Clara spat through clenched teeth, pointing in front of her. Gage grinned mockingly at the wolf, watching her sulk towards Clara.

"One shit disturber is enough for this group, don't you think?" she asked coolly when the white wolf stood in front of her.

Nahleese didn't look up from her paws, ears laid back against her head. Clara pointed ahead of her and whistled; the wolf made a chuffing noise and trotted ahead of the group with a moody flick of her tail.

Good gods, jealous of *Gage*? That wolf needed her head checked.

"Your friend's a bit hostile today," Gage remarked as he walked up beside her.

"She's always moody," Clara lied. He watched her face as she said this, a crooked smile pulling at his lips.

"Lie." Her eyes widened a touch, somewhat caught off guard by him calling her on it.

"Terribly annoying, isn't it?" he asked her dryly.

Clara smiled brightly before she flipped him off.

"Ooo, guess Nahleese isn't the only one who's a bit moody, is she, love?" he called after her as she walked away. He easily caught up to her again and kept pace with her.

"So what were you and Jared having such a hushed exchange about this morning?" he asked. Clara had been waiting for this question awhile now.

"Tips on how to properly cook a snake," she answered dryly, eliciting a single chuckle from him.

"All right, keep your little gossiping secrets, love." He wasn't terribly worried about their short chatter anyways.

Now that the wolf was off scouting ahead and not chasing away anyone who got too close to her, it seemed like the perfect opportunity to work on Clara. Her words from the other night still rung in his head every so often, and it bothered him. She was just a challenge.

It was only a game.

Straight flirting wasn't proving very effective to get past her guard. Romance was out as well; he could see now soft tactics were not something that would work on her. No, Fox was too clever for that, too sharp. He couldn't dig into her defenses; he needed to draw her out. As Gage reasoned out his approach, he found himself somewhat surprised by his eagerness in the pursuit of her. Clara's unmatched ability to tally him step for step in this game provided an intrigue he'd not encountered in anyone for a very, very long time.

"I couldn't help but notice your necklace earlier," Gage began, looking at the black cord that held the beautiful, violet pearl around her neck.

Her hand reached up to touch it, but she stopped herself and forced her hand back down, not answering the observation. *Interesting...*

"A beautiful trinket for a beautiful woman," he continued with a frisky grin, expecting her to roll her eyes since she was so used to this approach. Instead she looked at him guardedly, like she was trying to figure out what angle he was coming at her from. *Don't underestimate her,* he reminded himself, she was not the ordinary mark in any sense of the term.

"But you don't strike me as one to buy yourself jewellery." He watched for her reaction, keeping his gaze casual. She said nothing, keeping her face blank, a marker in and of itself that she was trying to hide something.

"Thought not—your lover bought it for you." It wasn't a question; he said it like it was a fact. A brash assumption.

"What?!" she sputtered. She almost laughed, stunned by how far off the mark he was. "No, he didn't!"

"Of course he did," Gage insisted, rolling his eyes as if Clara was being ridiculous for denying it.

"I don't *have* a lover," she informed him, sounding aggravated.

"Bet it was the contact. Fitz wasn't it?" Gage continued like she hadn't spoken at all. "The way he was all in charge and protective of his woman," he went on, as if it all made sense now, almost making her jaw drop at his sheer arrogance.

"I suppose he was some semblance of handsome," he continued, not sounding impressed by the man as he recalled him. "I mean, he's not me, but who is?" Gage shrugged.

"Fitz is not my lover; I don't take *lovers*." Clara said the word like it was dirty. "He's my friend, he has been for years, and thank the gods he isn't you," she finished with a glare.

She shook her head; after so many spot-on observations, it surprised her how wrong Gage had read into that one.

"Thank the gods indeed," Gage agreed, moving a step closer to her as they walked. "I don't want to be your *friend*." She was giving him things about herself he could work with now, and she didn't even realize it.

"Good, you'll never even get that far." Lonely with a disdain for love; this one had been burnt.

"How sad, to have never loved anyone," he remarked, watching her from the corner of his eye. Her green eyes briefly flickered down, so fast he almost missed it.

"Not at all."

Liar, he thought. For some reason, he felt a little twinge in his heart at the small revelation, to be burnt so bad that you wouldn't even admit it could have been love was... something approaching tragic. Gage caught the feeling and did his best to quash it; he was trying to get under her skin, not let her under his.

"Fitz," he said, as if the name tasted bad in his mouth to move the conversation along. "What kind of name is that anyways?"

"Like you can talk, Captain *Black-Gage*," she replied, taking a semi-playful, wholly sarcastic jab at him. Inside he grinned; he was in.

Wow, Clara thought, *way, way off base*. She inwardly laughed to herself; he was really losing his—

Wait.

She sobered instantly as she went over the exchange they'd just had in her head... That devious prick—of course his assumptions were going wide from the mark, so she would feel the need to *correct* him, telling him what he wanted to know about her.

He was using her pride against her, and she'd gone for it; Clara had actually taken the bait. She felt like walking off the path to go smash her face into one of the trees she'd gone past, instantly furious with both herself and him. But Clara had caught on now and better late than never.

"So no lovers, then," Gage said, unaware the game was changing under his nose, "explains why you like the game. You don't... *play* enough." He lingered on the word "play" like it was inherently naughty.

It was true that Clara had had only a few partners in her life, and only one had been emotionally intimate—she didn't like letting people get too close anymore.

"I get the feeling you *play* enough for the both of us," she replied with the same emphasis.

"Practice makes perfect, love." He shrugged, moving a little closer so their arms were touching as they walked.

"So how good are you at the game, Sinclair?" she asked, her tone a touch curious and almost... teasing.

"No complaints from other players," he assured her with a wicked smile.

"You care for any of them?" Clara asked casually, not returning the smile. He could feel the trap in that question.

"I never choose a partner unless something special is there," he said somewhat evasively, though honestly as well, trying not to sound as casual; he didn't want to lose her now.

"And what something would that be?" she asked, sounding amused. He fixed her with a roguish look; Gage smelt an opening.

"I'll tell you," he said, "if you let me whisper it in your ear." He watched her raised brow climb a little higher as she looked at him.

"Why?" she asked a bit warily, yet still looking a little intrigued. Gage couldn't help but notice that wasn't a no. He tried to not let his smile widen; he had her.

"Because it's a secret, Fox," he said, like that was the most obvious reason in the world. He made a ridiculous show of looking around as if to make sure no one saw them; it almost made her laugh, as he no doubt hoped it would. He pulled her aside a mere two steps, moving them temporarily out of view of the others behind a tree.

She didn't resist, even when he moved her so her back was to the tree, him cradling the space before. He briefly looked around the edge of the tree to check how far the others way, a bit dramatically, an attempt at getting her to further drop her guard with a bit of humour.

She was smirking when he looked back at her, still looking relaxed. Carefully, he leaned in to test his ground, teasing as he used his damaged hand to brush away a lock of her reddish-gold hair.

Clara didn't pull away as his breath tickled her neck and his lips hovered millimetres away from her ear. There was no tension in her at all, no signs of discomfort at having him so close, it emboldened him enough to slip his arm very carefully and slowly around her waist as he breathed into her ear.

"I look for the passion in them, Fox. That is something too precious and rare to ignore."

Clara felt that whisper, hot and intimate on her skin, raising the hair on the back of her neck. She didn't push him away, and he knew if she wanted to she would have.

Gage cautiously pulled her closer to him, in such a way that it was almost unnoticeable but most definitely happening.

Clara glanced away, around the tree to see William and Peter deep in conversation, a little ways away still but quickly approaching. Jared and Squint weren't far behind them.

She was drawn out of this observation by the gentle feel of his teeth nipping her ear to regain her attention, sending the strangest shock-wave right through to her core, making her draw a surprised gasp. *Pay attention, Clara.*

He heard the sharp breath and gently pulled her even closer until she was almost against him and still she didn't stop him. Gage pulled his head back to look at her face and see if it revealed anything. At the look in her eyes, curious and just a little unsure, he felt a leap of victory in his heart.

What surprised him then was that wasn't the only thing he felt, something else was filling him then... It almost felt like desire.

Just a game? A small voice murmured in the back of his mind as he dipped his head in to press his lips to hers...

Inches away from completing the kiss, Gage felt something sharp press against his stomach. He froze, eyes flickering down to see her hand holding that wickedly sharp blade she kept sheathed at her waist, threatening to spill his guts on both their boots with a flick of her wrist.

His eyes moved back up to her face, gone was the wide-eyed look of someone be-spelled by charm, now Clara's defiant green eyes were smug and just a touch cool.

"Do you know what your problem is, Sinclair?" she asked him in a whisper that touched his mouth.

"You don't play the game enough with other players; you're too busy with the pawns," she told him, moving her face that much closer to his so she was almost saying her words into his mouth.

"So much so you've forgotten when an opening is too easy to be right." Her smile held just as much potential to cut as her blade when she pulled back, a touch of anger in it that he thought she would be so easy to work.

He'd lost her sooner than he'd thought, and his expression hardened. A part of him was furious that she'd bested him, angry that he'd let *her* pull *him* in to make this point. The other half of him? Perversely excited, because he had no idea what she was going to do next.

Clara could have simply shut him down—true—done away with the theatrical threat, but he could see she very much wanted him to understand her, and she obviously felt something dramatic would better get her point across.

"I. Am. Not. A. Pawn." Clara enunciated each word very deliberately, her eyes two green flames in her face.

It was a fire to match in his blue eyes, and enough potential to burn them both. He damn well better learn this lesson the first time round with her; she didn't make a habit of repeating herself.

What angered Clara the most was that she did want him a little (just a little), and she couldn't have that; it was too much of a risk.

Little did she know the same thought was running through Gage's head at that moment.

"Of course not," he said, pulling his head back with a cheeky nod. She stepped out of his arms, resheathing her blade at her waist just as William and Peter passed the barrier of the tree and looked their way, on the cusp of catching them in the act of the precarious embrace.

William's intent eyes bounced between Clara and Gage, instantly sensing something off; he didn't miss how Clara's hand was just straying from the hilt of her blade. He glanced back at his captain with a cautious question in his eyes.

Gage responded with an almost imperceptible shake of his head.

William met Clara's stare with his hazel eyes, slightly narrowed, a bit less friendly.

"Problem?" Clara asked coolly when he still said nothing.

"No, Just William, Miss Clara, remember?" he answered.

William might not talk much, but he was apparently something of a smartass when he did. Peter just stood there, totally clueless to the subtext of their exchange.

"Are we stopping?" Peter asked, sounding hopeful as he dabbed at the sweat running down his brow with his sleeve. The hopeful anticipation in his question managed to break some of the tension between them all, drawing her attention off the first mate.

"Not yet," she sighed to Peter, turning to continue on.

Peter groaned with disappointment before he forced himself to follow her. Gage remained behind a moment, sensing his first mate had something to say to him.

"Yes?" Gage said after another moment of silence, turning his eyes up to meet the face of his tall first mate.

"You tread too heavily around that woman, Captain," William said quietly, eyes moving to her back. There was a reason William was Gage's first mate—his keen eyes cut to the quick of the matter like his blade did to his enemies.

"I do believe I've just learned that lesson firsthand, my friend," Gage nodded, looking after Clara and the adolescent stumbling behind her.

Clara chose this moment to look back at them. "Are you coming or—"

She was interrupted by the sound of a howl. Clara's head snapped in the direction of the sound so fast it looked painful.

"Was that—" Gage began to ask.

"Yeah," Clara called back in a tense voice, "she's found something."

She took off in the direction of the sound. William and Gage shared a brief look before running after her.

"Wait up!" Peter called when they sprint past them.

When they caught up to her, she was kneeling down on the ground. Nahleese was pacing almost nervously, head swinging this way and that, her blue and amber eyes scanning the ground.

“Sonuvabitch,” Clara hissed from between clenched teeth as she examined something.

“What’s wrong?” Gage asked warily, feeling a pit growing in his stomach as she stood, face hidden behind the curtain of her long fiery hair.

She didn’t answer him immediately, looking at the path ahead.

Gage didn’t see what she saw, but then again that was what he paid her for. “Fox,” he said firmly, trying to get an answer from her.

Clara looked back at him at last, and what he saw made his blood run colder through his veins. She was worried, and when the Guide was worried, things were bad.

Clara gestured with a nod for him to move aside with her. The games were being put on hold apparently. They moved a little ways away from the group, who watched, exchanging uneasy glances.

When they had some semblance of privacy, she held up her hand to show him something. Gage looked at what was in her palm and squinted, trying to make out what it was she was showing him. They appeared to be flaky and long, hollow-looking tubes...

“Snake skins?” he said at last.

“They’re everywhere,” Clara told him quietly, not hiding how much this disturbed her.

“If I had to guess, I’d say there are four or five mating balls up ahead. Big ones.”

“How do we get past them?” he asked.

She was already shaking her head. “Sinclair, you don’t try to go past mating balls. Even if I was willing to gamble on which breed of snake I might run in to, it wouldn’t matter; that many snakes at the height of their mating aggression? We would not make it out alive.”

Gage watched how she tried to keep her posture relaxed while the others watched them quietly converse, trying to hide the fact she was stressed. If they could hear how she was speaking however, it wouldn’t matter how relaxed she looked, they would know—just like Gage knew.

“Options?” he asked, adopting the same relaxed manner; last thing they needed was for his crew to panic.

"Two," she told him, taking a deep breath. "The safer of those two—I use the term 'safe' loosely here, by the way—is we go back to the lookout point and wait a week or so for their cycle to end—"

Already Gage was shaking his head. "I don't have that long, Fox. My men are loyal, but if I'm gone that long, they'll assume I died and leave port. If they leave port without me, it could take me a very long time to get my ship back."

"Let me finish before you decide," she said, holding up a hand to stop further interruptions. "I'm not sure I could keep five pirates alive in here for a whole week; I've never tried. The second option is another path, one that will take us to Torin in the same amount of time if not a bit sooner..." Clara trailed off and looked down at her feet, like she was trying to find the right words to convey something. She didn't want to go that way; she really, really, *really* didn't.

"But..." Gage prompted.

Clara took another deep breath before looking up to reveal her expression, to show him how serious this decision was.

"It's dangerous, Sinclair; everything is dangerous here granted and there are never guarantees for survival... but I'm honestly not sure if I can get everyone through that route alive," she said quietly, to be sure only he heard.

Gage was silent for a long moment.

"Do you understand what I'm saying?" Clara asked, holding eye contact with him.

"You're saying this way lies death, that way lies death, and ahead of us certain death," Gage replied with a hint of sarcasm.

"That would be the gist of it yes."

"Oh joy."

Clara was silent, waiting. She ultimately left the decision to him on their course of action, because she had faith she'd survive the Dark Forest; it was Gage and his crew's lives to gamble with—they'd given him that right when they chose to follow him. Gage thought about his options for another moment. Then he looked at Clara, *really* looked at her, weighing her out in a way he'd not yet given her the courtesy of, as it was long overdue.

He'd seen her skill with a blade, how quick she was on her feet, and her resourcefulness, how adept she was at dealing with what the forest threw at her; this was her home. Things may be deadly in here, but so was she—and more than that she was clever.

"Take us the second route, love."

Gage watched her gaze shoot to the crew at his decision, uncertainty in her eyes. He reached out and gently turned her face to look at him; if he could see the worry in her gaze, so would they.

"Don't underestimate yourself, Fox; in here, I'd always choose to bet on you."

Truth, she thought, stunned to see he really meant that as his hand dropped away from her face. She'd not had such blatant certainty and... blind faith thrust upon her in a very long time. Clara felt the weight of the lives she had to carry through the Dark Forest more heavily in that moment than she could ever remember having felt before.

She wished she could have the same certainty he did; perhaps if he knew what lie ahead he would struggle as she did. But Gage had made his choice, so she took her worries and her doubts and she shoved them all aside; Clara didn't have room for any of those things where they were going; his resolve would have to become hers. Speaking of things she didn't have time for...

"No more bullshit, Sinclair; I need all my focus," Clara warned him, referring to the power playing from earlier.

"Agreed," he said simply. He watched as Clara seemed to assess his sincerity on that for a moment; then as her lips turned up in a decidedly mad-looking grin, like now that she'd decided she was going to court disaster she was determined to at least enjoy the date.

"All right, let's go spit in the face of death, then, shall we?"

Eleven

Clara hadn't wasted time once the decision had been made. She'd reached into her pack and pulled out a bundle of rags, untangling them hastily and quickly handing one to each crew member.

"We're taking another path," she said as she shoved the burlap like fabric into each of their hands.

"Why?" Squint asked, looking at the fabric almost like he was suspicious of its purpose.

"Too many snakes ahead; we go that way we die," she explained briefly, not wanting to go into too much detail. It was a delicate line she'd walked a hundred times before, giving them enough information to help them survive but not enough to spook them. Spooked people did stupid things, and stupid things got spooked people killed.

"Is it safe?" a young voice asked curiously. Of course it would be Peter to ask the question she didn't want to answer. And to Clara's surprise she didn't have to; Sinclair was answering it for her.

"Safer than the way that leads us through a sea of venomous snakes."

Gage held his hand out as she came to hand him a piece of cloth, only to see there was only one left. He watched her as she looked at him and then at the rag with a grimace, arching his brow. "Hope that's not terribly important."

"Only if you want to live," Clara sighed as she ripped the rag in half.

"Try not to lose it," she told him, stuffing the slightly larger half into his hand like she was being deliberately gruff with him.

"Lose a gift from you?" he asked, as if he could scarcely imagine such an event. "I perish at the thought," he teased, slipping the cloth into his pocket.

"Wow, this 'no-bullshit' rule is going to be really hard for you to follow, isn't it?"

Gage held up his hands in a gesture of surrender. "Last one for now, promise."

"For now?" Clara repeated, catching the implication.

"Can't expect me to hold off forever, can you, love? Pirate," he reminded her with a wink.

She actually almost smiled even as she rolled her eyes; it took a little tension out of her; but she had an odd suspicion that that had been his intention. "New rules," Clara said, looking away from him to face the others. "You smell something sweet and pleasant, you press the rag to your nose," she told them, holding up her own bit of cloth.

Squint sniffed his and blanched away in disgust. "Smells like shit," he complained.

"The pleasant smell is the scent of corpse grass, and unless you're Nahleese, it'll kill you," she continued pointedly, everyone's glance briefly turning down to the wolf who was pacing nervously. "The rags counteract it."

Clara glared at Squint, not in the mood for his usual crap. "But if the smell bothers you that much then by all means, enjoy the fresh air." That smartened him up pretty damn quick.

"Corpse grass?" William repeated with a convulsive swallow.

"It wraps around you and pulls you down, poison fumes kill you, then it eventually feeds off the rotting corpses," Clara explained off-handedly before noticing his paling complexion. Ah, right—his last entanglement with Dark Forest vegetation had been rather traumatic.

Before she could do a little damage control on that slip, William was suddenly indulging in an uncharacteristic outburst.

"Is there a reason you feel the need to make horrifying creatures more terrifying by giving us a run down on how they'll slaughter the lot of us? Honestly woman, would it kill you to keep some information to yourself?" William looked as if he wanted to go on, but Gage was giving his first mate a decidedly unamused stare, and William noticed that fairly quickly, already faltering.

"Mr. William," Gage said.

"Yes, Captain?"

"Stop talking."

"Yes, Captain."

Clara retrieved a corked glass vial from a pouch on her pack, round and small enough to sit comfortably in the palm of her hand, filled with some clear liquid. She uncorked it, plucking a nearby bloom that she crushed between her fingers and sprinkled it in before recorking it. Clara shook it up a little, and immediately the water began to glow, giving off a bright blue light. She quickly tied it to a loop in her pack as she gave the last of her instructions.

"Watch me, and don't fall behind; if you do, look for the light, and don't call out to anyone. Do as I do, step where I step, stay very close to each other, and when we reach the path, no talking. Absolute silence: predators hunt by sound where we're headed."

She turned her back on them, staring off into the distance like she was measuring the steps between them and the new great perils ahead. Clara pulled the straps onto her shoulders, took a deep breath, and faced everyone once more with a more schooled expression.

"Does everyone understand the rules?"

There was a collective nodding throughout the group. Clara stared at them all a moment longer and made peace with the fact that she would try her damnedest, but in all likelihood, she was probably going to lose at least a few of them to this path. She took the lead just as she heard Jared's voice calling out a question.

"How do we know when we're on the path?"

Gage saw her lips press into a tight thin line before answering.

"You'll know, trust me."

They reached the path all right, and just like Clara had said, they all knew when they were on it. The underbrush seemed to thin out, replaced by a boggy moss that turned each step into a battle to keep from sinking into the spongy earth. The sunlight had been choked out by the sheer density of the leaves that greedily clawed at the sky, hoarding any ray of sunshine available.

The result of such was a place of dim shadows, tall trees with thick, scarred trunks left bare underneath their own canopies. A fine mist clouded the air that only thickened the farther they tried to peer into it, like gauzy veils that wrapped about the trees to create entire walls of obscuring fog.

Nahleese took the lead, head low to the ground, each paw placed delicately on the path, her ears perked for danger. Peter was behind Clara as she had insisted he be, then Gage, Jared, William, and Squint—all walking in a single-file line so close together that a misstep might knock them all over.

Their eyes were trained on Clara and her careful movements, made easier to follow by the light swinging from her pack. Gage noticed the deeper they traversed onto the path, the more unnaturally quiet it became until the loudest sound he could hear was his own heartbeat.

An unease settled about the men making them skittish, and he saw that even Fox could not hide the tension she carried in her shoulders as she navigated their eerie path. This forest may have been her home, but even she couldn't get out of this place fast enough. Gage noticed William's hands shaking as Peter looked about him nervously, the distracting tension causing him to stumble.

He caught himself before he fell, returning the resulting inquiring look from Clara a bit sheepishly.

She couldn't help noting how the whites of his eyes were all too visible when he did. She smiled and winked at him to try and ease his nerves a bit, watching him flush red as she did. Gage arched an eyebrow at her over the kid's shoulder as if to say, *Really, Fox?*

Clara casually flipped him off, returning her attention to the path ahead. It seemed they could keep the banter going without even speaking now as they moved on and the silence continued to condense on them.

A sweet scent began to tickle Clara's nose like she'd been expecting it would for some time. Her eyes swept the path ahead until she saw the tall blue strands of grass that came about waist height on her, cluttering the path in front of them. She pressed the rag to her face and turned her head to make sure the others did the same.

Only to see most of them were already near smothering themselves with the cloth.

If the circumstances had been different, Clara might have laughed; apparently she'd made her point just fine earlier. They were going to have to walk through a thick patch of the stuff, and she grit her teeth; she hated corpse grass.

She waded into it slowly, feeling the grass clutch to her like the hands of an infant, trying to hold her in place. The sensation never failed to send a shiver up her spine. She made brief eye contact with Gage, his dark stubble and high cheekbones hidden behind his rag. She held her hand up and made a waving motion while jerking her head to indicate the path ahead of her.

Just keep moving no matter what.

He looked at the grass clinging to her thigh, then nodded to show her he understood. Briefly Clara wondered how they had become so adept at reading one another so quickly. She surged forwards and did her best to ignore the feel of corpse grass trying to get a decent hold to drag her down, or the way her feet bumped into the remains of whatever creatures the grass had managed to snare. Sometimes those "remains' bumped against her.

The pirates waded in behind her; the rustling of a few sudden movements penetrated the quiet, the sound of someone jerking, surprised by the animate nature of the grass. It was nothing loud enough to draw attention, but it put her more on edge all the same.

Gage watched as Peter followed behind Clara bravely, pushing on ahead while trying his best to ignore the grasping reeds, and he smirked behind the reeking rag—it seemed the boy had as much faith in her as he did. Gage was distracted from this observation when he heard a whimper behind him; in the silence, it approached something close to deafening.

A glance back revealed Squint had frozen on the spot in the middle of the grass, falling behind and leaving a gap between them. Something had crawled between him and the group with a disturbing heaving movement. It looked a bit like a coyote only uglier, with a misshapen head and ratty-looking fur. It was the first hideous-looking creature Gage had seen thus far, though he wagered it hadn't always been so.

It was clear it was dying, trying to escape the predator growing under its feet. The scent the grass was shedding had obviously weakened it, and it collapsed in front of Squint. He watched the reeds slowly wrapping around it, pulling it silently down, sinking it slowly into its roots, small animal convulsing in its death throes.

It was enough to push the pirate over the edge; Squint stumbled backwards from the cocooned animal with horror in his eye; even the rag pressed to his face wasn't enough to smother his whimpering as it grew in volume. Squints head whipped back and forth in a panic, looking for escape as he pulled the rag from his mouth to flail and bat the reeds away from him. He was about to lose it in a big way.

Clara's head whipped around to look back, alarmed by the sound. However she didn't go on full high alert until he pulled his sword and started to hack at the grass, his struggles and grunts seeming to fill the space between them to bursting.

Her wide eyes met Gage's, conveying one clear thought with just a look. *Stop him before he gets us all killed.*

He was already moving, quickly and quietly as he could towards his crewmate, Clara could already see his mind was becoming hazy as he dragged the sweet poison air into his lungs rag all but forgotten in his other hand. He wasn't thinking clearly, now swinging the blade indiscriminately, wide eyed and panicky. Nobody but Gage and Squint were moving, frozen by fear and the strangling grip of tension it brought.

Just as Gage moved into range, Squint swung at him, a blow that would relieve him of his head. Clara's breath caught in her throat, hand outstretched in a useless silent warning.

Gage's gloved hand came up to meet the blade, the silver gauge blazing to life as the needle spun in almost a blur. Where most men would have lost said hand, instead the blade corroded, going up in ash almost instantly so that Squint was left swinging nothing but the empty hilt of his sword.

Gage grabbed Squint's shirt, yanking him forward and shoving his ragged cloth against the man's nose and mouth, holding his own breath. He shook Squint twice, hard enough to rattle his teeth as the pirate's mind seemed to clear, rank but clean air filling his lungs again. Squint stopped clawing at the grass long enough to look at Gage, hyperventilating into his rag.

When he was sure he had his attention, that he was focused, Gage pulled the rag from his crewmember's face so he could replace it with his own. He kept his fist bunched in his shirt as he did.

Clara couldn't see his face, but she felt the fury from where she stood. Judging by Squint's expression, it was a murderous level of rage.

Gage briefly considered killing Squint right there; he had almost gotten them all killed. Instead he pressed one finger to his lips, then he very deliberately put the gloved hand on his shoulder, fixing his crewmate with a piercing, unmerciful gaze to be sure the meaning of the gesture was not lost on him.

Squint nodded quickly—message received loud and clear.

Gage grabbed his arm and shoved him forwards roughly to get him moving, looking to Clara to convey the crisis was over.

Only Clara's head was whipping from side to side, scanning the area in the deafening hush, like she were holding her breath, looking for the impending danger—for those few whimpers and panicked struggles to damn them all.

Everyone watched her scanning, tensely waiting for all the hells to rain down on them. After a long uneasy moment, Gage saw her let the breath out just as quietly as she'd held it, and everyone seemed to breathe out with her. *Must have had a lucky star over us,* Gage thought, shooting Squint another icy glare.

That's when he saw the wolf's white head pop up suddenly, ears perked, alerted by something.

Clara caught Gage noticing this and quickly followed his gaze. Nahleese stood stock still, ears twitching and her nose to the air. Clara felt her muscles lock; that was not a good sign.

The wolf didn't move for a long moment, ears turning to the left before its large head swivelled in that direction as well. Clara looked with her to see if she could make out whatever had the wolf's avid attention.

Just beyond the reaches her eyes could penetrate the mist, a large shadow moved. It was massive, a hulking shape that seemed to slide through the fog and the shadows as water moved over rocks, only a great deal more quietly.

Clara's heart stopped. Even if she'd wanted to utter a curse she couldn't have, not because that would draw the monster she knew cast that shadow in the mist, but because her jaw was clenched so tightly she didn't know if she could even open her mouth.

It didn't take long for everyone to notice that something lurked in the swirling smog. She felt a wave of fear pass over the whole group like it was a tangible thing. Good, now they could all be as painfully aware as she was. Slowly she crouched, prompting the others to do likewise.

Clara's eyes never left the shadow, especially when it stopped moving. The shape in the fog halted as if listening, its interest piqued. The tension was so heavy, so thick and palatable in the stillness, everyone felt like they were going to be crushed by it.

Clara heard the sound of breathing becoming strident and irregular with fear over her shoulder, the sound muffled only somewhat by the rags. She wanted to yell at them all to stop *breathing so loud,* a tad hypocritical since her heart was beating louder than any breath they drew, racing traitorously in her throat. The corpse grass wrapped around her legs and began to curl around her forearms, her feet starting to sink into the mossy earth as it pulled on her. The sound of the pirates drawing every shallow breath just a bit too fast let her know she wasn't the only one getting a bit tangled.

Leave before we can't you son of a bitch, she thought, willing the monster lurking in the mist before them to go.

The shadow held position, and she could almost feel those eyes she knew to be blind sweeping, ears listening with that lethal, unflinching focus. The shadow of its head raised to the air, as if scenting something interesting.

She dislodged the corpse grass on her arms as she reached very, very slowly to draw the curved blade at her side, the other hand stuffing her rag into the pouch at her waist in favour of grabbing blade at her wrist. Deep down, while she held her breath, she knew if it came down to a close-quarters fight with the creature listening for them, in all likelihood she'd be dead very shortly thereafter.

Gage watched her put the rag, protecting her from being poisoned, away in favour of arming herself and knew things were very close to going horribly sideways. Whatever that shadow was, their group hidden from it by a thin veil of vapours, Clara was far more afraid of it than the corpse grass she was now shoulders deep in.

Gage filled his lungs with a deep breath before stuffing the rag into his shirt and drawing his sword, the feel of its grip in his hand steadying his nerves a bit. If she was getting ready to fight, he would be prepared to back her up. The seconds ticked by agonizingly slowly as everyone watched the shadow and prayed.

Just when Clara and Gage thought they would have to either trade their blades for their rags or breathe in the poison, the shadow silently moved deeper into the mist and disappeared.

A few more moments of silence passed, all of them sinking just a little deeper as the reeds strained to drag them down. Clara almost gave into the hysterical urge to start giggling as she quickly cut free from some of the corpse grass twined about her legs. She was thankfully able to resist when she sheathed her blades and pressed the cloth back to her face to filter the poison from her first gasp of air.

Clara just sighed, looking back to see that she was not alone in fighting the urge, a relieved mirth in Peter's eyes as he used his hands to rip away the corpse grass's hold on him. She could see William's hands shaking violently as he followed suit with the rest of them, and Clara didn't blame him; she felt a bit shaky herself.

Gage still looked wary, his eyes looking at the place the shadow had been as he put his sword away. She was surprised to see him doing so. Was he prepared to go into a fight with her? He was either much braver or far more stupid then she'd first thought. Either way she found herself, well, glad.

She was about to stand up, already looking to the path ahead, just in time to see it happen. Beside Nahleese, lying in wait, a snake was rearing back to strike.

Nahleese was so engrossed in the immediate threat that had been in front of her she'd failed to notice the much more subtle threat slithering up beside her.

There was no time—no time to react or even draw a breath; the only thing that Clara had time for was a single thought before all hell broke loose.

No!

The snake struck, sinking ivory fangs deep into the wolf's side. Nahleese yelped in pain, a sound so loud it cut the very silence from the air as it echoed through the trees. She fell out of sight into the mist, howling and snarling as she fought the snake pumping venom into her blood. Clara was already moving to her friend's aid, but just like that, a threat they'd all thought had been skirted returned with a vengeance.

The mist seemed to rip open as it leapt onto the path, a wingless, dragon-like creature with a hulking body that kept low to the ground, a long snout brimming with sharp jagged teeth, and a long, whip-like tail that could cleave a person's head from their shoulders. It was covered not in scales but in what appeared to be soft, deep blue feathers, so blue they were almost black.

Clara knew better, those feathers were sharper than her knives. This was the worst-case scenario, in her opinion as bad as it could get. This was what she'd been afraid they would cross paths with.

She'd called it a Maroth, an Ethonian deity of war and death, for a reason. Its wide, blind, milky eyes stared at them all, unseeing but knowing where they were all the same. There was no hiding now.

"RUN!"

Twelve

Clara's voice was like a sharp clap of thunder that sent everyone bolting in the opposite direction. Her cloth dropped from her hand as she shoved at Peter, urging him to move faster. He obliged, long legs carrying him past Gage, who didn't dare to look back at the predator that gave chase.

Regardless, a shadow soon cast over them as they ran for their lives, a darkness Gage felt the very weight of. Without thinking, one hand reached out to his left to shove Clara as hard as he could while using his opposite forearm to shove Squint just as violently, sending the man flying forwards and taking Jared down with him.

Gage was the last to move, throwing himself to the right and rolling out of the way of the claws that sank into the ground in the space where the three of them had been. The Maroths entire body whipped around, head moving from side to side as if deciding which of them to kill first.

Gage lay on the ground to its right with Clara on her back staring up at it from the left, both unmoving. Squint and Jared were scrambling to their feet behind it. Peter had turned back to help them, the damn little fool.

The noise they made all together was minimal, but it was a noise. Its feathered tail cracked like a whip behind it, a blur of speed towards Squint with the intention of decapitating him.

Peter's hand shot out and grabbed him by the back of his shirt trying to pull him out of the way. All too late. Everything happened so fast Gage couldn't track most of it.

It was just a blur, one strike, two strikes, and then the red-hot splash of blood colouring the air, mixed with two different screams. The Maroth's sleek head snapped around like a bird's, looking at Jared as he backed away so quickly he looked on the verge of tripping, not daring to take his eyes off the iron-feathered monster.

The Maroth thrust its head forwards, trying to impale him on its bristling snout. Jared lifted his pack like a shield at the last second, the contents flying everywhere as the feathers shredded the sturdy material like it was the most delicate of flower petals.

The impact sent Jared flying through the air—more blood, more screams. The combination incensed the creature, sharp, dicing feathers ruffling and filling the air with a sound akin to a hundred swords clashing. *She warned you, this is how it ends...*

As Clara had skidded into the dirt her adrenalin had finally ramped up to send her brain careening into the all too familiar hyper awareness that had saved her life more than once, pupils dilating, heart racing. *Do something!* She caught sight of Peter, blood splattered on his face, on his shirt, clamping his hand over Squint's mouth to muffle his screaming in a desperate attempt to save them whilst he dragged the man back.

But the Maroth was already locked onto them, the closest prey making noise once more. Those diamond-hard feathers almost seemed to point in Peter and Squint's direction. She saw the blood splattering them both, not sure which of them was wounded or how bad and suddenly the words felt as if they were ripping out of Clara's throat.

"Climb!" she screamed. "Get in the trees!" she ordered so loudly and forcefully it hurt her own ears.

Her voice brought upon her the Maroths single-minded attention, giving Peter the chance to drag Squint into the trees further from danger. That had been half the idea of course, to draw its attention to give everyone else a chance. However it felt like a terrible one when that monstrous head turned her way, milky blind eyes staring right through her, nostrils flaring as its jaw dropped open to expose rows and rows of jagged teeth.

"Oh shit."

She had just enough time to throw her pack away from her so it wouldn't slow her down and then she was rolling, the Maroth's snout tearing into the ground where she had just been, so close the feathers on its face lightly brushed her cloak and ripped the fabric apart like it was rice paper.

Every strike landed where she had been only milliseconds before, the Maroth's hot breath burning her skin while her world spun, deaths fingertips scratching against her skin, barely evading it every second...

William's hand wrapped tightly around Gage's arm, staggering him with the sheer force his first mate forced him up with. He'd barely gotten his bearings before William was darting to a nearby tree, clearly expecting him to follow. He should have, but he found his gaze sweeping the area looking for Clara instead, quickly spotting her fire-blond hair whipping around as she continuously rolled herself just barely out of the monsters killing strikes.

He felt his stomach drop into his feet, watching her barely staying a hair's breadth out of the grave. Without thinking, he was drawing his blade and moving in her direction, her looming demise sending his reason fleeing from his mind for a brief moment. His only thought was one that was as mad as it was impossible.

Help her!

That's when a second shadow cast over him from the mist, seconds before his ears caught the soft sound it made.

The sound drew his eyes behind him, and immediately he felt his pulse thumping even more loudly in his jugular, heart battering against his ribcage.

Another pair of milky eyes stared blindly past him from ten feet away and towards the epicenter of noise, a sound like that of someone lightly tapping silverware together as its feathers trembled with anticipation.

Most men, most pirates, almost any other person in the world would have seen this as reason to panic. But he was not most people; what he saw, even as the sweat broke on his brow, was opportunity.

The Maroth kept coming, jaws snapping, claws ripping up the earth where she'd been, the light brushes that it managed were enough to shred her cloak to tatters, and now some of her shirt. As the sharpness began to nip at her skin and coax blood to wet the earth Clara knew she had mere moments before she was a second too slow and then would be diced to pieces. She was dizzy, close to vomiting as she heard Jared and Peter screaming from their perches in the trees, trying to get the creature's attention off of her.

She couldn't tell if it was working or not, and frankly she couldn't spare any of her attention to find out, a sweet scent was now entering into the multihued blur that had become her world.

You've got to be kidding! her mind screamed as she rolled right into the grasp of corpse grass.

Clara tried to take a breath to hold her through the next minute, but that quick breath filled her head with flowers and made the world spin even more violently behind her eyelids.

Clara stilled in the cover of the grass, praying she could hold out on this one poison laced breath, as she remained silent and unmoving. Her vision was still churning as she looked to see the creature searching about blindly, distracted by the pirates whistling, yelling, and clapping of their hands, trying to give her a chance.

It hovered only a few agonizing feet away from her, motionless, listening. Clara's lungs were already aching for air as the grass began wrapping around her arms and torso, trying to cocoon her and drag her into the ground.

The Maroth refused to move, seemingly ignoring the sounds in the trees now, knowing the closer prey was on the ground and listening intently for it to give itself away. All this time she'd been so confident that no matter what she would always find a way to survive; for perhaps the first time, as fear seized her gut and crushed her insides with its vice like grip, she realized that maybe she had just as much to worry about as the rest who dared this forest.

Clara had to move. If she did, it would hear, and she'd be dead. If she didn't, she would soon be too tangled to escape and be just as dead.

You're done either way, just pick the best way to end it. That stray thought lacked bitterness, just a cold thread of words straight from some deeply dark and practical side of herself. It did her a world of good – because it cut through the fear by *really* pissing her off. Clara had survived too long in here to just *accept* death now. She'd find her godsdamn way out of this she thought, fingers curling into a thick clump of dirt.

Now or never.

Clara wrenched her body from the grass in one heaving motion, throwing the tight clump of dirt from her so it rustled bushes a few feet away. The Maroth's head snapped towards the sound as Clara shot to her feet and attempted to run for it.

She had too scant air in her lungs; the gasp she'd taken to save herself had been more poison than air. She stumbled forwards, her vision doubling as the world seemed to move in slow motion. Her legs gave under her, and she hit the ground hard, skidding a few feet on her back.

Instantly, the Maroth was bearing down on her, its feet crashing down on either side of Clara, trapping her between its front paws. That last thing her blurry eyes was going to see was the most glorious beast she'd ever seen pulling its head back to rip her apart.

Or so she thought.

"HEY!"

Sinclair? she thought, eyes searching for him, Maroth hesitating to tilt its head in his direction. She just made out a shape she thought to be Gage, strangely shouting at the trees before he hit the ground. What was he—?

Another great shape breached the mist, green-black feathers shining in the scant light as it stretched full out with long claws reaching ahead of it, flying where Sinclair's voice had been.

And where he no longer was. The next living thing in its path was the blue Maroth preparing to make Clara its meal. The green-black blur of feathers crashed into blue-black, sending a blinding shower of sparks into the mist as their knifelike exteriors collided, the sound of the impact like a thousand nails on a chalkboard.

Both creatures were torn from the ground, flying into the air and smashing into a tree that did nothing to slow them, splinters and diced chunks of wood flying in every direction upon impact.

The resulting shrieking was akin to having razor blades thrust into her ears, hands pressing to each side of her head to protect her hearing while her vision doubled so badly Clara felt like she was going to be sick. Then someone was dragging her up off the ground and forcing her to run, away from the chaos that shook the ground and sounded like a hundred men crossing swords.

The hand gripping her arm yanked her hard to the left, and she stumbled, back suddenly pressed against something solid while someone moulded themselves protectively in front of her.

With the help of the untainted air, the dizziness finally cleared, and she realized that her back was pressed against a tree. The warm presence standing in front of her, hands braced against the tree on either side of her head, was Gage. He was looking around the tree, watching the shifting shadows of the two beasts fight.

"You all right, Fox!?" he yelled just to be heard over the noise, looking into her eyes.

"Yeah!" She coughed, almost doubling over. She'd gotten one hell of a snoot-full of poison. Gage's hand was there instantly, propping her back up against the tree. Clara pushed the hand away, mostly out of habit; they didn't have the time to be coddling her—she'd deal.

"Yeah," Clara repeated a little more loudly, "just clearing my lungs!"

He nodded, accepting this as he shrugged something off his shoulder and gave it to her—her pack.

"Wouldn't want you to be without your endless bag of tricks, would we, love!?" he yelled, briefly looking from behind the tree to see if the battling Maroths were getting closer.

"You are the craziest pirate I have ever met!" Clara shouted at him.

"I prefer daring!" He gestured for them to climb the tree. "Shall we?!"

Clara laced her fingers together and hunched low to give him a boost.

"Ladies first!" he shouted, but she shook her head as a crash sounded closer to them and a wailing filled the air.

"Get in the tree!" she screamed.

He only hesitated for a moment before he stepped into her hands and allowed her to help him up. He quickly pulled himself into one of the higher branches before reaching his hand down to pull her up. To his surprise, she didn't take it, instead ripping off the vial that glowed so brightly on her pack.

"Fox, what are you doing? Get up here!"

She ignored him and quickly tossed him the glowing vial. Gage caught it with an incredulous look, realizing she had no intention of climbing to safety with him. Instead Clara backed away from the tree, drawing the blade at her wrist.

"My friend needs me. I'll follow the light back to you!"

Like that, she was turning to run into the mist brimming with uncertainty and danger, Gage's voice screaming after her.

"Fox! FOX!"

That stubborn, idiotic woman, he thought, cursing under his breath as he watched remnants of a shredded cloak and her copper blond hair disappear into the fog. That she was running off into mortal danger after he'd just saved her life strangely angered him. His eyes scanned the mist for the telltale flash of her hair, but the only thing he could see were the sparks that occasionally lit up the fog, signalling where the fierce creature's battle was taking place.

By giving him the light and making him her only beacon, she almost forced him to stay where he was; she'd tied his hands so to speak. Infuriating, clever woman. However those fireworks of violence were moving more steadily in the direction where Clara had run. She wouldn't be able to follow her beacon to him if she was in pieces.

"Goddamn it," he muttered viciously, dropping out of the tree and landing heavily on the ground. He shoved the light she'd given him into his inner coat pocket and ran in the same direction she'd headed.

The moss pulled at his boots with every step as he recklessly called Clara's name. He doubted she could hear him over the violent commotion churning the mist; then Gage stopped running.

He wasn't entirely sure why he'd stopped at first, something so briefly catching his attention he hardly had time to register it—had he heard something?

He closed his eyes for a moment and listened as hard as he could—ignoring the beat of his heart, ignoring the sound of the brawling monsters, the way the ground shook under his feet—and tried to pinpoint what it was that had pulled him to a halt.

A sound. Definitely a sound, he thought; a whining or perhaps something that could be likened to a whimper. It sounded close, extremely close. It didn't sound human, but it was certainly familiar.

He was drawn to the small helpless sound until the sweet scent he'd learned to fear tugged at his nostrils. He quickly chased it away with the rank cloth and walked into the sparse patch of corpse grass, the whimpering growing louder. While wading through, his foot bumped something rather solid in the grass, drawing his gaze down.

A cocooned shape lay at his feet, big and so tightly wrapped whatever it was had no hope of escaping. The only thing visible through layers of grass weaving its net of death was a few white tuffs of fur.

"Well, well," Gage muttered to himself as he knelt down carefully, swatting at the grass trying to wrap around him. He used his hand and three mobile fingers to pry the grass free and clear the reeds away.

The white head of Clara's wolf was revealed, her dull amber eye opening to peer at him while he tore the blue grass from her face.

"Aren't you a sad sight," he said, words muffled by the rag.

Her whimpering became louder, she lifted her partially freed head and struggled futilely to fully free herself, fear and pain colouring the pathetic sound.

"Shh, easy, easy, lass," he said soothingly, trying to calm her. Nahleese made a harsh yelping sound, indicating pain before her head hit the ground, that small struggle exhausting her.

"You'll be all right, girl, easy," he assured her in a pacifying tone of voice, patting her big head. It was a lie; he was fairly certain the wolf was dying.

The sound of ferocious snarling and the impossible sounds of a war circled around him, his eyes catching glimpses of shadows pressing on the edges of the mist in violent intervals. He was eerily certain the victor would soon cut through the thin veils of mist that separated them to collect the spoils. He would very much like to be heading in the opposite direction before that happened.

He glanced back down at the wolf lying in the grass, wondering if he should bother with Nahleese. She was dying after all, pulling her free wasn't going to exactly help her, and he needed to find Clara.

That golden orb blinked slowly up at him, each laboured breath shuddering through her with a painful difficulty, watching Gage watch her. A part of him said to just leave the wolf; his time would be better served looking for Clara and dragging her perfect, stubborn ass to safety.

But there was something in the wolf's eye as he murmured empty soothing words that watched him so carefully. Something about Nahleese struck him as impossibly... human at that moment, so afraid, understanding like he'd never seen before in an animal of what was truly coming...

He found it struck a soft spot he didn't know he had. Thank the gods no one was here to witness it. It seemed cruel even to him to leave

Nahleese to a slow death. He pulled his cutlass from its sheath, angling his body so she wouldn't see it; the least he could do was ease the wolf's passing he figured as he continued to pat her head. He moved his blade closer, positioning the point of his cutlass to pierce her heart and lungs for the cleanest possible death.

"You're OK, girl," he told her softly, even as her mismatched eye closed for a moment as she gasped, as if she knew despite his soft words he only had his steel to offer her.

"You won't feel a thing."

Just as he was about to end it for her, to drive the blade home, he noticed she still had something clutched between her teeth. He squinted, hesitating as he saw it to be the snake. Gage looked at the stripes along the bloody body of the serpent in the dim light, trying to make out the pattern of colours on its body.

Black, green, blue, white.

Black touches green...

Gage smiled. "Thank the queen."

He corrected the angle of his cutlass and began to cut away the grass trying to swallow Nahleese into the ground, patting her head more firmly as she raised her head and that amber eye and that midnight-blue eye opened to look at him, as if surprised.

"See, lass?" he said with a relieved grin, "Not even a pinch."

Gage quickly finished cutting her free before he sheathed his sword, took a deep breath, and grabbed a handful of her scuff, dragging her out of the corpse grass and drawing high whines of pain from Nahleese, who stubbornly clutched the serpent in her teeth.

"Sorry, girl, no time to be gentle," he apologized gruffly, voice strained.

He stopped and looked around; the mist seemed to have thickened. Regardless he tried to peer through it; there had to be someplace he could stash her where she would be safe for a short time until he found Clara.

The ground was bare here except for the moss and fallen leaves; they were both far enough from the grass that its deadly enticing scent could not reach them. He figured in terms of safety this may be the best he could ask for. He let Nahleese's scruff go and knelt down next to her for a moment, placing a reassuring hand on the wolf's flank.

"Don't go anywhere now, darling," he said, almost swearing the wolf rolled its eyes as he got up and began jogging away.

He was only five feet from the wolf when he heard the groaning, a second before the earth suddenly gave under his feet and he was falling. His body tumbled down a steep slope he'd been unknowingly walking the edge of, jostling his every sense before a blinding dull pain stabbed into his shoulder when he hit a wayward stump. The pain went right down to the few fingertips he could feel.

He pulled both arms in and braced himself, unable to stop as rocks in the ground bit all along his body on the way down. Finally he hit even ground and slowed enough to throw an arm out to stop the tumble, finding himself in a very shallow puddle of water that was cold and bracing.

The very first thing he did as he collected his senses was pat his front pocket, feeling for the sharp edges of the object there. He felt it through the leather of his coat and relaxed very slightly.

His eyes were squeezed shut and teeth grit, hand reaching up to grasp the throbbing stabs of pain in his shoulder. He knew that pain: dislocated.

"Sonuvabitch," Gage hissed between clenched teeth, feeling the cold water seeping into his clothing as he clenched his eyes shut—he hated this forest. The pain retreated a little while his hand gave the joint some support, allowing his other senses to focus past the pain. He could just barely hear Nahleese howling, as if trying to call out for someone. He really hoped that the person she was calling for heard it.

His brow wrinkled with confusion; what was that smell? It wasn't the deadly scent of corpse grass. This was different but somehow still eerily familiar—what was that? He opened his eyes and waited for the spinning to stop, letting them clear to get a better grasp on where he was.

A yellow sky?

All his clearing vision could make out was the colour at first, yellow, like the highlights the sun brought out in Clara Fox's hai—Gage felt his blood freeze.

"Bloody hell..." he whispered.

Slowly, very, very slowly, he reached into his inner pocket for the bright vial of light...

Clara scoured the ground for Nahleese with a recklessness usually reserved for the suicidal. Ignoring the gnashing of teeth and explosions of sparks that moved dangerously in her direction, she tried to sort through the violent sounds for even the smallest of whimpers to locate her friend.

Please, Nahleese, she thought desperately as she searched, a frantic feeling of dread invading her entire body. How would she tell—

No, she couldn't even finish that question.

Please, please don't be dead.

That's when she heard the most beautiful sound she'd heard in all her life, mixed in with the shrieks and the sharp clashing, Clara heard the sound of a howl.

She shut her eyes, ignoring everything else, trying to pinpoint it. Clara picked the direction where it sounded the loudest and ran as fast as her legs would carry her. The howling trailed off, but Clara kept running in the direction she hoped to find her, pausing to look for anything that resembled the shape of a wolf.

Just when the dread began to return, that perhaps she'd gone in the wrong direction, she saw something. Near a patch of corpse grass, the earth had been disturbed; the moss was shifted like someone or something had been dragged. She only had to follow the trail a few short feet before she saw Nahleese sprawled out on the ground.

Before Clara knew it, she was collapsing by her friend's side, her fingers weaving into Nahleese's fur and trying to find the deep puncture marks from the snake. Nahleese lifted her head slowly at Clara's touch, dead snake clamped in her jaws.

Without thinking, Clara snatched it from her mouth, examining its body. Black touching green. Clara almost felt like sobbing with relief as she buried her face into Nahleese's flank.

"Don't you *ever* do that to me again. You hear me?" she sighed into her fur. "Never again, you are *not* allowed to die."

She wasn't sure she'd ever been so relieved in all her life. Then a thought occurred to her in the midst of her respite. Who dragged Nahleese from the grass? It certainly hadn't been Nahleese's own doing; she was clearly too weak.

The wolf suddenly whined as if hearing her unspoken question, feet kicking at the dirt like she was trying to propel herself forwards. Clara lifted her face back up from her friend's flank, watching the wolf's head drop back to the dirt and huff with frustration.

"What is it?" Clara asked, looking ahead of her.

Nahleese kicked her feet again and huffed even more loudly, a pain-laced whine edging the sound, the venom making any movement painful and cluing her in to just how important it was to Nahleese that she draw Clara's attention to something.

Squinting in the direction Nahleese tried to move, she could just make out a missing chunk of a ledge. She never would have known a ledge was even there had the dirt not crumbled away to reveal it. It looked like it had given under someone's weight.

She crawled carefully to the edge to examine the place where the dirt had fallen away, getting the impression of a steep hill but not expecting to make out much through the fog.

Which was why she was surprised to see a small light flickering at the bottom. Her light. She felt her stomach drop into her feet. *That fucking idiot.*

Clara got to her feet and quickly covered Nahleese under some moss and leaves, not much for protection but the best she could do with time running short. The fight had begun to sound more vicious, if that was even possible. The winner would soon be made clear.

"Stay," she ordered. Nahleese growled in reply, carrying a distinct tone of annoyance before laying her head back down on the ground.

Carefully, she made her way down the steep slope, drawing closer and closer to the bright light. The closer she came, the more the outline of a man became clear through the fog.

When she reached the bottom, the silhouette had filled out enough for her to make out Gage, like she'd never doubted it was, lying in that scant little puddle. Curiously, he didn't look at her; though she could tell he knew someone was approaching, something else holding his attention enraptured. She quickly realized what.

Yellow little blooms hung everywhere in a canopy of hundreds, petals all trembling in warning as each Spitter aimed at the heat source lying smack-dab in the middle of their midst.

"Sinclair," she hissed.

"Fox," he said through clenched teeth, sounding inappropriately lighthearted considering the danger he was in, eyes shifting to take in her slow approach.

"So glad you could make it."

"You just couldn't stay in the godsdamn tree, could you?"

Thirteen

"Seriously," she said, eyes scanning the riled state of the vicious blooms, "how do you keep getting into these situations?"

"Just lucky I suppose. If they go off?" His tone was questioning, light despite the fact his body was vibrating with tension as he lay there, cradling his one arm. He was hurt; she was really starting to hate this day.

"That puddle will be your final resting place," she answered him honestly, easing in a little closer while trying to spot a safe way to pull him out without killing them both.

"Not a terribly fitting fate for a famous pirate, love," he quipped, muscle in his jaw clenching tighter. He watched as she seemed to pluck a match from thin air and light it, the flame eating away at the vapours as it flickered to life.

"Love the improvements to the outfit by the way." The "improvements" he was referring to were of course the dirt stained fabric, tattered and slit in parts to reveal the flesh along her arms, legs, and torso.

"It's the 'I survived' look," she told him sarcastically. "Really big with the peasants—every year." She watched the flowers while the match burned. Not one turned in her direction. "You're too hot," she said, dropping the match, the flame dying with a hiss as it hit the water, leaving it a little darker.

He laughed apprehensively, "Now you notice."

"Really, now?"

"Might not get another chance," he said with a minuscule, one-shoulder shrug. She'd seen him use charm and sexuality to disarm, coax, manipulate, put someone at ease, and even as a weapon—but she'd yet to see him use it to cope with fear. If flirting helped him keep his grip however, she was all for it.

Clara herself could practically taste her own pulse in her mouth as it thudded through her like a drum; of all five pirates, the one she never thought she might lose in this dangerous course change was him. Why did that thought bother her so much? Why did her heart clench and burn her blood with adrenaline at the possibility he might die here?

"Oh, I don't know," she said, circling slowly. "I'm sure you're going to have plenty of chances to annoy me later."

"Is that what they're calling it these days?" he asked, grinning, the expression looking strained on his face as his eyes followed every careful step she took.

"Among other things I'm sure," she answered with a forced grin of her own. Clara felt him examining her face as she went back to trying to figure out how she was going to get him out, every idea fizzing out like the small flame that had clung desperately to the match when it hit the water.

Gage groaned, his teeth clenching together tighter in pain, eyes closing when she moved out of his line of sight. He didn't dare move his head to follow her progress, especially when he realized she was humouring him.

"Bloody hell, now I know I'm in trouble," he muttered to himself. "Any ideas, darling?" he asked louder, voice finally showing his struggle to remain calm.

Not a damn one, she thought.

"None worth mentioning," Clara answered instead, finishing walking the perimeter of the flowers and finding no safe opening she could exploit to save his life.

"Can you crawl?"

"One way to find out."

He let his shoulder go slowly, eyes opening to focus on her. He began attempting to wriggle towards her. Clara saw the trembling of the yellow petals become more violent at the attempt to escape.

"Whoa, whoa! Stop!" she said frantically, holding up a hand as if he needed the visual cue to stop him. He was still again, both watching with baited breath for him to be impaled with a thousand little barbs. The trembling subsided a little, not much but a little.

"The water," Clara said to herself, then louder, "it's the water—it's keeping you just cool enough to protect you. You move, you disturb the water, and you look warmer."

"So what do we do now?" he asked. He was so close; she could literally take five steps and be by his side. Yet he was so very far away, because those five steps fell under an umbrella of death.

If Clara took those steps, she killed them both. If she didn't, eventually those spurs would fire anyways and he'd die; the water couldn't protect him forever. All her experience in the Dark Forest told her one cold fact in that moment, that there was nothing she could do to get him out. He was going to die there.

Clara didn't look at him; she knew he'd see that knowledge in her eyes. She was trying to think of something, anything to say to him, but no words came.

Gage watched her staring at the flowers, but he could see she wasn't really seeing them—she was just trying to not look at him, and he felt his stomach slowly dropping into his feet.

"Clara," he said softly when she didn't answer him, "Clara, look at me."

She didn't. He saw her lips press together like she was bracing herself before closing her eyes for a moment. Suddenly that same belligerent voice that had been chastening her while she laid in the grass was in her head now, more forceful than she'd felt it in a long time. She had not lost a damn client yet, so this insufferable *bastard pirate* would not die here today and ruin her perfect record, he simply would not—she'd eat glass first.

Clara finally looked at him then, opening those hard, determined, dark green eyes that burned with newfound resolve and just a touch of anger.

Surprisingly, he sighed in relief at the hard look.

"Scared me there for a moment, Fox. Thought you were giving up."

"Not really in my nature," she said with a shake of her head. He laughed again, laying his head back in the water. "So I've gathered."

She had a brief moment to again wonder why it felt so utterly unacceptable to her that she might have to watch him die. That moment ended when the silence abruptly returned, so heavily Clara felt as if she'd been struck deaf. The water stilled, and the sound of their breathing was suddenly the loudest sound in the forest.

"I think we have a winner," Clara said quietly, eyes scanning the mist warily.

With all the ruckus that had somehow quickly become background noise, Gage had forgotten just how oppressive the silence was. It was made even more unbearable on his now-ringing ears by just how sudden the absence was of almost any sound.

"Perhaps it's moved on," he whispered to her, sounding hopeful after a few long minutes passed in uneventful hush.

Clara caught the lightning-quick flash of a shadow pressing against the mist in her peripheral, but when she looked, it was gone. She saw it again, on the other side of her this time, but once again when she snapped her head in its direction, the shadow had disappeared from sight.

It was circling.

"I'm afraid we're not that lucky," she whispered back.

"Would you be terribly offended if I said I hated this forest?" Gage asked through clenched teeth, raising his head to look at her. The petals shivered almost in anticipation at the small movement.

The Maroth didn't attack, small glimpses of shadows moving around them the only indicators it was there before disappearing into the mist soundlessly; it started to feel like they were surrounded by a horde of the creatures.

"What. The hell. Is it doing?" Gage panted as loudly as he dared, the sharp, aching pain making his breath come to him in short gasps now.

Clara raised open hands in a helpless gesture of 'I have no idea.' Her brow wrinkled, it was just circling them, why would the Maroth just circle? They were being almost suicidal just exchanging these few hushed words, yet it still wasn't coming in for the kill.

Gage's face was a mixture of tense, pain-laced curiosity at Clara's shared uncertainty.

She shrugged, not the most encouraging gesture she knew, but she honestly didn't know. Gage's expression seemed to light up with a cautious idea.

"Hunts by sound, right?" he whispered so softly she practically had to read his lips to understand. "Don't know about your ears, love, but mine are certainly ringing."

Genuine surprise filled her face. That made sense; with how sensitive the Maroth's ears were and the beating its loud fight had inflicted to said ears it was most likely a bit off kilter, having trouble picking out exactly where they were. Not a bad deduction on Gage's part.

That unfortunately just made it worse, knowing it was still going to find them eventually. She could practically feel it moving through the mist like a heat...

Clara stopped. An idea so insane struck her then she almost had to give her head a shake. It was a plan that was either going to go brilliantly or backfire horrifically, unfortunately it was now the only gamble she could think of that might result in any success.

"Do you trust me?" she asked him, gaze fixed deeply into the mist as she slipped her pack off her shoulders.

"Don't have much of a choice, do I?" His voice hissed between grit teeth, jaw too tense to open.

"When I tell you, make as much noise as you can," she said, skirting the edge of the puddle and the flowers as quickly as she could so she was now to his right. She gently tossed the pack so it landed halfway between them both with her holding one of the straps.

"What, no rope in your bag of tricks, love?"

"You want me to save your ass or not?"

Gage turned his head slowly to look at the pack before his eyes glanced to her.

"You're either very clever or very crazy," he told her, letting his grip on his injured shoulder go once more to grasp the shoulder strap firmly.

"Have to be a little of both to survive in here," she said, flashing him a brief wide grin.

"Now," she ordered, digging her feet into the dirt and tightening her grip on the strap.

"Over here!" Gage yelled, voice echoing harshly.

"You want a taste of pirate?!" he shouted into the mist, the shadow casting itself thickly into the mist now as it slunk closer to the sound of Gage's voice.

"Then come get a bite you preening peacock!"

Something fell from Clara's pack as his grip tightened on his strap, drawing her eyes as it plopped into the water, seeing Gage had shook something loose. It was the sack of gold coins he'd used to pay for her services.

Gage heard the sound as well and looked to it for a moment. When he saw the bag of gold, his eyes widened. His gaze met hers, and it was crystal clear he knew exactly the decision she was faced with. In the next five seconds, she could grab the gold and escape or grab Gage and escape, but she couldn't do both.

The shadow was left behind in the mist as once again it cut through, revealing the winner had been the original Maroth of the blue-black feathers, once again hurdling towards them with a blood-lust that burned the air. No words could be said in time to convince her of anything—no bargains, no plays he could utilize to save his life, no time. Clara saw in his eyes that he wasn't laying any bets on her choosing him. The earth trembled under them as sharp claws battered the earth. Their eyes held for one long second in those brief seconds before it all came together.

Gage looked away from her and to the oncoming threat, his knuckles turning white as he held to the strap anyways, daring to hope.

The Maroth hurled towards them, eager and hungry, mouth opening in anticipation like a black hole with teeth, feathers rattling as it came at them with all the force and speed of a hurricane.

It was in such a frenzy, so focused on its prey, that as it barrelled under the canopy it didn't notice the scent of all the Spitters above it. The flowers abruptly shifted to the new, far larger source of heat under them, petals fluttering almost frantically.

That split-second shift was all Clara needed to either make the grab for Gage or her gold. She'd made her choice. Clara yanked the pack as hard as she could, giving Gage the momentum he needed to roll out of the way just as thousands of black spurs began raining down on the Maroth.

A blood curdling screeching, almost more violent than they'd heard in the fighting before, resumed full force, Maroth dropping on the spot. It writhed in pain as a thousand spurs sheared off its protective feathers, into its eyes, finding their way into any and every small opening of unprotected flesh through its many feathers.

Water and dirt flew in every direction as it flailed and convulsed on the spot, tearing at the earth while its claws struck out to rip the flowers from their canopy, destroying everything it touched.

Gage wasn't sure how but they were running, his arm cradled to his chest as his legs carried him forwards with Clara at his side, matching him stride for stride. Their feet dug into the steep hill, and they clawed their way in an adrenaline-fueled haze to the top.

When they reached the summit, they promptly collapsed over the edge he'd fallen from. They stayed like that for a few moments, gasping for air, collecting themselves while the Maroth's screams turned into mewling wails. Clara rolled to her back and Gage followed suit, neither looking at the other. After another minute, Gage felt compelled to say something.

"You, lass, are bloody amazing."

"I like to think so."

"How was it for you?"

"For the love of the gods, Sinclair, shut up," she snapped, sitting up and brushing her hair from her face.

When he didn't sit himself up, she grabbed him by his shirt and pulled him upright, drawing a pained laugh from him, his hand automatically going to steady his arm from being jostled.

"That bloody smarts like a bastard," he hissed between humourless chuckles. Her fingers lightly pressed around his shoulder joint. "It's dislocated," he told her quickly as even her light touches set his teeth to grinding.

"Yes, it is," she agreed, putting one hand on his shoulder blade just behind the joint and the other firmly taking hold of his forearm.

"You left the gold," he said softly while she confidently took to tending him.

"Yeah," she said simply. Why the hell had she done that? Chose Gage over gold? Clara didn't have an answer. At least not one she liked.

"Interesting choice," he said, sounding overly blasé, a host of implications coming with just those two words.

"Don't flatter yourself, Sinclair," Clara said, forcing herself to roll her eyes.

"Cold hard math. Don't let the money man die; you need to be alive to replace that gold," she smirked. She watched his face harden in an instant.

"Like hell—"

Clara pulled down as hard as she could on his forearm, using her other hand to manoeuvre the joint back into place before releasing her grip on his forearm. There was a loud sickening pop as the shoulder joint snapped back into place.

Gage cried out in pain before snapping his mouth shut, trapping the sound in his throat where it was less loud and slightly less agonized; black spots and explosions of light eating away at parts of his vision.

Clara caught him before he could roll forwards, holding him upright as she felt him let out the breath and start to gasp in shallow fast breaths.

"Slow it down, Lucas, deep breaths," she instructed calmly, still holding him up in her arms. It was the first time he'd heard his first name on a woman's lips in what felt like an eternity. In a way, it hurt more than the shoulder did. Strangely it also gave him the focus to do as she instructed.

He took in one deep, shaky breath and let it out slowly, then another and another. She watched his face for a moment, using her hand to swipe a bit of his hair out of his face to see his eyes.

It was only when he looked at her as if he was surprised by the gesture that she realized how intimate it had been. She quickly flashed him a bright insincere grin to distract from the impulsive action.

"Was that good for you?"

"Hilarious," Gage wheezed sarcastically. Seeing he had collected himself, she got up and pulled him carefully to his feet. She unclasped the all but shredded cloak she wore and removed it from her shoulders, tearing a long wide strip from the ruined fabric.

"Speaking of interesting choices, you pulled Nahleese from the grass." She started to fashion something from the material, eyes focused intently on her work.

"Well, I need you, and you need her—seemed prudent." He shrugged, then winced at the movement. "Gods, not doing that again anytime soon," he muttered through clenched teeth.

Clara couldn't help but think that it was a strange thing to lie about. That hadn't been why he helped her. Nahleese was a great aide and a better friend, but Clara didn't strictly *need* her to get through the forest; she'd made the trek hundreds of times without her. In fact, with her hurt she would most likely be considered a hindrance. She knew Gage knew that.

"Be grateful it was the arm with that famous disabled hand of yours and not the good one," she said, slipping his arm carefully into the crude sling she'd made, sliding it over his head to hold his arm comfortably in a rest position.

"You're going to need it to carry Nahleese," she said, patting his good shoulder with a smirk.

"No good bloody deed goes unpunished," he muttered to himself.

Clara followed their tracks back to the rest of the group as Gage carried Nahleese over his good shoulder. The Maroth's yowling was softer than the loud jarring sounds of fighting; it filled the mist with an unnerving foreboding that Gage tried to ignore.

For Clara, the sound put her at ease; any creature hunting would be compelled to ignore them in favour of the injured and dying Maroth.

When they found the others, her and Gage both saw his crew had at this time seen fit to climb out of their trees. Clara might have scolded them for this but soon saw their injuries were punishment enough.

Jared looked green as William tried to help him drink from his canteen, propped against a tree and drawing strangled breaths. She'd gamble his ribs were broken. Peter was taking care of Squint, pressing a piece of cloth he'd ripped from his shirt to the man's hand to staunch the flow of blood, he looked short a finger. Hot blood dripped off Squint's chin from a deep gash that looked to have deprived him of his famous squint eye. Peter himself sported a laceration that ran from his shoulder right across his chest to his opposite hip, not nearly as deep as Squint's but worrisome nonetheless.

Clara got to work as quickly as possible; the fact that the Maroth was no longer intent on killing them all in no way meant the danger had passed, time was not on their side—everyone had to be as near fit as quickly as possible.

Gage put Nahleese's unbalanced weight down on the ground as gently as he could (difficult with only one arm) and went to Jared's side, pressing a hand to his abdomen that nearly bugged the man's eyes out of his head.

"Well, Jared, apparently lady luck is on your side—you've only cracked ribs today."

Gage glanced back to ask Clara for something to wrap them with and saw she was already ripping her ruined cloak down the middle and tossing it to him.

"That should do it," she said. Gage nodded his thanks before he shoved the tattered cloth into William's hand.

"Wrap his ribs and get him up," he ordered.

"Yes, Captain."

Clara was already next to Peter, pulling him away from Squint and giving him a lightning-quick once-over.

"Doesn't hurt," he told her as he looked down at the long, bleeding wound. "I'm cold," he said almost absently.

"That's the wonderful work of shock, Peter." Clara looked into his eyes and saw enough of a spark in them that she decided the shock was more a blessing than a problem. She pushed the bits of her torn and ripped cloak against the gash, making him flinch.

"Hold this there," she ordered before crouching down to attend to the more seriously injured Squint. She gently grabbed the ripped piece of Peter's shirt he was using to bandage his hand to get a better look at the damage.

Squint had been deprived of his pinkie, ring, and middle finger, his palm deeply split down the middle.

"Gonna have to flip people off with your other hand from now on, Squint," Clara said lightly as she pulled a strip of cloth from the front pouch of her pack and tied the ripped shirt on the wound tight enough to draw a loud curse out of the man.

"I'll be sure to remember that," he growled under his breath, unsteadily allowing her to grab his arm and pull him up.

Her job had been near impossible to begin with, with most of the party now sporting injuries it had just become that much harder.

Gage heard the moans of the Maroth dying out, the thin cover of sound fading by the second.

"Plan, Fox?" he asked with a raised eyebrow.

Clara was brief, he saw she didn't have much time for anything else.

"We need to run. I know they're hurt, but we no longer have the luxury of being sneaky."

Nahleese was shakily getting to her feet, panting loudly like she could diffuse the pain through bigger breaths. Clara quickly knelt in front of her, holding each side of her big head as those large mismatched eyes looked at her in pain.

"Nahleese, don't push yourself," she said softly.

The wolf's eyes were piercing in that moment. As much as Nahleese listened to Clara, nobody could make the wolf do anything she didn't want to do. She did as she damn well pleased, her gaze relaying about as much to Clara. Nahleese pulled her head out of Clara's hands and limped to take up rear position behind the pirates getting to their feet and lining up.

Nahleese knew what she needed, and for that Clara was eternally grateful.

"I'm starting to see a resemblance," Gage remarked dryly, watching Clara get to her feet.

"She okay?" Peter asked, blood still seeping through the rag and down his chest.

"You just worry about yourself," she told him. Clara quickly hopped over to him and pressed his hand harder into the makeshift bandage. "The red stuff is supposed to stay on the inside."

"What can I say? I'm a rebel." He tried to smile, though it was came across more as a painful grimace.

"Everyone's a comedian today," Clara sighed exasperatedly. She heard someone unsheathing their sword, she knew who it was before she even looked.

Gage gave the blade a test swing that whistled through the air, wielding the sword as if it were an extension of himself rather than a separate thing. His crew followed his lead, and for the first time in her life, Clara caught herself being actually relieved that she wasn't the only one with a weapon.

"If it moves or gets close to you, kill it," he ordered. Those ocean glacier eyes of his turned to her. She'd never seen so much... fire in such a cool shade of blue before.

"Care to lead the way, Fox?" he asked as a grin tugged at his lips.

Craziest damn pirate she'd ever met. Since Clara almost grinned back while drawing her own blade, she wasn't entirely sure what that said about her.

"Thought you'd never ask, Sinclair."

Fourteen

They ran like all of hell was on their heels. Night had begun to close in, Clara could feel it in the slight chill filling the air as they all careened headfirst into the dangers littering their path.

She held her breath—having lost her rag— as they tore through patch after patch of corpse grass until she was dizzy. The one stroke of luck she had on her side was the corpse grass didn't span far, but holding your breath and running are not easy things to do together.

She led them along the path they were most likely to survive, true, but even then, every step was like balancing on the edge of deaths knife. Nahleese pulled up the rear; any pirate that started to fall behind was quickly encouraged forwards by the nearness of teeth on his backside.

Swords cut at the bush, beheading flowers and stabbing at half-seen creatures. Clara cleared more than a few wayward beasts with teeth and sinister death traps from their path, but the attempts from a few butterfly-spiders the size of pups and other equally disturbing critters seemed paltry in comparison to the Maroth now.

The less injured helped those that stumbled or were slowed by pain. Squint was pulled along by William while Jared wielded a blade and Peter kept them both up to pace, holding his makeshift bandage against his chest.

The more they ran, the more creatures of the forest seemed to come clawing at them from the mist.

Gage's blade was the most lethal of the entire party; any creature that caught his eye was felled in an instant without him missing a step. He didn't know it, but he'd saved Jared from being melted by an acidic secretion twice, cutting some unsavory plants from the path before they could spew their insidious acidic fumes.

Everything was trying to kill them; a collective decision had been made to make an effort to repay the favour. Nicks and jagged cuts collected on them all with every mile they made alive; blood trailed behind them as surely as it stained their skins.

Gage grit his teeth the entire run as every step jarred his shoulder into an almost unbearable aching, keeping Clara in his sight the entire time. She cleared their way, Nahleese limped after them and covered their backs, and Gage? He and his men made mincemeat of anything in between.

Clara was just throwing her curved blade, spearing a butterfly-spider that she'd caught in her peripherals, trying to drop from the high branch of a tree down on them with fangs extended. The knife impaled the creature, impact moving it off target so it hit the ground instead, legs scrabbled at the moss in pain while its beautiful wings fluttered against the boggy mess. Its guts wet the moss under their feet but they spared it hardly anything more than a passing thought, they just kept running. More things were coming out of the woodwork for the injured crew every minute.

Just when Clara thought they weren't going to make it before nightfall, just when she thought they were going to have to make the last stand any of them would ever make against the dangers darkness brought, the moss and fog began to lift.

Her heart soared as she demanded more of her body, pushing it to carry her faster to what she knew must be the end of the silent path. Gage pulled up beside, matching her stride for stride, as if he could feel the edge of this hell with his fingertips and was straining to grasp it with all he had.

Just when doubt began to worry into all their guts that they might be wrong, that there was no end in sight, they suddenly broke through the mist, into the bright greenery, seeing the last touches of orange fading from the sky.

Gage felt a thousand miles high, a cry of triumph almost escaping his lips. The sound of their feet pounding the earth out of the shadow of the silent path was like applause, even mingling as it did with the now angry shrieks of the monsters that might devour them.

Clara felt no relief, she did not slow her pace nor let her gaze stray from the target ahead of her, even as she felt the multiple pursuers slow at the invisible barrier that marked the border between the silent paths private horrors and the regular fare of the Dark Forest's terrors.

William looked back, multiple eyes gleaming out at them all from the swirling mists and darkness of the silent path, pacing, watching them all run into the fading light as if that barred them somehow behind the haze of their boarders.

"They're not following," William wheezed, stumbling to a stop, bracing one hand on his knee as he pulled the blue cap from his head to wipe his face.

Everyone slowed at this realization, their breakneck run turning into a borderline drunken stumble forward, a ragtag group of blood-smeared men with their heads turned back in an awe-like horror to where they'd just emerged from.

"They will be," Clara huffed to herself, sparing only a glance back. She saw Nahleese limping through the grass, fur matted, eyes glazed as she panted violently for air, holding her marker at last place as if to prove that all had made it.

It was a good omen Clara thought as she finally stopped a far ways away from the silent path to grab something that lay at her feet.

Gage watched as she strained and pulled until slowly a large door, disguised as part of the earth under her feet, swung open. She let the heavy door in the ground fall open, revealing a dark hole.

"The sun is almost set! Move!" she yelled to them all, hurrying them as her worried eyes turned to the last slivers of light in the sky.

When the sun went down there were no paths of less or more danger, the forest turned into one great spanning free-for-all forest of death and feasting.

She watched them all collecting what was left of their strength and pushing themselves forward, sweat and blood streaked men racing at a hobble to her against the sun. Jared was first, descending into the darkness, then Squint, William...

Gage reached her next, but instead of following his men he took post next to her, looking back to the stragglers.

Nahleese limped next to Peter, nudging him with her nose to keep him going as he looked close to falling. His hand twisted in her flank, and for a moment Clara thought it was to keep himself upright. A moment later she realized Nahleese wasn't the only one lending encouragement. The wolf's legs seemed to betray her as she stumbled, coming very close to actually falling—saved from doing so only by Peter's firm grip.

But then Nahleese stopped walking, as if all she had the energy, the will for, was keeping herself upright. Peter came to a stop with her, yanking on her flank

"No, no, no—we're almost there, girl, come on," he encouraged softly, panting just as violently for air as her—holding that blood soaked scrap of fabric to his chest to slow bleeding. Clara nearly choked when she realized it didn't even occurred to Peter to leave Nahleese behind.

The sun was almost gone, the last rays of light all that was between them and the hordes of horrific monsters pacing the boarders of the mist behind them.

"Move lad!" Gage shouted, waving Peter forward.

Nahleese raised her great white head to look at Peter, yanking on her flank to move her. Gods, they were so close.

"Run, damnit!" Clara shouted at the pair.

With a great effort the wolf heaved herself forward, Peter and her closing the space separating them from safety with seconds left to spare. Only then did Peter let go of Nahleese, slipping past Clara and Gage into the hole.

"Aren't you just the damsel in distress today?" Gage mocked as he knelt down to the trembling, haggard wolf.

Nahleese snorted at him in response, a slight growl on the edge of the noise. If he didn't know better, he'd think the wolf was telling him to go to hell as he scooped the beast up with his good arm and, with a great effort, onto his shoulder once more before Nahleese could collapse.

Gage quickly carried the wolf down the narrow stairs in the ground.

The sun disappeared, and Clara was witness as a writhing mass of hungry shadows spilled from the mist like a wave just before she jumped in after him, heaving the latch closed with a loud click, the sound of her latching and bolting it filling the darkness.

Clara held the door closed despite the fact it was locked, and soon the sound of claws scraped against the wood and dirt while it rattled and shook, with snarls and sounds that would do damage to any man's calm.

"Fox," Gage said, voice strained with the same tension squeezing his gut.

"It'll pass," she answered, voice hard, arms shaking as she strained to keep the door secure.

The creatures railed against the door for a time, but it was as short as it was intense. Then the barrage faded, interest apparently quick to wane, accepting them as their escaped quarry.

"It'll hold," Clara's voice told him, slowly releasing her grip on the door.

"Go, I'll be right behind you, watch your step," she advised him as he began to descend the narrow steps.

It was a bit perilous, carrying Nahleese, but he made it eventually. As he hit the bottom step, his eyes were aided by a single candle someone had lit, revealing their lodgings for the night.

He was surprised as he crossed a threshold to see it was wide and open, a great cavernous room carved out of the earth, a twelve-foot-high ceiling braced with planks of wood. Numerous candles were mounted into the dirt walls for light (being lit, one by one, by Jared) that brightened the place considerably with their yellow, flickering flames.

There was a round, wooden table in the corner with eight chairs (three occupied by his wheezing injured companions) and a narrow hallway just beside it. He smelt water, heard it too; perhaps there was an underground stream nearby.

He walked in, examining the space with some awe before slowly laying Nahleese down on the floor. A crude, makeshift cabinet had been built along the wall; a few shelves encircled the space holding a few unlabeled bottles. Had she built all of this?

Right then, Clara walked into the room from the narrow stairs, her faithful pack in her hands—hands that were shaking. Gage saw how tense every muscle in Clara's body was; it was a surprise she could even move her limbs with all that tension still coursing through her.

"I feel sick," Peter said, pale faced and looking close to vomiting. Squint echoed that sentiment by falling to his knees and dry heaving.

"We all do, it's the running lad," Gage assured him as William pulled Squint back to his feet. Gage himself was still trying to catch his breath and not looking so hot, and for Gage that was saying something.

Clara's eyes took them all in, how they were covered in nicks and gouges and various injuries that had painted many of them red; they all looked gruesome. Peter wasn't the only one feeling ill. She felt it too, and she was very used to running.

"It's not the running. He's been poisoned," Clara said bluntly. "We all have."

She could have dropped a pin, and she was pretty sure it would have hurt their ears to hear it hit the ground at that moment.

"What?" Jared finally said, as though he'd misheard her.

"There was no way in hell we could do what we just did, which was complete madness, and not be tagged by multiple poisons," she said as she moved to a shelf and began rooting through a few tiny wicker boxes and some tin jars, searching for something. Finally she went to each of them, carrying small rolled balls of various herbs, bound together with a bit of string, and handing one to each of them, giving a certain size amount to each. She felt her fingers swelling already, she had to hurry.

"This should counteract it. Chew it; don't swallow," Clara ordered.

"This negates all poisons?" Squint asked on a wheeze, still very out of breath, his lips starting to turn unnaturally blue.

"Most, if you get it in you early enough."

"What if we have one that this doesn't cover?" Jared demanded. He didn't realize it yet but black veins had begun to show around his eyes. Squint noticed and he was paling even more at the sight. If Jared's eyes started to bleed he was going to die.

"Have any favourite gods?"

"I see you've a mastery of assuaging fears," Gage muttered, chewing the bitter herbs with a scrunched-up face, using his sleeve to wipe some blood from his cheek.

"This is what I was referring to earlier," William added, making an obvious effort not to look at Jared.

Clara had to disagree, though she didn't say so aloud—she hadn't told them that the careful combination of herbs she'd given them would speed the effects of any poison it couldn't dissipate. It was a mercy, because any poison she couldn't cure was one that would take their life in a very slow and cruel way.

"How long till we know?" Peter asked, wide eyed gaze fixed on her.

Clara popped the herb into her mouth, starting the countdown in her head.

"Five minutes."

The time seemed to drag on forever, no one moving, the sound of their panting filling the space, pain beginning to line the creases of their faces as tension over took adrenaline. They could have attended to their wounds, should have, yet it seemed an unvoiced consensus that silence was preferred, stillness—no matter how much it wore on the nerves.

Clara kept her expectations low, expecting to lose two at best and everyone at the worst—even herself.

One minute.

Two minutes. The swelling in her fingers dissipated.

Three minutes. Jared's eyes cleared, Squints lips reverted to normal.

When they hit the five minute mark and they all still stood, Clara honestly thought she'd miscounted the time. She counted out another minute just to be sure and still no one dropped dead—and she knew no one was going to.

"Looks like you're all good."

More than a few knees turned wobbly at her declaration, tension draining away to leave behind fatigue and relieved joy.

"I need a bloody pint," Squint said through clenched teeth.

"Just one?" Jared asked, like he wanted several himself.

"Well he might have trouble grabbing two," William observed dryly, glancing to Squint's mutilated hand.

Squint took Clara's advice and flipped him off with the other hand.

Gage grinned at his men, turning to Clara as if he expected her to be doing much the same.

Clara however looked around at all of them less like she was actually seeing them and more like she was looking for the next thing that was coming to attack her. She was still running damn hot on adrenaline as she moved to do whatever next task she had set herself.

Gage slipped into her path to halt her, putting his hand over hers to halt their trembling.

She hadn't even realized they *were* trembling.

"Fox," he said firmly, getting her to really stop for a moment and look at him. "We made it—breathe."

At first she just stared at him with a blank face, misted with droplets of blood (hers or not he wasn't sure), not really taking it in. Then she let out a breath she hadn't realized she was holding; it felt like she'd been holding it from the moment they'd started to run. But she could breathe now, because... they'd... made it?

Everyone was silent again as the realization seemed to slowly dawn on them—they had survived. It settled more fully on Clara it seemed, because she broke the silence by laughing.

"We... we actually *made* it." She giggled, grinning the first sincere smile he'd ever seen on her face.

It was a contagious thing that seemed to spread to his lips as well as she laughed hard enough to make her eyes shiny with tears. It spread from her to Gage, then to the rest of the crew, laughing through the pain, sweat, and blood. They laughed till their sides hurt, slowly managing to get a hold of themselves one by one.

Clara was one of the last, she let out another half sigh, half laugh like she still couldn't believe it. Yes, they'd made it; they had just survived the suicide run to end all suicide runs. And she hadn't lost a single one of them, not even Nahleese—it was one of *those* days.

"Well then," she said to Gage, wiping a tear from her eye. "Drinks on you Captain."

Clara had managed to coax Nahleese to a secluded corner and onto a bed of straw, where she curled up and closed her eyes, taking some much needed rest. Clara disappeared down the hall once more while everyone used the water bubbling up into a basin mounted on a wall near the stairs to wash the blood from their skin and cuts.

She emerged a few minutes later in a simple pair of trousers and a fresh white shirt. She flittered about from shelf to shelf collecting things, pulled two chairs into the corner, and one by one Clara treated their wounds with the balms and bandages she kept in the reserve of her little safe havens.

She cracked a very small clear jar open and began smothering exposed wounds with the thick clear gel, miraculously closing them within minutes and making them look weeks old instead of hours, if not making most of them disappear completely.

Squint's hand now looked as if he'd been missing fingers for a solid year. She used the gel on his face as well, but there was only so much it could do.

"That eye is useless now, I'm afraid, Squint," Clara told him bluntly.

He shrugged. "It was my bad eye anyways. At least now I look as mean as I feel."

"Cause you looked so cuddly before," Clara said, patting his shoulder. "Gonna have to get a new nickname, or start using your real one."

"My real name's Quint," he grumbled. Wait a minute. He'd been *Quint the Squint* this whole time?

"You're screwing with me, right?" Clara asked, starting to smile.

"No," he replied grumpily, glaring. No wonder he was such a prickly jerk.

"Well, you just forget I said a damn thing, then," she said, just barely holding her laughter back. "And cheer up, you're alive."

"You seem pleased about that," Squint noted, observing her with his now singular eye.

"If you'd have told me a few days ago that I would get five people through the silent path at a loud, dead run I'd have laughed hysterically and told you to get your head checked," Clara said, a bit of giddiness still in her voice.

"Ah, professional pride then. Too cold for anything else, huh?" he remarked. She could have taken that personally, but she had Squint figured for a one-note man, and that note was abrasive—be it to his crewmates, friends, captain, or otherwise—and he knew it.

"Well it's certainly not cause I like you, Squint. You're kind of an asshole." Squint blinked at her for a second, then he actually laughed, a brusque sound that shook his whole body.

"That I am, that I am."

She reexamined the gash that went across Peter's chest, shoulder to hip, now a thick, ropey, pink scar. She attended him mostly in a silence that seemed to be making Peter squirm, his body so tense she was pretty sure a musician could have used him for a lute string; but she couldn't find the words she felt needed saying to Peter.

"I appreciate you sticking with Nahleese," she told him at the same time he blurted out, "I'm sorry for trying to kiss you!"

Clara and Peter blinked at each other, them Clara snorted out a brisk laugh.

"In the past kid, but if it makes you feel better, apology accepted."

He sagged, relaxing a little at last.

"You did really good today, little Rebel. You should be proud of yourself," she told him sincerely. He puffed out ever so slightly.

"Thanks. What is that ointment stuff?" Peter asked, sounding awed as he examined the new scar with her.

"Bought it from a gypsy who worked magic spells into the herbs," she told him. "Cost me an arm and a leg. It's one of the very few bits of magic that works in here, though, so worth it."

"Magic doesn't work here?" he repeated, sounding stunned. She forgot sometimes that not everyone was on the same page as her, she didn't really tell people much more than she thought they needed to know.

"Most magic," she corrected. "Mild healing balms is pretty much it. Nothing big or fancy will work in here," she said, shrugging. Clara saw him draw his hand along the scar again, and she punched his shoulder lightly.

"I hear bar wenches love scars, Rebel" she said with a wink. He smiled at the new nickname she'd pinned him with.

"Do, uh, you like scars?" he tried to ask casually, as if just trying to make conversation.

Subtlety was clearly not Peter's art, but that was actually kind of cute. She was also in a very good mood, getting everyone through alive thus far and all, hence why Clara took the open opportunity to toy with him just a little bit.

"Are you calling me a bar wench, Peter?"

"What?" he almost yelped in alarm. "No! No not at all!"

"What do you mean no? Do you have something against bar wenches?" she demanded, trying to swallow her smile as she watched him try to back pedal.

"Of course not! I just, I mean, do you want to be? A bar wench? I mean, no, of course you don't, uh—" He pushed his unruly, shaggy brown hair from his face, trying to think of something to say that wouldn't get him in trouble. He looked at her, helplessly mute before he realized she was grinning from ear to ear.

"Just messing with you, Rebel."

He opened his mouth, closed it, and then opened it again. Finally he laughed. "You know what? You are a bar wench," he said at last, standing up from his chair.

Clara just chuckled, giving him a slight push to send him on his way.

All the pirates now sat around the table with their flasks of rum; someone had apparently brought a deck of cards, and they were just beginning to deal out a hand. What they were playing Clara had no idea; she'd never had occasion to play cards with anyone.

She sat comfortably in her chair a moment and just watched them: William dealing out the cards, Jared trying to sit in a way that alleviated the pain of his cracked ribs, Squint figuring out the best way to utilize his hand with the lack of fingers, and Peter pulling a chair back to sit in. Wait a minute. Where was—

She felt a hand gently touch her shoulder and jumped.

"I've never seen such simple attire flatter someone so well," Gage's husky timber informed her playfully.

"Dammit, Sinclair, don't do that," she snapped, turning her head up to glare at him.

His hair was still wet, making it as black as ink, tossed even more carelessly about his face in a way that somehow made him impossibly more... attractive, in a laid back sort of way; skin scrubbed clean and down to his simple loose fitting shirt she could have easily said the same of him. Clara roughly shoved his hand off her a moment later.

"Did I spook you, darling?" He grinned with mock surprise, taking the seat across from her.

"I didn't think that possible," he admitted.

She could say no, but she'd be lying, and chances were he'd know she was lying so it all around seemed pointless. "Even a blind pig finds an acorn once in a while. What are you doing?" Clara asked as she watched him carefully remove the sling from around his neck.

"Don't you want to check how your patient is doing?" Gage pouted.

"I already know how this patient is doing. The fact that he's being a pain in my ass is a sure sign of recovery," she told him brightly.

"The shoulder hurts like the dickens, Fox. Could you not at least... *examine* it?"

He lingered on the word like it was the most sensual three syllables to have ever passed his lips, raising the hair on the back of her neck. Gage was too smooth for his own damn good sometimes.

"If you couldn't flirt, I'm pretty sure you'd wither up and die," Clara said flatly, "and that'd be a shame, because I'm pretty sure you'd be less fun to look at. Shirt off," she said, the last with a lidded gaze and a smirk.

Gage was a bit taken aback at the smile she gave him—playful, challenging. He'd grown used to flat-out snappy denials to his charm. She was trying to throw him now; she'd have to do better than that.

"Are you saying you like to look at me?" he asked, undoing the buttons of his shirt with deliberate slowness.

"To borrow one of yours, it's not a bad view," Clara said, like she didn't notice what he was doing before she helped him get his arm out of his sleeve and allowing him to do the rest himself.

"You know if there's anything else of mine you'd like to borrow..." he trailed off as he dropped the shirt on the floor. He was now sitting before her with his exposed broad shoulders, lean, toned muscles from years labouring under a hot sun to manoeuvre a ship over an unforgiving sea, a slight sheen of sweat still clinging to his bronzed skin.

Her grin was wide and amused as she ran her eyes down the length of him, taking in every glorious inch. Clara could see why so few women turned him down, but she'd continue to be one of those few.

"Hmmm, can't think of anything," Clara said, bringing her gaze back up to his with a mock look of puzzlement on her face.

"I could make a few suggestions," he offered, leaning forwards in his seat and waggling his eyebrows at her.

Clara laughed, shaking her head at him.

"Oh, Sinclair, you're just a big pirate whore, aren't you?" She reached forwards and gently kneaded the muscle around his shoulder, his skin hot to the touch.

"I prefer accomplished lover," he amended, wincing slightly at the soft yet brisk examination.

"Who wouldn't?" Clara asked sarcastically. She couldn't describe what it was that was different about this exchange, but it felt less calculated, more natural. A camaraderie-like feel had begun to invade their conversations of late, a few walls coming down in the lull between making those big strategic moves.

Strangely she felt like the quips they exchanged were like ones you exchanged with... a friend? Friend didn't seem like the right word, too casual, not strange enough perhaps, but it was surely something along those lines.

"Ooo, such disdain," Gage replied, clucking his tongue like she were a misbehaving child, bringing her back to the conversation as she finished the examination.

"How long do you plan on pretending you don't like me even a little, love?"

"Who's pretending? How bad is the pain?"

"Well, nothing more painful than the blatant disinterest of a beautiful woman, is there?" Gage leaned back in the chair as if to give her a better view of him. Clara pretended not to notice. She pretended very, very hard.

"You're a big boy, I'm sure you'll recover. Is it a shooting pain when you move the arm or just aching?" she clarified in a deadpan.

He put his elbow on his knee and rested his head on the back of his gloved hand, looking up at her with an overly exaggerated wistful gaze, ruined by the spark of mirth in his eyes.

"Simply *aching*," he said softly.

"Stop molesting innocent words so they sound naughty." His grin almost split his face in two as they sat there just looking at each other, doing nothing for a moment or two.

"There was a reason you demanded I take my shirt off, correct?" he asked when she did nothing.

"Of course; seeing what all the fuss is about," she told him airily.

He shook his head, chuckling. "Why, Fox, I do appreciate such an implication."

"What implication?"

"That you care to find out," he said with his signature wink.

She rolled her eyes before dipping into her little green pack and pulling out a jar of white ointment, opening it, and rubbing some between her hands.

"Where did you learn all of this?" Gage asked curiously, prying more into the enigma that was her.

"Fitz taught me the basics," she admitted freely. "From there, I either just kind of figured it out as I went or I paid for the good stuff," she said, nodding to the ointment jar. She started to rub the ointment over his shoulder, chasing away some of the bruising and the pain as she gently massaged it in.

"Trial and error?" he asked, amazed at how the pain melted away under her touch.

"Well, when you have as much time as I usually have on my hands, you find ways to pass the time; I can't tolerate boredom."

That was not nearly as satisfying an answer as he'd hoped for, but then again he wondered why he cared to know that at all about her. He wanted to ask more questions about her, but Clara's touch was beginning to distract him. It was gentle but firm, adept as if she'd done this a thousand times before. He found himself feeling strangely jealous at the thought of her practicing, most likely on Fitz, he thought, finding himself almost contemptuous towards the other man.

Her hands weren't soft but there was something pleasantly tender in her touch as they smoothed down his arm and over his shoulder. She never lingered too long in one spot, but still, jolts of electricity ran through him, mixed at times with sparks of pain. It was very telling though that he found he didn't mind. Gage did want her, as much as he played her, tried to get in her head; that had always been true, and he'd made no show to hide it. He'd wanted and had many women, but this desire Clara had ignited in him was different, growing by the day. He wanted her... around. As much as he wanted her physically, he found he genuinely liked her quite a bit. And he knew he couldn't afford the feeling, yet here he was, bantering with her—making it grow.

"You were brilliant out there today," he said, surprised by how much he meant it.

"You weren't so bad yourself," she replied, brushing off the compliment. "That move with the Maroth was nothing short of inspired, if you don't mind me saying so—saved my ass."

"Is that a thank-you?" he asked with a raised eyebrow.

"Nope," she said stubbornly, her tone making him laugh.

"You saved my life, I saved yours—you owe me gold," she reminded him, pointedly.

"But of course," he acknowledged, obscurity on his face causing her a moment's pause before continuing.

"However... you saved Nahleese today," she said, tone deceptively casual. He didn't say anything, waiting for her to continue. "So... I appreciate that," she finished at last, refusing to look him in the eye as she said it, the closest she'd come to a thanks without actually saying the words.

"Sorry, love, didn't catch that, could you say it louder?" he asked, cupping a hand to his ear as if to hear her better.

"Yeah, I'm not saying it again," she told him coolly.

He chuckled. "You're one of a kind, Fox."

She didn't know what to say to that, especially since it was dangerously close to sounding sincere. She took the safe route out.

"Did you ever doubt I was?" she asked, making light of the compliment. Clara realized she was still massaging his shoulder, even though she didn't need to be, and briskly finished applying the balm before pulling back.

The feel of her hands somehow lingered on Gage's skin in a way that distracted him more than a little.

"Better?" she asked.

Gage rolled his shoulder, looking pleasantly surprised. "Much."

There was a cry of victory from the table mixed with a few groans of the losers of the latest hand.

"Captain! Someone needs to teach Peter a damn lesson in losing, whaddya say?" William called out from the table as Gage turned his attention to his crew playing a game of shimmy.

Clara took advantage of the distraction, leaving her seat to start searching one of the shelves for some of that moonshine Fitz always made just for her. Gage was not oblivious to how Clara jumped on the opportunity to "excuse" herself and took it as her version of a dismissal.

"I'd say prepare to be made fools of." Gage grinned, grabbing his shirt and getting up from his seat to join them at the table.

A few hands were played as they drank their rum and generally celebrated the fact that they were all alive. They should have been exhausted from the run and their trials, but truth be told, there was still too much adrenaline in them all to let them sleep. So they tried the age-old way of calming nerves or alleviating boredom, a good ol' game of "pirate shimmy."

Gage hadn't really expected Clara to join them, and she of course lived up to that expectation. His eyes flickered to her every now and then as she stayed unobtrusively in the corner near the sleeping Nahleese, sipping at an unlabeled bottle from her shelf and cleaning her knife. It seemed he wasn't the only one who was keeping an eye on her.

"Miss Clara, care to join us?" William called out to her, watching her expectantly. Everyone seemed to try to look at her without actually *looking* at her then to see what her reaction would be to the invite.

She, however, didn't bother looking up from what she was doing.

"I don't know the game."

"We could teach you," Peter offered eagerly.

Clara smirked at the sound of Peter's voice, but her eyes never strayed from examining the edge of her knife. She didn't fraternize unless she had to; that was a rule, and she had to keep to it. Especially with these pirates, because despite her efforts? She was actually starting to like a few of them.

"Thanks, Rebel, but I think I'll pass," she told him kindly.

Gage smirked to himself for a moment; it was too good an opportunity to pass up. "Leave her be, lad," Gage told Peter. "Lasses of the world generally don't play cards, and if they do, they don't do it well," he informed him with a touch of condescension in his voice. He almost felt her eyes spear him from across the room.

"Beg your pardon?" he heard her ask coolly. He did his best not to smile wider or look at her, focusing on his cards.

"I find that women are no good at card games," he repeated casually. He must think she was an idiot.

"Wow, if you were any more transparent, you'd disappear altogether, Sinclair," she said, shaking her head as she went back to what she was doing. He shrugged, an action that now caused him barely any pain.

"Care to prove me wrong?" he asked.

"Not especially, no."

"It's all right, Captain, wouldn't be terribly fair to her," William said, obviously catching on quickly.

"It's not a woman's game," Squint chipped in crustily.

"Definitely," Jared agreed quickly.

The pirates looked to Peter expectantly. When he didn't say anything, William rolled his eyes and kicked him from under the table.

"Ow! I mean, yeah, they're hopeless really," Peter added finally, struggling to think of something. William face-palmed and shook his head with a sigh.

The fairly annoyed attempt to not submit to goading was suddenly a highly annoying itch. Clara gritted her teeth together and glared at them all, well aware of what they were doing.

The pirates were trying to look like they were casually dealing out the next hand and not shrinking under her glare for a few minutes. Gage however boldly held her gaze, grinning. She wanted in on the fun; she just didn't want to admit it.

"It's just a game love."

The edges of her lips just barely quirked upward, those twin green jewels of fire in her face meeting his eyes.

"Isn't it always?"

Clara weighed it out before she finally stood, the desire to make them all eat their words overriding her desire to follow her own rules; besides, just one card game, right?

"Fine."

She dragged her chair behind her up as she approached, William and Peter both moving to give her a space at the table. Flipping her chair around to straddle it, she put her bottle down to her right and stabbed her knife with a dull *thunk* into the wood to her left.

"What are the rules?"

Fifteen

Clara lost the first two hands, trying to get a grip on how it was all played. The next two hands she knew they let her win in an attempt to keep her interested.

"Would you look at that, she can play after all," Jared had remarked as she took a swing from her bottle.

Clara had laughed at that. "Bullshit, you gave that game away. You're all a bunch of flatterers and liars."

"Us? Lie?" William asked, his attempt at sounding appalled ruined by a small smile.

"Offended?" she asked lightly.

Gage levelled her with a wicked grin. "Personally I'd be offended if you thought we were honest, love."

The hands after that? Clara started to win for real; she was pulling even on the scratch card with Gage and Peter, both who seemed like the two most adept players of the game. Of course this is where the others quit pity-playing and started playing like the pirates they were.

"If he plays a six on his second turn, you skip the next player," Squint tried to convince her, ensuring her unable to play a card. He was the third one of them to try to implement a bullshit rule to slow her streak of good luck, two games now being played at once: a card game and a game called, "see-who-can-put-one-past-Clara."

"Nice try," she said, laying her next card down and taking another drink.

"Can't play royalty on the fourth turn," Jared tried next round.

"Actually I can, which means you're out." Clara smiled sweetly, laying the card down dramatically for his benefit.

"The rules say he's still in if he gives up a card," William said, trying to see if he could slip a less self-serving falsehood past her.

"Just William, you couldn't lie to a three year old—give it up," she told him, shaking her head.

"How do you do that?" Peter asked, laying down a card.

"Do what?" Clara asked, being deliberately obtuse.

"Know when people are lying?" he asked curiously. Gage watched her, wondering how she would answer.

Clara shrugged. "Just do."

"No special trick?" Gage asked, turning his eyes back to his cards.

"One," she admitted after a moment.

Everyone waited for her to explain further, but it appeared she didn't feel the need to enlighten them as to what that trick was.

"I'm sorry, we are still playing cards, right?" she asked when no one played a card.

"What's the trick?" William asked, unable to hide his curiosity. She smiled at him but said nothing.

Gage laughed at her coyness. "Don't bother, William. Lass loves her mystery," he told them all, using his two good fingers on his left hand to pick a card from the deck. "And I know the only thing Miss Fox loves more than that is a gamble."

Clara's eyes slowly strayed from her cards to him, interested. "And I bet you have just the one in mind."

"If I have the winning card in my hand, you have to tell us your secret."

She was already shaking her head. "Not a chance."

"How about you reveal one thing about yourself no one knows?" Peter suggested eagerly.

Clara seemed to consider this a moment before she examined Gage's face carefully; he remained neutral and unreadable. She looked down at her own cards, finding it was a hard hand to beat. He didn't have it; he didn't even think she'd take the bet.

"All right," Clara agreed, nodding at Peter. "I call your bluff, Sinclair."

His face remained completely neutral as he used his thumb to flick the card from his hand onto the table, giving her time to look at it before he grinned.

"Shimmy," he said as the entire table groaned and threw down their cards.

Clara grit her teeth. *Son of a bitch.*

"Pay up, little Fox," Gage said smugly.

Everyone waited quietly, curious as to what she would tell them all. She'd had a bit of drink now, enough to make her slightly looser with her tongue than she was normally, she picked a bit of information that at the moment seemed harmless, yet was something she'd never told anyone.

"The very first creature I recognized in here was a fox, just roaming about in the heart of the Dark Forest like it didn't know it should fear for its life. That's how I ended up picking my last name." It wasn't until it was out of her mouth that Clara realized just how much that tiny bit of information revealed about herself.

"Wait, you picked your last name? Didn't you have one?" Peter asked.

Gage watched her smile at the kid, but it looked uneasy on her face.

"No, Rebel, it was just Clara back then."

"Didn't your parents have last names?" Peter pressed, clearly very interested and not bothering to hide it as Gage was.

"The bet was for one thing no one knew, Peter, not two." There was a quiet that bordered almost on awkward, as no one really knew how to respond to that, finding her tidbit only raised even more questions about the Guide than before.

"I'd have picked something with a little more theatricality myself," Gage said, making a show of shrugging the new information off, "something that matched how very handsome I am." He gave her a sly look. "Ah, but perhaps you did—Fox."

"And on that note, I'm out." Clara yawned, rolling her eyes. She stood and was surprised to find herself wobbling on her feet; had she really drank that much?

"All right there, love?" Gage asked, noticing her lack of coordination as she stumbled.

"Fine," she told him, quickly telling everyone the arrangements.

"This room is general sleeping quarters. I bid you all good night." She made for the hallway to the left of the big open room.

"Where are you going?" he asked curiously.

"To my room," she said in a tone that implied everyone else should stay far from it. Clara nearly stumbled, hand going up to grab the door frame to steady herself.

She tossed a quick glance over her shoulder towards Gage, seeing he was watching her closely, she tried to brush off the stumble as nothing and sent him a predictable warning glare.

"If nothing's on fire, don't bother me." Clara disappeared into the hall with Gage still watching after her.

A niggling feeling of unease was in his gut, like maybe, just maybe something was wrong. He did his best to shrug it off. He could smell the moonshine she'd been drinking even though the bottle was across the table from him; anyone would be a touch unsteady after some of that.

Why did the feeling remain, then?

Clara leaned against the wall, limbs feeling heavy as she just tried to get to her room. Something was wrong; there was no way she should be feeling this—she hadn't drank nearly enough to intoxicate herself this badly.

She stumbled into her room, nearly tripping into her waiting cot. She couldn't get herself up, trying to push herself up into a sitting position and finding herself completely unable. Something was very wrong.

Dread filled her stomach as her hand fumbled up to the back of her neck, and her fingers groped for what she was afraid to find.

Her fingers brushed against a hard-shelled lump she knew wasn't supposed to be there, firmly attached to her.

Nightmare beetle.

When the hell—

Oh gods, the gun, some of the bloody oil must have rubbed off on her cloak and into her clothes, maybe even her skin.

"Shit," she slurred, trying to reach into the pouch at her side to slick her fingers with alcohol, but her limbs couldn't seem to do as her brain ordered, numbly veering off course and missing.

Clara tried to again but her arm failed to comply to her command at all this time, her entire body seemed to be cut off from the screaming of her brain as she lay there paralysed.

She felt herself falling impossibly forwards as her vision of the dirt wall disappeared, replaced by the fears the nightmare beetle would feed from.

Unfortunately it would feed well.

A small child waking up in a forest in a white night dress, surrounded by tall trees and the sounds of the wild, vicious and unfamiliar. Where am I? *She thought, looking around as the heavy weight in her stomach seemed to get heavier with fear. She didn't know.*

Her fear only grew when she realized she didn't know who she was, that she remembered nothing before waking up here in this place.

She knew her name was Clara, she knew she was ten, but that was all she knew.

What's going on?! *The sounds of creatures in the night stalking unseen in the bush made her heart thump uncontrollably in her chest.*

"Hello?" her voice called into the dark night, tears running down her face. Gods she hated the dark...

No one answered, and she was too terrified to call any louder for fear of something hungry finding her. Too scared to move, too scared to do anything but cry and wonder why she couldn't remember anything about herself or how she got there.

Hiding, hiding for days, terrified to venture out from the nook of a tree she'd stumbled into for warmth. Knowing she couldn't stay, the dread of knowing she would have to venture out if she was to have any chance of surviving. Worse—knowing that her imagination wasn't getting the best of her; there really were monsters in these trees.

Running, running as fast as she could with the hot sun beating down on her, angrily brushing away tears as the trees nicked at her. Falling and forcing herself up, noticing strangely how most of the terrifying creatures seemed to ignore her and being grateful for it.

Relief, oh the relief, when she breached the edge of the forest into town. She was out! How she'd been thankful for her escape, how she'd promised she'd never go into that horrid place ever again. Remembering how that suffocating dread had begun to build in her as she walked aimlessly past towns and farther from the trees. A voice screaming at her that she couldn't leave the forest, a nagging feeling that inexplicably told Clara she had to go back, to stay there. She knew it was important, she knew that feeling was right and true—she may know hardly anything else, but Clara knew this. She didn't have to strictly speaking; she knew she could leave if she tried. But she was supposed *to be there.*

Standing back on the edge of the Dark Forest, so frightened, wishing so desperately she didn't have to walk into those gods forsaken trees again before doing just that...

Eight years later, the forest and its many deadly creatures growing more vicious with each year. How she'd learned to love it; the thrilling, dangerous, beautiful place she lived; embracing the uncertainty, rolling the dice of survival every day with a smile and a blade. It was love the crucible or let it eat her alive at this point...

The sound of a little boy crying at the forest's edge she was just emerging from, finishing a trek. Seeing an olive skinned boy being beaten by some larger boys. Chasing them all off with hard slaps and a boot in their asses to teach them all a damn lesson.

She reached down, grabbing the small boy's hand and pulling him upright.

"You all right, kid?"

"I'm fine," he'd told her, wiping his tears away as quickly as possible on the back of his sleeve. Messy brown hair, eyes the colour of slate, and a stubborn frown fixed on his small face.

"Who asked you to butt in?" he'd snapped angrily at her, trying to wipe away more tears and the streaks they left on his round little cheeks.

"Is that your version of 'thanks for the help,' twerp?" she'd asked sounding thoroughly annoyed.

"I don't need your help," he'd told her impudently, a statement ruined by the trembling of his lower lip, kid was no older than seven.

"Yeah, I saw how you had them on the run," Clara had replied, rolling her eyes at him.

Those slate eyes flickering from her to the forest.

"You came through there?"

"I live in there." The satisfaction of watching his jaw drop.

"Only monsters live there!" He'd thought about that a moment. "Are you a monster?"

"No." she answered with a bit of annoyance, turning away from him. "Go home, kid," she'd yelled over her shoulder, heading into town. He was waiting for her when she came back, looking as if he'd not moved from the spot where she'd left him.

"I can't go home," he'd told her softly upon her return. He'd hesitantly asked to come with her to a new town. "No one wants me here," he'd confided.

"Pretty sure your parents do," she'd assured him.

"I don't... have any," he'd said, looking away from her.

Ah, that would be why he couldn't go home, no home to speak of. It had tugged at her heart, she knew the feeling of being alone and homeless, knew it far too well. She held out her hand to him.

"Clara Fox, the orphan," she'd said as way of introduction.

He'd given her a small smile before taking her hand and shaking it firmly. "Eric the orphan," he'd said, returning her introduction.

"Nice to meet you, Eric the orphan," she'd grinned.

Oh god, how that memory made the dread in her grow, how the venom tricked her mind into thinking this time she could change the outcome, this time if she just tried...

She'd been scared, taking him through the forest. Clara had never taken anyone with her before, and she found she was actually very good at it. She'd meant to leave him with Fitz, but Eric never wanted to stay with him. He followed Clara like a lost puppy and never let her out of his sight. She pretended to be annoyed, but it never seemed to discourage him.

"Promise you won't leave me behind," he'd demanded when she was trying to go into town without him one day.

"I didn't think other orphans were this annoying," she'd deflected.

"Neither did I!" he'd spat back, making her smile. Sharp kid, *she'd thought, ruffling his hair.*

"Fine, I promise, ya little twerp."

I can change the ending, her poisoned mind assured her. *I can change the past...*

Two years later, he'd started calling her Mom. She'd never been so frightened of a word in her life, never been so afraid of being unable to live up to a title before. You'll fail him, Clara, you don't know how to be a mother...

A long time passed before that fear and that feeling faded. Realizing she loved the kid, loved him like she'd never loved anyone or anything in her whole life, and scared of that feeling.

A year later, coming to a decision, deciding she didn't care what she knew. Knowing she had to be in this forest wasn't enough to keep her here any longer, knowing she could leave if she tried and deciding to leave with Eric. Clara had decided to trek back to where Fitz was and never come back to this dangerous, thrilling place she'd learned to call home.

I can change this!

"Did you hear that?" Eric had asked, looking curiously down from the railing of one of their many rest points in the forest. It'd been a long day; she was tired and to be honest she hadn't really listened that hard, if at all.

Listen to him! Stay awake! Watch him! Something bad is coming! Clara's mind seemed to scream, but there was no change—the memory just kept playing out, exactly the way it had in the past.

"No, sorry, kid. Let's get some sleep, okay?" He'd nodded, but she saw him look a few more times as they settled in for the night, like he was still hearing that something, his attention strangely drawn to it.

Waking up with a start that night, ice in her heart, knowing something was horribly wrong. Getting up and finding Eric's bed deserted, the fear growing when she saw a pulley rope hanging down like someone had gone to the ground. At night.

Oh god, find him! *Leaving the safe point, finding his abandoned, bloody cloak in the dirt. Flinging herself through the forest, through the dark like that very first time, frantically screaming his name into the night, uncaring if she was heard, eyes wild and horror swallowing her whole.*

You failed him again, Clara.

"Eric! ERIC, WHERE ARE YOU?!"

Gage was tired. He lay there on his bedding roll, wanting to sleep, trying to sleep, but for some damn reason he couldn't stop thinking about his fiery blonde down the hall.

This wasn't unusual, the thinking about her part. Since he'd met her, he always seemed to be thinking about her in one form or another. This was a bit different however; he couldn't shake that feeling, a feeling that told him something was not right.

He groaned and rolled over for the hundredth time, trying to ignore it. *She's fine, bloody fine...*

Gage sighed after a few more minutes of this nonsense, succumbing to the desire to check on her and forcing himself to get up. He snorted. Check on her? Since when had he become the type to check up on anyone?

He'd go under the pretence of trying to annoy her some more, which he trusted wouldn't be too hard to believe or accomplish. Gage was sure he could throw out some innuendo that would save him face in the very likely case all was well, then his only job would be to try to keep his head attached to his shoulders.

He stumbled in the dark of the hall, following the light of the candle still burning in her room—perhaps she was still awake, then?

He braced himself against the door frame of Clara's "room" and looked in, just big enough for the cot she was lying on and a shelf mounted in the wall, holding only a few books. She was lying with her back to him, facing the wall, her boots still on. She looked almost as if she'd just fallen onto the thing and fell asleep. Besides the odd position, Clara looked fine.

"Gods, Fox, you call this a room?" he called out softly, tone teasing. He expected her to start, to roll over and threaten his life for daring wander near here. However she didn't react to his voice, didn't stir at his words.

Peter had informed him just how light a sleeper Clara was; his footsteps should have been enough to wake her. That's when he knew something was more than a little off.

"Clara," he said louder. Not a twitch.

He walked in and sat down on the edge of the cot, grabbing her shoulder and rolling her over. She moved limply, reddish-blond hair spilling over her face.

"Clara, wake up," he ordered loudly, feeling his stomach clench to the size of a raisin in the time it took to draw a breath. Gage carefully swept her hair out of her face and found her eyes open, a slightly translucent cloudy film marring the deep green of her eyes.

Eyes wide with terror.

"Ah hell," he muttered, cradling her head in his hand as he pulled it forwards to see the black insect responsible for her paralysis, firmly secured at the base of her skull.

"There you are, you dirty little bastard," he muttered to the critter, gently putting her head back down on the pillow to reach for his flask; she'd said alcohol burned the parasite.

"Drinks still on me then, huh love?"

He quickly grabbed Clara by the shoulder and pulled her into an upright, sitting position. He wrapped his left arm around her tightly, securing both arms very firmly to her sides and using the few functional fingers of his left hand to grip her tightly.

He remembered how Jared had reacted when Clara had removed the nightmare beetle feeding off him; she'd need to be restrained as well. He had the briefest thought cross his mind that he liked how she felt in his arms.

When he was sure he had her tightly enough in his arms, her head leaning on his shoulder, he uncorked his flask with his mouth and poured it directly onto the shiny black beetle. There was a high-pitched whine before it turned white and fell onto her pillow, its bushy legs waving in the air as it died.

Ten seconds later, Clara was screaming.

"ERIC!" she shrieked, thrashing in his arms, trying to free herself from his grip.

"Fox, calm down!" he spat through gritted teeth, trying to hold her and very nearly failing as she fought violently to get free of his embrace.

"ERIC?!" she shouted frantically. "Eric, where are you?!" She fought him like something wild and terrified until he wasn't sure he could hold her much longer.

"Damnit, Clara, it's me!" Gage snapped.

Clara seemed to realize then where she was, her struggling ceasing all at once like some grief had sucked all the fight out of her. "Eric?" she called out softly one last time, her voice breaking down into a sob.

Gage was stunned by the sound of her tears, the raw emotion as she began to cry into his shoulder, seemingly unable to stop herself. He eased his grip on her now that she wasn't fighting him, fully intending to let her go, but he found his arms lingering around her shoulders.

That's when Peter came stumbling through the door frame, looking worried.

"Clara! Are you—"

Gage glared at him as he held her. "Get out," he hissed between bared teeth, shielding Clara a bit more from the lad's view.

Peter looked wide-eyed at the two for a brief second. "Is she—" he began to ask.

"Now!" Gage snapped viciously, sending the boy scurrying away with only a brief, worried glance to Clara, who barely seemed to register he was there.

It was when she still held onto him after that that he realized just how vulnerable she was right then. For maybe the first time in his entire life, his first instinct was not to lunge to take advantage of it.

In the newfound silence, Gage's hand hesitantly reached up and stroked her soft curls, her shoulders shaking while she cried.

"It's okay, it's okay," he told her softly. "It wasn't real, it's over," he tried to sooth her.

She laughed, a truly wretched sound through her crying. "Not real," she repeated shakily "I *wish*." Clara hiccoughing in distress on the last.

He let her cry for a time, let her get some of the poison this pain had obviously allowed to fester in her out.

"He was the boy you lost in here, wasn't he? Eric," he said after a moment of silence, Clara still allowing him to hold her.

His tone implied she need not answer if she didn't wish to, so Clara didn't answer at first, growing so still in his arms it was like she was barely there at all. When she finally did say something, it was barely above a whisper.

"My son."

She knew as soon as the two words fell from her mouth she shouldn't have said them. He was Captain Black-Gage, the ultimate pirate, the manipulative, constant game-playing bastard.

It was too much, it tipped the scales far out of her favour, upset the balance of power. It was something she shouldn't share with him of all people. But Clara did, and she didn't push herself out of his arms because she needed to be held for a moment. Because it hurt *not* to be.

Why hadn't she really *listened* when Eric had asked? Why hadn't she woken up? Why did he leave to search in the dark? Those questions had kept her up many nights for even more years. If she'd done any one of those things, he'd be alive, and how she had hated herself for failing to do any of it.

"I'd told him," she whispered. "I'd told him, 'don't go out at night, Eric. It's too dangerous,' and he didn't lis—" she cut herself off before her voice cracked. "I don't understand why he went out," Clara finished after a moment.

Promise you won't leave me behind.

"He was ten. He'd... he'd be almost eighteen now." God, why was she telling him all this? *Shut up!* Her brain screamed. The silence after that was heavy, feeling longer than it actually was.

"It was my wife. Anna," Gage told her, voice sounding loud when it broke the silence. "She had her soul flame ripped out by a Wielder, who proceeded to snuff it out in front of me."

He glanced down at her face, seeing the confusion there he elaborated. "That's what Wielders call someone's life force; it resides in the heart, it's why the damn thing beats—it's your light, all that you are," he explained, finger lightly tapping on her chest above her heart. "Skilled Wielders can rip it from a person's body, literally holding a person's everything in their hands. It can be used for a whole manner of magics apparently—one of the Scarlet Queen's favourite trophies I hear."

That almost made Clara physically ill, the *thought* of anyone doing that to anybody alone was horrifying—cruel and despicable.

"But he used it for nothing; he simply smothered it and killed her."

"Why?" she asked tentatively.

"He wanted her, she didn't want him, and if he couldn't have her... well, I'm sure you know how that song goes."

Clara was stunned by the volunteering of this information, almost entirely unsolicited no less. Gage said it unemotionally, as if quoting facts from a history book. Not like it was the most painful event in his life, knowing she died for loving him over another.

"Then, because that was not punishment enough for her refusal, he cursed my hand. The paralysis was slow at first, but it claims more of it each year," he said, holding it up to look at the gloved hand. "My glove is what Wielder's call a 'power-lock.' It slows or renders certain magic impotent; more specifically the progressive nature of curses; at times, I can even vent the vile nature of that curse onto other things. I have more time now, but regardless, one day it will kill me."

Clara slowly pulled out of his arms, and he let her, her tearstained face searching his. That was why his glove had worked earlier in the journey: power-locks were not spells—they were meant to suppress magic.

His jaw was tight, mouth pressed into a thin line; they had not been easy words for him to say. But he'd said them, showed her the raw wound in his heart just because at this moment she was unable to hide hers.

"To sum it all up bluntly, life can be a wretched harpy at times," he said, taking his flask out and popping the cork one-handed. Gage took a swig before offering it to her.

Clara shook her head, but he didn't withdraw the flask.

"No, take it. Trust me it helps," he insisted. She hesitated only a moment before she took it, hands still shaking a little as she had a sip and handed it back, feeling the burn all the way down her throat.

Say something, Clara thought, but what really was there to say in the face of that kind of pain? In the face of his seemingly inevitable fate?

Gage was about to say something when he took his flask back, something possibly inappropriate to shake that haunted look from her face, hush Anna's memory and his long-running predicament from his mind.

When she caught his eyes, he found the words somehow stuck in his throat. They stared at each other for what felt like an eternity, not speaking, seeing each other far too clearly.

"If you kill the Wielder, will you live?"

"He is not a man easily slain—I've been searching for the means to do so for a very long time..." he trailed off.

"But yes, if I kill him I will be spared my fate." The words were so empty she was surprised there wasn't some kind of echo in them. Clara felt like those words on bad days, hollow. She also felt his quest had an upside he wasn't seeing.

"I could have saved Eric if I'd listened to him that day." She'd never admitted that out loud to anyone before, it tasted bitter, it cramped her tongue in her mouth.

"At least you have someone to blame other than yourself." Clara did not. Every single day, she knew the blame lay squarely on her own shoulders.

"Do I?" he asked quietly.

Clara made sure she had his attention fully on her before speaking. "Yeah. You do."

And she meant it; he could see that. A silence surrounded them, and it was possibly the most intimate thing either of them had shared with anyone in years.

Clara cleared her throat loudly, growing uncomfortable. "So yeah..." Clara looked away, "Don't be a wuss about it." It was a *truly* asshole thing to say and she knew it; that was the point, to shut this... connection down as harshly as possible.

His face locked down instantly, both hiding away that genuine humanity they'd touched in one another.

"I won't if you won't, love," he replied coolly.

But those words weren't really what they were saying to each other and they both knew it. They were telling each other that this, whatever it was, couldn't be more than a game; as it had always been. This could not venture into anything real for them. What they were agreeing to as they closed themselves off once more was that they were going to pretend, just like they had before, that they weren't seeing each other as they were; that they weren't connecting—that they never had.

And underneath that, both were a little afraid that even though they both agreed on this that there still might not be any going back.

Gage reached up and quickly flicked a tear from her cheek, surprising her.

"But whatever the matter, I dislike it when a lass cries." He said it with a bit of an almost uneasy laugh, as if unused to sincerity, trying to erase the past ten minutes.

Clara wiped her face off quickly as he stood.

"Should you like I'd be more than happy to stay and comfort you," he told her, flashing her a seductive smile.

The tension between them broke, back to how it had been before they'd been terrifyingly exposed to one another. She actually managed a laugh at how predictable the line was, same old Lucas Sinclair.

"Get out, you floozy," Clara said, turning away from him, in tight control of herself once again.

"Ooo, harsh words, Fox," he said over his shoulder, disappearing into the hall.

She crushed the bug on her pillow and threw its husk spitefully into the corner before she curled up on her cot again, feeling strangely cold now that she was alone.

Clara didn't sleep for a long time, too busy walling up old ghosts.

Gage left her narrow hall to find Peter standing by the table.

"She... okay, Captain?" he asked hesitantly, making it obvious he'd been waiting up.

"Did I give you permission to wait up, Peter? Fox is fine," Gage growled to him coldly. "Get your ass to bed," he snapped.

Peter didn't ask anything else, the mood of his captain obviously less than hospitable and far from indulgent.

Gage lay down on his bedroll, glaring at the ceiling. His mood had turned nearly the moment he'd left Clara's side. He wasn't actually angry with Peter; the kid was simply a convenient outlet. No, he was angry with himself, that he'd actually felt compelled to comfort her. Gage couldn't afford to care; he didn't *want* to care. He wouldn't damn it. His hand reached up to touch his jacket pocket, and his expression hardened further.

She was the Guide, he was Captain Black-Gage, and they both had one job. Nothing about that was going to change; he didn't owe her a damn thing. That was the mantra Gage lulled himself to sleep with that night: *he didn't owe her a damn thing.*

Sixteen

When Clara emerged from her room, she was surprised to see Gage sitting at the table, absently sharpening his cutlass. He kept his eyes focused on the task at hand as she entered the room even though Clara knew he was well aware of her presence.

"The captain that never sleeps," Clara said by way of greeting.

"I'm an early riser. I assume we move soon?" Gage's tone implied it was less a question and more a firm suggestion. Being very straightforward today she noticed; it was almost disconcerting.

Clara shrugged. "We move whenever you like, the shortcut we were forced to take shaved half a day off the journey, so we have time to rest if you like." She looked around at all the sleeping pirates to see the only one stirring was William, eyes opening blurrily at the sound of their voices.

"However we should be in Torin just after midday if we get moving in the next half hour," she finished.

"Then I suppose we move in a half hour. William," Gage's voice sternly calling his name seemed to rouse the man fully from sleep as he sat up, tall frame moving slowly, hazel eyes still foggy with sleep.

"Yes, Captain?"

"Wake the men," he ordered.

"Yes, Captain," William said, slowly getting to his feet.

Gage slipped his file into his pocket as he stood and stretched while his first mate woke the others. He strode over to where she stood until he was just in front of her.

Clara watched him carefully but did not pull back from his presence.

"A harsh reward for such a splendid job getting us all through alive," he said a bit gravely. Her brow wrinkled with confusion

"What is?" she asked. He put his hand against the wall next to her face as if it was the most convenient place to lean.

"Parting with me as your 'view' so early," he said innocently. It was not an expression he wore well. She had expected some awkwardness to be between them for a little bit at least, but it seemed Gage was already back to form.

"I'm sure I'll struggle through my disappointment," Clara replied sarcastically.

"You'll miss me," he told her, as if he'd have put money on it.

Clara almost wouldn't have bet against him. She rolled her eyes as she opened her mouth to reply with yet more sarcasm, but he continued before she got the chance.

"I know I'll miss you."

Clara would have laughed if he hadn't said it so sincerely, if she hadn't seen the truth in those words. Her and Gage looked at each other in silence for a long moment, saying nothing. Clara spoke first, trying to make light of what he'd said.

"Until the next pretty face comes along I'm sure." Gage just continued to look at her, like he hadn't heard what she said. It wasn't as calculating as usual; it was like he was really looking at her, like he had when she'd laid out his choices before the silent path, a touch of something unfamiliar in his eyes. It unnerved her a little, but maybe that was what Gage wanted.

"Make use of the basin while you can," she said, looking away first as she hurried to change the subject, pointing to it for emphasis. "Fill your canteens," she advised, moving past him.

He watched her walk away from him, a rare pensive look no one saw aimed at her back.

Clara dropped her stuff on the table before going to nudge a snoring Peter with her foot. He started, eyes flying opening to look up at her in blurry confusion.

"Come on, Rebel, you got a forest to conquer." She told him to fill his canteen before turning back to the table, where Gage was standing waiting for her. She found it just a little odd that he still seemed to have some wish to speak with her, what else did they have to talk about?

When she approached, he held out a small bag to her; closer inspection revealed it to be the glice powder she'd given him a few days earlier.

"I believe this is yours," he explained, dropping it into her outstretched hand. It almost felt like he was saying goodbye in a strange way as she took it back, a door between them trying to close though in truth neither really wanted that. Clara smiled knowingly, the expression her own version of a bittersweet farewell.

"And you didn't blind yourself with it once, you must be proud," she joked.

"Hmm, very," he told her, walking away to go pack his roll.

The early morning sun was already hotter than hell when they got to walking. Though Nahleese kept pace with Clara near the front, she was still moving slowly, not entirely recovered from the venom.

She guided them past the usual dangers, which, despite their very real lethal potential, felt mundane in comparison to what they'd already faced. Clara reached for her canteen at one point and unscrewed the lid, tilting it back to take a drink. No water touched her lips.

"What the hell?" she muttered to herself. Clara came to a stop and let Nahleese take the lead. She hadn't bothered to fill it because she'd barely drank any water from it the other day, it should have still been full. Clara examined the canteen for a moment before she saw the cut that ran along the bottom, a thin slit that had allowed all her water to leak out. *When did that happen?* Clara wondered.

Those damn Maroth feathers must have nicked it during the scuffle the other day. She frowned; most of the time Maroth feathers cut clean because they were just so sharp—this cut looked a touch jagged. She waved it off; could just be the angle it caught the canteen at. Nahleese had circled back, bumping her head against Clara's hip as if asking why she'd stopped.

"Hope you're not thirsty, girl," Clara sighed, patting her big head. Thankfully it was a short trek, otherwise she'd be running the risk of dehydration today.

"Problem, darling?" Gage asked, pulling up beside her and looking around warily for the reason she'd paused.

"Not your darling, Sinclair," she sang back irately, screwing the lid back onto her canteen as she wrapped the strap around it. Clara couldn't help but notice how close Gage was standing to her and how Nahleese felt no need to growl at him for it. It seemed he didn't fail to notice this either.

"It seems we have a truce," Gage observed offhandedly, like he'd expected this outcome all along. He could be so full of himself sometimes.

"Doesn't mean she likes you," Clara told him.

"So you say. You know it's going to be a tad difficult to drink from that canteen when it's at the bottom of your bag," he said as he watched her stuff it into her backpack.

"I'd get about as much water from it either way; damn thing sprung a leak," she muttered.

Gage held his canteen up. "Ask, and ye shall receive," he offered with an innocent smile.

She'd ask Gage for his charity when hell froze over, and he damn well knew it.

"Pass," she said, rolling her eyes and walking ahead. Gage didn't bother her much after that; maybe he did feel some awkwardness after all. Either way she needed her focus, they'd be parting company soon. Strangely that thought made her a bit... sad?

Dammit she was thirsty, she thought glaring up at the sun. Why did it have to be so hot today? Then again if it had to be hot to assure an uneventful trek she'd take the heat. The trees and underbrush began to thin out and a few minutes after that they broke past the tree line completely, free from the reach of the forest.

"Congratulations," she said, mouth feeling dryer than cotton as she turned to watch everyone stumble out. "You survived possibly the most dangerous trek I've made in the last four years and met a third of its most dangerous critters." She gave them all two sarcastic thumbs-up. "You must be good luck."

Peter was the only one who laughed, the rest of them were all a little quiet and not overly enthusiastic.

"Well, don't look too excited, boys," she said, giving them all a queer stare.

"We're tired," Squint muttered.

Clara just shook her head and looked ahead of them to see their destination laid out before them, Torin. The shipping town was vast even from where they were, alabaster stone almost blinding as it reflected the noon day sun. It was a beautiful place, despite the fact she knew the Scarlet Queen's mark was branded into the city gate – the black armoured horse rearing up. But instead of examining the unique view of the city before her, Clara looked to the ocean, glittering, stretching far and disappearing into the distance. She was going to get to see it up close today. Gage found himself almost smirking a little when he saw how she gazed out on it, the wonder that gleamed in her eyes for a just a moment before she hid it.

"A lovely trek, Fox," Gage said, unscrewing the lid of his canteen as it hung on his hip. "Let's never, ever do it again," he suggested, taking a long drink.

Gage caught her watching him drink from the corner of his eye and could tell by the way she swallowed she was damn thirsty now. He also knew she'd probably eat her boots before asking him for a sip, but he'd already known that. Gage strode up next to her, already fishing his empty flask from his side and handing it to her.

Clara took it, knowing it was empty, and gave him a sardonic look. "Gee, an empty flask, thanks."

He ignored her as he poured water from his canteen into his flask. "To getting us through," he said, clinking his canteen against the flask and taking another drink. It seemed Gage, for once, wasn't going to make her ask. Having waited the entire trek for her to do so, she had made it abundantly clear she wouldn't.

"To getting us through," Clara repeated slowly, saluting him with the flask before tilting it back against her lips. It had the aftertaste of rum, but it helped quench a bit of her thirst, the water gone all too quickly.

"Your turn to lead, Sinclair," she told him, handing the empty flask back. Clara looked down at Nahleese, who was sitting a few feet away and panting. She knelt down next to her and scratched under her chin. "You know the drill."

Nahleese got up and walked back to the edge of the trees, finding a shady spot to lie down and wait as Gage took the lead.

"What's a matter, Sinclair—harbour not good enough for you?" Clara asked.

"I don't like my ship in any port without me on it, safer to drop anchor out of town," he explained as they breached a spatter of trees and bush to reveal the sheer side of the cove where the ship had weighed anchor.

The sails had been pulled up as the large ship rocked gently on the ocean; the ship sidled right up to the cliff face so that dropping a plank of wood was enough to let anyone easily walk aboard. The wood gleamed a distinct cherry oak colour that was rich and pleasing to the eye.

"She's a beauty," Clara said, eying the ship. "Kind of colourful for a ship called *The Grey Ghost* though."

"Something wrong with that?" His tone dared her to take a shot.

Clara smiled. "Not at all," she answered innocently.

He let that one go, as someone on his famous vessel spotted their approach and start to holler.

"Captain! You're alive!" the man yelled.

"I don't die easy!" Gage shouted back. "Drop us a bridge!" he ordered.

"Aye, aye, Captain!" the man yelled back.

Gage looked back and saw Clara looking out at the ocean again; he knew this was the closest she'd ever been.

"Everything you thought it'd be, Fox?" he asked.

"I don't know what I thought it'd be like," she admitted as Peter stepped up beside her.

"Looks like it goes on forever, right?" he said with a smile, obviously happy to see it again. Clara smiled at his enthusiasm.

"Yeah," she agreed simply. She heard the plank hit the ground, giving them a bridge to board the ship.

Gage gave her a slightly playful bow. "After you, milady."

Clara wasn't sure why, but the grin she was wearing froze on her face. Nothing actually happened in that second, even the invite aboard his ship was nothing she hadn't expected, delivered in the manner that could only be described as "Sinclair."

But at that moment, Clara felt every warning bell in her head go off at once, almost deafening. Something was wrong. She turned her head to look around her, taking everything in. The shifting of gazes, where everyone stood, the subtlest of tensions in them...

"I'm good here," Clara replied after a moment.

Gage frowned and somehow made it look attractive, like he was sincerely unsure of the reason for her refusal. "You still want your gold, correct?"

Clara smiled at him; it wasn't an entirely friendly expression. "Oh, I'm not leaving without it," she assured him, "but I like my feet to stay on solid ground."

It was brief, so brief for a second she thought she almost imagined it, but she saw... disappointment fleet across his face. Something was wrong.

Peter looked back and forth at the two, unsure as to why suddenly there was a strain between them.

There was a brief silence in which Clara took in everything around her again, Gage in front of her, Peter by her side, and the rest of the crew at her back. A look passed between Jared and William, lightning quick that she caught from the corner of her eye.

Clara shifted her position casually so that she could keep her eyes on the pirates behind her and still face their captain.

Something passed through Gage's eyes then; he hadn't missed the stance shift.

"Jumpy, Fox?"

"Do I have reason to be?" she asked casually, though her eyes were trained on him far too intently for casual.

"Not that I can think of," he said, raising an eyebrow. Obscurity. Clara felt a weight drop in her gut.

"All the same I prefer solid ground," she told him, forcing a smile. "The landlubber in me I suppose."

"Very well, William, go—"

"No, not him," she said, cutting him off abruptly, "send Peter for it." William's expression didn't so much as twitch under that blue cap of his, odd. *Wrong.*

"My, my, Fox, terribly suspicious today," Gage remarked, still smiling.

"Send Peter for it," she repeated, tone bordering on making the words an order.

Peter glanced at her curiously. Clara answered the look with a blasé shrug, like this was all perfectly normal.

Gage smirked, the expression filled with a bitter knowing as she returned it with the usual sharpness, even though her insides were screaming at her.

"As you wish. Peter, get Miss Fox her gold."

Peter ran off to carry out the order. Clara felt like every hair was standing up on the back of her neck as she looked after him, disappearing onto the ship. It was unbearably quiet for a long moment, all eyes on her.

"So, any plans on what to spend your hard-earned money on, love?" Gage asked, voice cursory as he crossed his arms. He looked so totally at ease that it was hard to believe she hadn't imagined all the signs. Clara truly wished that could be the case, but she wasn't naive enough to convince herself it was as she continued to look after a long-gone Peter.

"I think we both know you've no intention of paying me today, Sinclair." Clara said quietly, hand hovering inches from the hilt of her blade.

The tension soared in an instant; she felt it thicken the air she was trying to breathe as the pirates at her back physically tensed. Clara met those ice-blue eyes of Gage's just in time to see them harden like diamonds, and she knew she was right.

"What was it?" he asked finally. At least he didn't have the gall to try to outright lie to her.

"Besides the lack of truth on your face? They're too tense," she said, indicating the other pirates with a nod. The forest was long behind them, but they were still acting like there was a threat. In all fairness, there was; they were looking at her.

"The only one acting relieved was Peter; I assume the only one not privy to the plan?"

Gage actually looked away from her for a second and sighed.

"Kid's a bit too honest; he'd have given it away," he admitted. "But that would be why you had me send him aboard," Gage guessed, looking back to her, unsmiling now.

"Youth has a tendency to stay my hand," she confessed, "and *none* of you deserve that courtesy."

Clara felt rather than saw William and the others try to close in a little bit, pulling the ring cutting off her escape a little tighter. Her head snapped in their direction instantly, forgetting Gage entirely as her hand took to fully resting on the hilt of her blade.

"After all my hard work to keep everyone alive, you're *really* going to make me kill you all?" she hissed. Oh, she was *mad*; she should have seen this coming a mile away. But she hadn't—because she *liked* them.

Even now Clara didn't want to kill them, knowing if things went bad she might have to, angry that she was forced into this corner. Angry that this betrayal *hurt*.

"Back up." The words fell from her lips like a snarl.

"Stay where you are, lads," Gage ordered alternately, voice harsh.

Clara returned her glare to him, and Gage met the fire in her eyes with the resolved arctic calm of his own.

"Is the gold really worth dying over, Sinclair?"

"If this was about gold, you'd be on your way by now." She felt the confusion showing on her face, if this wasn't about gold...

Then it hit her all at once.

Dangerous cargo?

Not to you, no.

Any... let's say unwilling passengers?

If we go, we all go willingly...

Gage knew the exact moment she pulled it all together, looking floored by the revelation. Clara laughed after a moment, managing to somehow make the sound bitter and menacing at once.

"Oh," she said, voice almost emotionless as everything suddenly made sense. Her glare swept over them all; if looks could kill, they'd have died on the spot. Gage hadn't lied, but he certainly hadn't told the truth—she'd lost the game as soon as she'd taken the job, and Clara hadn't even known it.

"I'm your cargo," she said at last. Gage remained silent, denying nothing.

"I've gotta say, *Black-Gage*, that is one ballsy job to take," she told him with a nasty emphasis on his moniker, "especially on me." Her tone turned decidedly dangerous on the last.

"You're out of the forest and outnumbered; don't make this harder than it has to be," he said quietly.

His betrayal should not have hurt her this much, but gods it did. Clara had known from the moment she'd laid eyes on him that he could not be trusted, and she'd done it anyways. Somewhere along the way, this had stopped being a game, she thought as she stared at him; at least it had for her. Thankfully her anger burned hot enough to engulf the stabbing pain in her back entirely.

"I think it was you who once said you never admit defeat. Guess they cut us from the same cloth."

Clara drew her blade, and the tension in them all snapped tighter than a drum; the others drawing their swords in response.

"Clara!" Her name was a warning on his lips as he uncrossed his arms and held them up as if to pacify her. He didn't want this to get ugly; he didn't want her hurt, but if Gage didn't stall, he might be forced to and it would go badly for them all. And he *really* didn't want to hurt her.

"You want me on your ship, you're gonna have to drag me," Clara declared fiercely brandishing her dagger. "That you thought you could walk me on is insulting."

He'd made no move to even to arm himself; he just watched her, eyes flickering to the knife only briefly before settling on her face again.

"Honestly?" he said, keeping his voice level and calm. "I didn't think I could walk you on, and I knew forcing you would probably be messier than it was worth. You're a fighter to your core, Clara." He said it like it was something he admired. All he had to do was stall her a bit longer, and her and his crew could be spared any harm...

Clara heard something hit the ground at her side and looked down to see she'd dropped her knife on the ground. Her hands were suddenly numb.

"So I took precautions," he said as she looked at her hands, alarmed.

A wave of dizziness washed over her, and she stumbled a bit, trying to stay on her feet.

"What the hell..." Her hand came up to her face like she could steady herself and the sudden onslaught of dizziness. Oh gods, the water—

"It was in the flask, not the canteen," he explained when she looked back to him, shocked.

The canteen...

"You *bastard,*" she hissed, taking a knee as the drug sapped at her strength.

I know, he thought as he watched her hang her head, eyes clenched shut and teeth gritted as she fought the grip of the sleep draught.

"When it kicks in, it works fast, Clara." he said gently, walking towards her, intending to collect her.

Her eyes flared open and peered up through the curtain or her fire yellow hair as he approached, the ferocity in them making him hesitate a moment.

"Then I best make the time count." Her hand reached into the pouch of glice powder hanging at her side.

"NAHLEESE!" she shouted. From a nearby bush, a white blur rushed, all fur and teeth with a vicious snarl proceeding it.

Chaos broke loose as Clara threw the powder, Gage raising his arm to protect his eyes just in time, the rest of his crew were not so lucky.

There were screams as the power burned at their eyes, stumbling back as they were blinded. Nahleese tore into Jared's leg, dropping him to the ground screaming and wetting the wolf's muzzle with his blood while the others reeled back in pain.

Nahleese didn't bother getting too messy with him; she was next to Clara in a heartbeat, and she grabbed her flank. The wolf was off, helping her run through the opening she'd made for them into the bush.

"Son of a bitch!" Gage cursed. He thought she'd left the damn wolf behind.

He didn't waste time ordering his crew to get off the ship and get her back; he just drew his sword and ran after her.

Stupid, how could you be so stupid? Clara's mind berated her sluggishly as she held onto Nahleese, the wolf giving her enough support to keep her feet moving.

Nahleese always knew to follow at a distance when she went off with clients, and this hadn't been the exception, even being as weak as she was. If they could just get back to the trees...

It became clear very quickly that Clara was not going to make it that far, not by a long shot. Gage was right; whatever he'd given her it was working fast. Her legs gave under her, and she went to her knees hard; she didn't feel it nearly as sharply as she should have. Darkness was eating at the corners of Clara's vision now, trying to pull her down.

She let Nahleese go and braced her hand against the ground to keep herself from falling over and cursed. She could hear a commotion from where they'd both run from but she didn't pay attention to it; she knew they were going to find her.

Nahleese was circling her, whining as she nudged her roughly with her red-stained muzzle, trying to get her up.

"I can't," she told the wolf, hating the sound of her voice as she said it. The wolf seemed to sense this, coming around to stand in front of her. She licked Clara's face as if to reassure her before she went to stand at her back, putting herself between Clara and any pirate dumb enough to make a run at her.

Nahleese might get a few of them—in fact that was a guarantee—but there was no way she could protect her from them all in her condition and Clara knew it. She had seen Gage wield that sword of his, and that glove was a hundred times more lethal; it was not a fight she wanted to risk Nahleese's life on.

"No," she almost slurred, arms shaking as the struggled to keep herself upright on her knees.

"Your sister would... kill me if anything happen to you."

Nahleese's mismatched eyes only spared her a brief glance, but it was clear she had no intention of leaving.

"Go."

Nahleese didn't move, almost pointedly ignoring her.

Clara grit her teeth and reached behind her, summoning what strength she had left she grabbed Nahleese by the scruff of her neck and yanked with all her strength to move her. If Nahleese hadn't been weakened herself it would not have been enough, but as it was...

"Go!" Clara ordered harshly, almost throwing the wolf from her.

Nahleese stumbled a little ways from her before looking at Clara, a high-pitched whine conveying her distress, eyes less sure from only a moment ago.

"Go. Home," Clara rasped, less strength in the words now.

If Nahleese returned home without her, Fitz would know something was wrong; he most likely couldn't do anything but at least he'd know.

Nahleese whimpered once more, hesitating for a few more moments before she finally turned and ran.

Clara foggily watched her go, vision blurring as her friend disappeared from sight.

Gage tore through the bush, sword drawn. Why couldn't she have left that damn wolf back at the tree line? He didn't want to have to kill the mutt, but he seriously doubted that Nahleese would leave him much of a choice.

He heard his men searching for her when he stopped to listen, hoping he'd catch some indication of where she'd run to. Gage knew she wasn't going to get far, but as usual, she'd gone for it anyways.

"Go!"

His head swiveled to the left as his ears picked up the sound of her voice. He ran in that direction, sword at the ready. Gage eventually found her kneeling on the ground as if unable to stand on her own, just catching a flash of white disappearing into the scant shrubs.

Had she sent the wolf away? Slowly he sheathed his sword and carefully walked around her, keeping an eye out just in case the wolf was hanging around. When he was sure Nahleese was gone, he crouched down in front of Clara so he could look into her eyes.

She looked back hazily, a touch out of breath as she braced herself with her hands to stay upright. She was fading fast.

"That was foolish," he told her coolly.

"Burn... in hell," she spat weakly in response, the green of her eyes marred only by the strands of hair hanging in her face.

Gage said nothing as he watched those eyes roll back before closing, reaching forwards gently to catch her by her shoulders before she hit the ground. He sighed, just holding her against his chest for a moment. Of all the questionable things he'd done in his life, he knew in that moment, without a doubt, this would be one for which he hated himself the most.

"My dear," he said out loud at last, picking her up with him and throwing her limp body over his shoulder, "For this, I've no doubt one day I will."

Seventeen

Squint was just helping Jared up when Gage returned, carrying Clara over his shoulder. It seemed Squint had managed to protect his one eye from most of the powder. Jared and William were not so lucky, tears running down their faces as the blindness and pain seemed to be receding.

"You got her," Jared hissed between clenched teeth, blood soaking his pant leg as he squinted, trying to see.

"No thanks to you fools," Gage snapped in reply.

"Need help carrying her?" William asked, eyes bloodshot but still clearer than Jared's, especially since he seemed to actually be able to make out the slumped form that was Clara. Say what they will of her capture, she'd aimed to make them pay for it.

"I've got her," Gage said. "Someone grab that and bring it," he ordered, famous black-gloved hand pointing to her backpack, silver gauge glinting in the sunlight.

"It's a narrow plank to the ship, Captain—" William tried again.

"I said *I've got her,* William," Gage growled, silencing the man instantly. "Now get aboard and make some use of yourselves before I decide to leave you here."

He walked swiftly past them, over the plank and aboard *The Grey Ghost,* striding across the deck with her on his shoulder past his men who had been on the ship, jaw tight—a warning the men failed to notice.

"Who's the woman, Captain?" someone called out.

"That can't be the Guide can it?"

"I think it is!"

"I'll be damned. She's a hot piece of ass," one of the pirates remarked crassly.

Gage ground his teeth together so hard he felt as if they might crack, his temper on a hair trigger—despite being an enemy captive that kind of disrespect to her sat... *very* ill with him. His gloved hand flashed out, snaring the man who'd made the comment by his shirt. The shirt burnt off the man, blackening and decaying to shreds right off his body at the touch.

Before the man could even react with any kind of horror that same hand grabbed his wrist and, with one solid jerk, threw the man so hard he hit the mast, head bouncing off the unyielding wood and collapsing unconscious into a crumpled heap.

"Anyone else have an observation they'd care to share?" he snarled at the men.

Absolute silence met the vicious inquiry.

"Good. Cast off before I throw one of you lot overboard!" he ordered, his tone sending everyone scrambling to obey the order. Their captain was in a foul mood, a strange sight considering he had his prize.

"Captain?" Gage turned towards the voice to see an alarmed-looking Peter staring at him.

"What happened?" he asked, coming forwards to investigate. "Is she okay?"

William smoothly interceded before Peter could continue approaching his volatile captain.

"She's fine, lad," he assured him, putting an arm around his shoulder and steering him away. William shot his captain an unreadable look over his shoulder.

Gage didn't meet it, nor hear the rest of William's overdue explanation. He opened the door and carefully headed down to his cabin.

He delicately laid Clara down on his bed, cupping that back of her head with his hand as he did, brushing her hair out of her face. She looked peaceful as she slept, reddish-blond hair fanned around her face over his pillow. Gage knew that would change quite drastically when she woke.

He sat on the edge of the bed and was reminded of the other night, sitting with her while she was lost to her private horrors. Gage shoved the bothersome thoughts from his mind as he checked her pulse.

It beat strong and steady under his fingers; he hadn't expected otherwise, but it eased his nerves to be sure. Gage sighed and rubbed his face. That he needed to steady his nerves at all pissed him off; how had he let her get this deep under his skin?

He unlatched the button of his front pocket and reached in to pull out the object he'd been safe guarding—a medium-sized shard of a mirror. He was about to tap the surface when he stopped himself. Quickly he reached over and put a few locks of hair over her face again, obscuring her features somewhat.

He looked into the mirror again and finally tapped it. A second later, Airalyn's pale red eyes were staring back, white hair once more in some elaborate style, and a black feather collar around her slender neck that only exaggerated how very pale she was. Though he could only see her from the shoulders up, she was no doubt dressed in a hauntingly beautiful black attire.

"I thought you might be dead." She said it like that would have been a minor inconvenience. Truthfully, he'd have been highly suspicious of any warmth from her.

"Greetings to you as well, Your Majesty," Gage replied cheekily with a bright fake smile.

"I was expecting your call sooner, Lucas," she said dryly.

"I tried, but I'm afraid anything of a magical nature is dampened in the Dark Forest," Gage explained.

"Suppose I should have expected that. Do you have him?" the Scarlet Queen asked, the first real spark of interest lighting in her pale red eyes.

"I suppose I forgot to mention, the Guide is a woman," Gage corrected. "I was surprised as well," he continued at the look of disbelief on her face.

"All this time I'd been told the Guide was a man. My contacts will have to be dealt with for this mistake." The way she said those words left no doubt as to exactly how she planned to "deal" with them. "Let me see her, then," Airalyn ordered, leaning a little closer to her mirror.

Gage shook his head, and the refusal definitely did not sit well with the queen.

"Let me see it first," he demanded firmly.

Her eyes narrowed at the order in his tone. She held up her hand, a cloud of black smoke seeping through her fingers before dissipating to reveal an ancient-looking short blade, crudely fashioned handle from some kind of antler with a just as crudely made blade—jagged edges.

But the feature that marked it as what he was looking for was the strangely elegant "V" that looked almost as if it was stitched into the metal, spider-thin scorch marks that almost seemed to pulse all along the edges of the letter.

"The one weapon that can kill the Mage, your wife's murderer, as agreed," she said, holding the blade closer to the mirror for his inspection.

He felt his heart beat quicken at the sight of it. This was it, what he'd searched so long for was almost within his grasp. It was all drawing to a close, after a hundred years he would have his revenge.

The blade disappeared in another cloud of black smoke, leaving only the Scarlet Queen and the hard expression she aimed at him.

"Now show me, Lucas," she ordered coldly. Reluctantly Gage turned the mirror so it was pointed at Clara.

"I trust she is mostly undamaged?" he heard the queen's annoyed voice ask as she surveyed the unconscious woman.

"She's in perfect health," Gage assured her, turning the mirror back to face him. He could tell the queen disliked how short a look she'd gotten at her soon to be captive.

"How do I know she's really the Guide?" Airalyn asked, tone suspicious.

"I would be suffering a slight case of death if she were anyone else."

"Ah, yes, how was the Dark Forest?" Airalyn asked, almost sounding amused as she leaned back in some chair, wherever she was, more comfortably.

"It lives up to its reputation," he said, mouth thinning to a hard line. "Six people barely made it through; I highly doubt the girl will be able to lead your army through it. In fact, I doubt even half of your forces would survive the venture," he informed her, ever sure of her designs for war.

The queen laughed—not the reaction he'd been expecting.

"Oh, Captain, I've no intention of using her *skills* to guide my men through."

Gage couldn't entirely help the confusion that filled his eyes. "If you don't want her to guide your soldiers through, exactly what use is she to you?"

Airalyn's eyes narrowed, and he felt an involuntary chill run down his spine; he reminded himself he had to be careful with her.

"Why so curious?" she asked. Gage managed a blasé shrug, looking as if he didn't much care if she answered or not.

"I assure you, it's professional curiosity." She looked at him for another minute before bestowing a dainty smile.

"What do you know of the Dark Forest?" she asked.

"More than I knew three days ago," he answered.

"Well it was once a normal forest; one day as my forces marched through it to take Ethona's kingdom, it was suddenly filled with horrors that massacred just over half my army and proved at a later date to be completely impassable. Do you know why?" she asked, knowing full well he didn't.

She was enjoying flaunting her knowledge to him, even as she also flaunted a past failure. It was one of the Scarlet Queen's flaws, he noticed: she wanted everyone to know how smart she was, how capable. In that sense, he'd learned how to play her like a fiddle, when to commend her for her own cleverness, when to withhold interest and when to charm her.

"Enlighten me?" he invited with a smooth smile, not hiding his intrigue.

"The entire forest has had an enchantment cast on it," she told him.

He was legitimately surprised for a moment, an entire forest under an enchantment? He'd never heard of such a thing, nor of anyone who could sustain such a powerful act of magic. He wasn't even sure if the Mage could pull that off.

That would explain why magic didn't work there; any other curse or spell would be smothered almost instantly by all that buzzing power. The only reason his curse had any effect was because it was so tightly focused in such abrupt bursts, a simple pressure valve release.

He watched the Scarlet Queen's expression grow less dainty and fragile-looking into something harder, bitterer.

"The forest is still the only path for a successful invasion, even more so since it has been written off as impassible and as such is still mostly unfortified, the one upside to this whole fiasco. But it has set me back nineteen years, wrought havoc on the strength of my army and once cost me a new profitable kingdom that is the gateway to my greatness; a kingdom that should have bowed to me many, many years ago."

It was the look of fervour as she said it, that spark in her pale red eyes that exposed the raging megalomaniac inside her, laid bare all too clearly how this queen would never have enough power. She truly believed she deserved every subject, every resource, every obedience and every influence the world had, whether it was offered or not. That spark of madness in her eyes told of the inferno inside; she truly believed there should only be one throne—and that she should sit on it.

"She has made me look weak—no more," she said, her tone imparting a great seething hatred.

"What does this have to do with her?" Gage asked nodding to Clara, as if to speed her along. She glared at him, obviously not appreciating his casual manner or address but continued in spite of this.

"This was no normal enchantment, Lucas. Enchantments are not like spells or even curses. Magic that complex needs something to root it down, an anchor if you will." The bitter anger drained from her face, and something like an empty joy filled her red eyes.

"A living anchor," Airalyn finished.

Gage looked away from the mirror and back to Clara.

"Her?" he said, eyes wide with shock.

"So it would appear," Airalyn agreed, eyes narrowing on him, cross that he would not turn it so she could gaze with him at her prize. "I suspect this enchantment had multiple casters and for some reason they picked her to bind it; the enchantment is so massive I'm surprised it hasn't killed her to be honest."

Airalyn almost sneered then, an ugly look that exposed her desperate, bloodthirsty wish.

"Perhaps that is testament as to why they chose her," she pondered aloud, curiosity overtaking the dark look, finger tapping her chin. "Either way this problem must be dealt with."

Her mood swings could give a man whiplash, Gage thought to himself.

"All that time spent on objects, then rumours of The Guide began to surface and I knew, as impossible as it was, they had to be the anchor." That was why only she could get through the insanely dangerous forest she called home; she was holding the whole damn place together.

"I assume killing her won't break this enchantment?" Gage asked, cautious to keep how he felt about that prospect from his voice.

"If it were that easy, I'd have had you stab the bitch three days ago," she sneered. Despite her snide answer, Gage felt a brief moment of relief.

"I spent too long searching for an object rather than a person, so the opportunity to simply break this enchantment via assassination has passed. If she dies now, I lose the ability to crush this enchantment, only further impeding my plans," she sighed, rubbing her temple with one hand as if this whole affair had potential to give her a migraine. One could only hope.

"It will be complicated but doable. In the end I will have and win my war, my power will finally be absolute over Ethona, and their riches will be mine." She dropped her hand from her head and smiled once more as if the prospect was almost too thrilling to think about, at how she could exert her influence over anyone who wished for the precious ores she would control, all too pleased with herself.

"Is she going to survive your meddling?" he found himself asking.

Once again, Airalyn's look was both curious and suspicious. "Why would you care?" she asked cruelly.

"I don't, just seems a waste of potential," he assured her, expression carefully conveying as much. The look in her red eyes then was more wolf like than he'd ever seen in Nahleese's mismatched gaze, as if she was searching for a chink in his armor. If ever there was a more merciless creature when it came to attacking any perceived weakness, he'd yet to meet it.

"Good," she said at last. She flicked her wrist sending a plume of black smoke that pierced the placid silver face of the mirror. It swirled around his gloved hand, sparks jumping and hissing as the silver weather gauge almost burned white.

He yanked his hand back almost instantly, but the smoke had already faded away, its purpose done.

"The hell have you done to my hand you crone?" he growled, examining it for change as she smiled sweetly at him.

"No need to be nasty, Lucas, just a simple spell," she said sweetly. "It'll allow you to pluck one soul flame right from someone's chest, separate her from hers as soon as possible."

He felt his stomach lurch at her words, feeling sick at just the thought of being bestowed with such an obscene power, so reviled he was tempted briefly with the urge to destroy his glove and the power-lock with it.

"As I am to understand it, you've seen it done before, so you already know what to do." Airalyn watched his face with an almost innocent, doe-like concern as she went on. "Don't look so dour; it won't kill her unless you intentionally snuff it out—it'll just make her easier to... handle."

He had no reply that would not be rough with anger.

"Oh, and don't wait too long, Lucas; I'd hate for my spell to interfere with the power-lock that has been scribed to keep that nasty curse at bay." She smiled coyly. "And who knows how long before that happens?"

The cold bitch was testing him. He let a sinister smirk spread over his face, one that he'd worn many a times just before delivering a fatal blow.

"I hardly think I will find out, I am not unaccustomed to going for the throat." He gave a cordial nod to the mirror. "As one generally knows when dealing with pirates."

She appeared displeased with his lack of reaction, but after a long moment satisfied by his answer at least. "Take it at your pleasure then—time is on your side."

The Scarlet Queen smiled wider, "See? I am not without my favours. I'll contact you later to arrange the meeting place." She raised her hand to cut the connection with a wave, then hesitated as if remembering something.

"Oh, don't lose it, Lucas; I'll want them both intact. Till next time."

The mirror went dark. Almost immediately, Gage dropped the façade as he surged to his feet and threw the shard of mirror away from him, hard enough that its sharp edge stuck into the wood plank of the floor. He glared at his hand, new spell faintly tingling, pressing itself against the original properties of the gloves power-lock.

If he could, he would have said he tried and failed just to imply her spell was inadequate but that wasn't an option, as Airalyn well knew, the bloody harpy. He began to pace the confines of his cabin just to burn off some of his rage. That she would attempt to coerce him in this manner galled him beyond measure—if she wanted Fox's soul flame, she should bloody take it herself.

Strangely, even that notion sat curiously unwell with him. Either way, he couldn't afford for this spell to counteract his gloves power-lock, surely he could play the queen into the idea that taking Clara's soul flame was an unwise play, get the spell removed and keep Clara sa—

He stopped pacing, catching the thought before he even completed thinking it; why was that a priority for him at all? Clara's well-being in the queen's hands had nothing to do with him or his revenge. If this came down to her or him and his revenge, it should be simple cold, hard math.

He slowly returned to stand over Clara, who hadn't stirred the whole time; the sleep she was in was too deep for tossing and turning.

Once more he brushed her yellow fire locks from her face. It was true, he almost recoiled at the very thought of it—the act, one he might not be able to reconcile. He'd done his fair share of terrible deeds, would be the one that left him wondering who Lucas Sinclair even was anymore?

"That's another, darker game altogether, isn't it?" he murmured to her sleeping form, "We do well to finish the one we're playing, even if you and I don't lose well, do we, love?" Why did he feel the need to speak to her when she couldn't hear him, let alone answer?

Gage had a little time to think on the task set before him, which unfortunately reminded him he'd have to secure her soon, because "not losing well" was going to be putting it mildly when she woke.

Clara's head hurt; she felt like she was pulling herself out of the fog of a massive drinking binge, a hangover already in full force. She kept her eyes closed, thoughts coming to her sluggishly. Her arms felt funny, like they were pulled above her. She let out a moan, *oh gods my head...*

What had happened? What was going on?

A sharp awful smell pierced the haze of her brain and seemed to tear some of the curtains of fog in her mind down. She tried to move her head away from the repugnant smell, but it seemed inescapable.

"Come on, wake up sweetheart," a coaxing voice said softly. Finally, she pried her eyelids open, waiting for everything to come into focus. The first thing she made out of the fog was Gage's face, pulling smelling salts away from her nose. Everything came back to her in an instant, and her first instinct was to lash out, but when she tried, her arm was held firmly in place.

She looked up to see each wrist was tightly bound separate above her, holding her up. She tried to lift a foot to kick him only to be thwarted in that attempt as well, feet separately tied down too.

"There she is," Gage said calmly, not even flinching from her attempt to attack him. *Thank the god,* he thought, putting the smelling salts in his pocket.

"Get your bearings, love," he said calmly as he eyes flitted alarmingly about her a moment, "deep breaths."

Clara's rebellious gaze landed on him and he almost felt his skin burn, her eyes once again had that glow about them, burning in those intensely dark shades of forest green. She watched him smirk.

"Had me worried, Fox; I was starting to think I'd put you under a sleeping curse by mistake."

When Clara said nothing Gage kept smirking, but he ended up looking away from her first. Yeah, she'd have a hard time looking her in the eye too right now if she were in his place.

He turned around for a second, giving her a chance to scan her surroundings more thoroughly as she became increasingly more aware and less sluggish.

She and Gage were in the ship's brig from what she could tell, a few lanterns hanging from the walls to shed their warm light in the dreary place, with no windows it was impossible to tell what time of day it was.

"Here," Gage said, turning back to her with a cup. He tried to press it to her lips, but she turned her head away.

"It's just for the headache; I trust it's in full swing about now? Look—" He took a small sip of it as she watched him from the corner of her eye.

"Safe. No ploys—my kindness buys me nothing now," he assured her as he held it close to her lips once more. Clara hesitated as he held it up for her expectantly, pain flashing across her face as that headache started to kick in.

"Come now, there's no reason for you to be uncomfortable."

She seemed to relent after a tense moment, turning her head back and allowing him to tilt the cup up to her mouth to help her drink.

"That's a good girl," he said, pulling empty the cup away. Clara spit it in his face almost as soon as he moved the cup, glaring daggers at him. *Spoke too soon,* he thought as he calmly wiped the liquid from his eyes to look at her.

"Suppose I had that coming."

She said nothing, face hard with her rage. Gage turned his back on her as he walked to a small table pressed against the bars of the cell.

"I'm surprised you sent Nahleese for the hills," he said, keeping his hands busy with something.

"If you sent her for help, I'm afraid it won't get here in time."

Still, Clara said nothing. He'd expected venom and threats from her; he deserved every bit of it after all. Her silence, however, was almost unnerving, it ate at him more than harsh violent words ever could. He wanted that, for her to spit insults, ask questions, something that would make this... easier.

"You've been holding out on me, Fox; your forest is so much more *yours* than you let on. Honestly, I don't blame you for your lack of forthcoming about it." He turned back to her as he said it and saw a flash of confusion cross her face before it was replaced with that hard resentment once more.

"Unless you don't know?" he asked, returning some of the confusion he'd seen on her face. How could she not know? From the flickers of emotion Clara tried to conceal with her anger though, he could see she had no idea to what he was referring.

But she didn't ask, though he knew she wanted to. Gage wouldn't tell her what he knew unless she asked; it was one of the few bargaining chips he had to get her speaking.

"Very interesting," he said instead.

Oh, did Clara ever want to know what he was talking about! But her pride wouldn't let her ask, especially considering it had already been bruised by her kidnapping. Clara looked at the wall to her left, further shutting him out by not even looking at him.

"You know most men would find that silence haunting and discouraging, but I am not so easily dissuaded from a conversation," he said, passing the topic over, taking the chance to speak on it away from her.

Clara's eyes flicked down to the floor stubbornly, then back to the wall, still saying nothing.

Clara heard him go back to whatever he was doing at the table as he spoke.

"You'll have to excuse the lodgings—"

It comes with complimentary restraints, what's to excuse? she thought sarcastically to herself.

"I would have had you confined to the more civilized comforts of my cabin—"

Her eyes remained two hard slivers of emerald, cast upon the wall and making no effort to disguise the thoughts burning in them.

"—but I get the distinct impression you'd try to kill me," he finished.

"Try" implies I'd fail, she thought briefly, unable to help looking at him to see he was watching her face over his shoulder.

"I thought so," he said as if she'd spoken the words out loud. "You know, most people would be curious at the very least as to the reasons for their... imprisonment at this point," he prompted, implying he would answer questions, still focusing on whatever he was doing.

Her silence prodded him further than anyone else's ever would have.

"Such as why, or who..." he suggested.

Clara didn't care about who wanted her or why; she knew she should have but she couldn't seem to actually find it in her to give a damn right now. Hell, she didn't even care about how much he was getting for this, maybe it was because she was too raw at the moment over something else—because there was only one thing she really cared to know, and she wasn't ready to ask yet.

A lightness around her neck drew her attention and looked down to find her the cord with the sirens pearl missing. She felt her heart tighten, already missing her ace in the hole.

Gage didn't fail to notice the alarm on her face when she saw this.

"I'm not taking any chances with you, love; if I've learned anything from you, it's that if it's pretty, it's dangerous. That rule applies to your baubles, I'm afraid. Also, pirates always take a trinket," he added on the last, attempting to goad her into speaking now.

Clara wouldn't give an inch, and after a minute, he decided to go another route.

"You'll not be harmed here in any way; my men have no wish to die." Still nothing. He hated her for having the ability to make him feel this guilt. He stopped what he was doing.

"Clara, just... just say something," he said softly. It remained quiet for a long moment before she did.

"What would you have me say?" she asked, deliberate words soft under the weight of her ire. "Better yet," she went on before he could answer. "Why don't I, the prisoner, just get one clarification?" she offered in that same voice. "Like—does your protection extend past the people you're selling me to, Captain Black-Gage?" she asked, words dripping with venom.

He was amazed at how she made his title feel like a slap. He didn't answer her; he didn't know *how* to answer her, and his nonresponse elicited a derisive snort from her.

"Your silence is *deafening*," she sneered, squeezing her eyes closed as her head throbbed with pain. When Clara opened them, she saw he was facing her, holding up the cup again. She realized he'd been mixing up another tonic for her headache.

"Have we changed our mind yet?" he asked.

"Did I miss a spot on your face?" she countered. Gage actually laughed at that.

"Good to see you still have your—"

"I thought it was real." Her voice was calm as she said the words, holding no inflection whatsoever, but they almost choked them both into silence all the same.

He didn't need to ask what she thought had been real; it didn't even sound like a question though they both knew it was. Those simple words had sucked the air out of the room for him.

Clenching his jaw, he put the cup down on the small table and met her eyes fully for the first time since she woke, crossing his arms.

"It wasn't," he told her emotionlessly.

Clara had never had her heart ripped out before, but she was pretty sure this was worse when she watched him say those words; lies weren't usually this hurtful.

"I can't tell if you're lying to convince me or to convince yourself."

His eyes hardened as she said it with his own anger at last as she turned her face from him.

"If it's any consolation, I wish you weren't lying," she told him quietly. That was true, but then how could the opposite be just as true?

"It's not a lie," he told her coldly, letting his own anger surface in him now. She laughed at his declaration, a sound so soft he barely heard it.

"Whatever helps you sleep at night, *Captain*," she spat, "God, I bet you never even had a wife."

He was very suddenly in front of her, looking into those eyes that could drown a man and burn him up at the same time.

"I did this *for her*, revenge for her murder! That's what I'm getting out of this, the one thing that can kill that damn snake of a Wielder," he hissed angrily. "And if it were you, if this was a revenge for *Eric*," he said, the name feeling hard and merciless on his tongue, "you'd do the same. Damn. Thing."

There was a charged silence after those words. He expected rage from her after bringing Eric into this, for daring to say his name outside the sanctuary of that one vulnerable moment.

Instead, her anger seemed to dissipate to some surprise. Clara searched his gaze with her own then, as if wondering if that was true, if this was the path she'd walk if the tables were turned. Clara's eyes turned down to her feet, and for a long, long time, she said nothing; just rolling those words around in her head over and over and over.

Finally, she leaned forwards, eyes still on her feet, until the ropes binding her stopped her from moving any closer, leaving their faces the space of a breath apart.

"No. I wouldn't," she whispered.

Gage found he couldn't find anything to say to that bold statement for a moment. He grabbed his gloved hand with his right and massaged it, as if he was mulling something over. Finally, he dropped it to his side, seeming to hold off on some course of action or decision for a bit longer.

"A hundred more years to your name might change your answer," he whispered back, turning his back on her and walking away to leave the cell.

A hundred years?

Gage was almost out of the cell when she found her tongue.

"You're right," she called out to his retreating back, the sound of her voice pulling him up short.

Gage looked over his shoulder surprised to hear her admit it, her gaze still downcast. However, it seemed that wasn't what she was referring to.

"Your kindness buys you nothing. But I promise you," Clara said, eyes flickering up to meet his at last, holding him briefly prisoner with just a look. "Your betrayal will cost you dearly."

When she said those words, there was absolutely no doubt in Gage's mind that she meant every syllable. The moment he'd known was coming from the start had arrived at last, they had become enemies of the bitterest kind. He didn't know he'd been dreading its arrival quite this much.

You've made this bed Lucas...

Gage tore his gaze from hers almost forcefully; she watched Gage go without a word of retort and was grateful as she closed her eyes, a warm wetness sliding silently down her cheek.

Clara would be damned if she let him see her cry.

Eighteen

Peter had to wait until mealtime to do anything. The rest of the day, after the true purpose of the entire trek had been revealed, William had kept him busy scrubbing decks, hauling rope and much more. Chore after chore after chore. They didn't trust him to keep an objective attitude about what was going to happen to Clara, what *they* were going to do to Clara.

He himself wasn't sure he could disagree with that assessment. The foul mood of the captain barking orders and threatening the crew more readily than usual made him think that maybe he wasn't alone. The one who'd made a remark of some insulting nature had a concussion; apparently, that had been him getting off lucky. The whole crew felt like they were on eggshells at the moment.

On one hand, Peter had his duty; on the other was Clara, whom he liked and owed his life to. She'd gotten them all through the forest alive; it just didn't seem right, but what exactly was "right" to pirates?

He did the daily chores, thinking the rest of the day about what to do if anything at all. Finally, the meal bell was rung, and the crew all hurried for the gruel that Cook had prepared for them. Peter quickly moved past the others with a few casual elbows, grabbing two bowls.

"One bowl a man," Cook had growled at him, holding a full ladle over one bowl.

"For the prisoner," he'd explained just as gruffly. Cook gave him a hard look before dipping the ladle back in the pot and filling the second bowl.

Peter made off to the brig as quickly as he could without running. Of course, there was a guard just outside the door, but he'd known there would be.

"Food," Peter said before the guard could ask him, shoving the bowl into the man's hands.

"Prisoner's too," he held the bowl up as if the older pirate might miss it if he didn't.

The pirate waved him away like further explanation was unnecessary and just a tad annoying, focus now on the food he thought he was going to miss since being given guard duty.

Peter opened the door and slipped inside, the door closing firmly behind him. Somehow he felt as if the tension was even thicker in here; maybe it was because he knew how the captain would react if he found out where he was right now.

Now that he was in, Peter felt for the first time hesitancy. How would Clara receive him? They were technically enemies now.

What was he even here for? To make sure she was okay? That seemed stupid; he could make sure she was unharmed maybe, but okay? Probably not. Ultimately, he didn't know why he was down here. Peter could hear the groaning of ropes being strained against and found himself concerned as to how he'd find her; if Clara was tied up... she'd be pissed.

He puffed himself up a bit and stood straighter, whatever the reason he'd come this far, in for a copper in for the pot. One step would be all it took, then he'd be able to see her; it wasn't a very big brig after all. He took that step slowly and peered past the bars into Clara's cell.

Clara's hands were tied separately above her while her feet were knotted down to the floor with more rope. She was wrenching her arms from side to side as if she was trying to wriggle out of her bonds, hair sticking to the sweat on her face like she'd been at it for hours.

Peter opened his mouth to call her attention to him, but he didn't get a chance. Clara's head perked up like she sensed him, eyes landing on him as she abruptly quit struggling.

At first, her features locked down, appearing guarded, then she seemed to recognize him, and her face showed genuine surprise.

"Peter?" she asked, sounding out of breath.

"Hi," he said, grasping at the first thing that came to mind. He felt like smacking himself in the face—Hi? Really?

Clara, as he'd belatedly come to expect, did not look terribly pleased to see him.

"Did your captain send you, Peter?" she asked carefully, eyes dissecting him even from this distance.

"What? No! If he knew I was down here... probably wouldn't be pretty," he said, almost shivering.

She gave a shake of her head to unstick her hair from her sweat-beaded face.

"Then you shouldn't be here," she told him as he entered the cell.

"I think this is where I say something about asking forgiveness rather than permission." He shrugged, trying to come off as casual and doing a half-ass job at best.

Regardless she rewarded the effort with a ghost of a smirk.

"Rah-rah, little Rebel."

He came to stand in front of her, and for a minute, they just looked at each other. Clara patiently seemed to be waiting to hear what he'd come to say. He realized, as Clara waited, that that was why he'd come. She'd known before he did. Yet he felt at a loss as he struggled to find words that weren't as pointless as "I didn't know" or "I'm sorry."

"I..." he tried, already trailing off.

"It's all right, kid. I know," Clara cut in, saving him from further searching for inadequate words.

"But I'm afraid we both know it doesn't matter," she sighed. "Any way you spin it, we're on opposite sides of the board now." Because he couldn't side with her on this.

She could tell he didn't know what to say to that, looking torn. Clara knew immediately it would be the easiest thing in the world to manipulate him, get him to untie her and tell her how many pirates she was looking at between her and Gage's cabin. It would be like playing a well-tuned fiddle.

Clara also knew it would take Gage all of five seconds to figure out who had helped her. She'd never get them both off the ship, so if she went that route she had to be damn well prepared to leave him at his captain's mercy, and she wasn't entirely sure Captain Black-Gage had any of that. It seemed a rotten way to repay a good deed.

"You should go," she told him again.

"You're... not hungry?" he asked.

Clara looked at the steaming bowl of... something in his hands and arched an eyebrow. In truth, the spoon looked more appetizing than the actual food.

Peter shrugged apologetically.

"Yeah, not the prettiest food, but hey, it's hot, right?" he tried awkwardly, holding out the bowl for her to see.

Even now, she wanted to smile at him but clamped down on the urge, less she encourage him. His heart was too good for this life.

"It looks like cruel and unusual punishment, I'll pass," she said, trying to dismiss him by looking away.

Peter made no move to leave. She caught him squinting up at the ropes restraining her hands above her from the corner of her eye. Clara didn't need to look with him to know they were red and raw of course; they burned with every yank and twist of her wrist. If she it kept up, they'd bleed soon.

Clara was about to say something to him when she saw he was putting the bowl of food down, face hard and resolute. He was reaching for something that glinted in his boot—knife.

"Peter!" she snapped, making him jerk with surprise at the force with which she'd said his name.

"Take your gruel, and get out," she growled.

"I'm not going to hurt—" he tried to assure her, but she shook her head again.

"Hurt me, I know. Do you know what cutting me loose gets you, Peter?" she asked him.

The answer was *dead,* of course, but she'd let him stumble to that implication on his own. She could tell this was not the reaction he'd been expecting. Peter looked so damn conflicted, torn between loyalty and what he thought was right. She knew one way to make this easier for him, but it involved being a bitch. Clara could handle that.

"Of course you don't—how could I expect you to think that far ahead?" she asked snidely. Clara could see her words were like a slap to his face, but it had to hurt or it wouldn't work; that's what she told herself to smother that spark of guilt in her chest anyways.

"Actually go ahead, cut my ropes so Gage can walk you off a plank to drown, or maybe he'll cut your throat—either way you'll be out of all our hair."

"What?" He sounded so shocked by her harsh words.

"Should I speak slower? I don't want. Your help. We're not friends Peter. You were fifty gold pieces to me, just a bag of meat I had to keep breathing long enough to get paid. So piss off, I'm tired of watching you use up valuable air," she sneered at him nastily.

Just go, kid, don't get mixed up in this.

"I know what you're doing," he said stubbornly, slowly standing upright again, leaving his little knife where it was, good start at least. She grit her teeth in frustration.

"I'm telling you to fucking leave, you pissant," Clara hissed at him coldly.

He stared at her for a minute, managing to look angry, sympathetic, and determined all at once. That was how they spent what felt like a full minute, a strange meeting of wills between them; about what she wasn't entirely sure. He flicked his eyes up to glance at her wrists, and then finally he picked up the bowl and turned his back on her.

Clara let out a silent sigh of relief, assuming he would leave in a hurt, angry silence. To her surprise however, he paused with his back to her.

"We've weighed anchor five miles offshore. One guard's at the door. Your things are in the captain's quarters, right above this room."

She couldn't hide the surprise on her face as he gave her the information that would aid her in her escape.

Peter said it like he saw no possible future where she didn't get out of this cell and wanting to aid her in some small way.

"Please try not to kill anyone... Good luck." He didn't look back at her once as he left.

Gage was last to get his bowl of gruel, busy with his charts in his cabin to keep his mind occupied. He ran into William on his way there, he had the feeling his first mate had been looking for an opportunity to "run into him" for some time now.

He moved past him, not really in the mood for a conversation, but William fell into step behind him anyways.

"A word, Captain?"

"Seeing as that's three already, why not?" That was all the leave (sarcastic as it was) William needed apparently, and he wasted no time cutting to the chase.

"You're on edge, sir. I'm not the only one to notice—have we run into a problem?" William asked carefully.

"If we had, would you not be among the first to know?" Gage asked as calmly as he could through clenched teeth.

"Depends on the nature of the problem," William replied cryptically.

Gage turned on his heel to face his first mate so fast he almost ran into him. Gage was not as tall as William was but he had a way of making himself tower over people, no matter how tall they were.

"Do you have something to say William?" Gage asked coolly.

His first mate did not flinch under his glare, a rare quality which had helped him rise to his current rank on the Grey Ghost. The way those hazel eyes seemed to look through everything they examined was useful, and at times a nuisance—William knew he had become split on this matter, because of her.

"Revenge has its cost... perhaps this is too—"

"Who is the captain on this ship Mr. Williams?" Gage asked, voice like ice. The blue capped sailor straightened, a bit of tension in his shoulders. The look William gave him spoke volumes to Gage, even though the matter was clearly not open for discussion. The first mate wanted his captain to think on this choice.

"You are, forgive me... Captain." William nodded his head and dismissed himself, leaving Gage, as he made his way to the kitchens, to struggle with this by himself.

Cook poured the greasy-looking slop into Gage's bowl with a nod of respect and no chat. He had barely eaten anything for a good while now that he thought about it, stomach growling even at the unappealing looking food. Clara probably hadn't had much either...

He frowned. Somehow his mind always went back to her. *Why shouldn't it?* he thought, looking back at his gloved hand; he flexed the few fingers he had left to find the middle finger had ceased to move at all, due to his admittedly tantrum like folly earlier. He knew magic was fickle; the spell could take anywhere from an hour to a year to begin truly interfering with his glove. All the same, he shouldn't be playing with fire by ignoring the threat the complication posed. But here he was, filling his plate with gruel like the problem didn't even exist. *Go do what needs to be done Lucas Sinclair.*

Yet...

"Cook," Gage barked, snapping the man to attention almost instantly. "Take what's left down to the prisoner," he ordered, going to sit at the table.

"Didn't Peter already do that?"

Gage turned on his heel so fast he almost spilled the bowl of gruel onto the floor.

"What?" he snapped.

"Peter," Cook said, already trying to back away from his captain. "He already took her some—"

He cursed, already dashing out of the dining area. There was a reason Peter was being kept far from Fox; she'd wrap that damn kid around her finger in a heartbeat. She'd probably already convinced him to free her.

Gage nearly jumped down the stairs as he came upon the brig, lone guard just finishing his supper ration.

"Captain—" he greeted, standing. Gage moved past him without even a glance, throwing the door he guarded open and striding in, one hand on his blade. He very nearly ran into Peter, who appeared to just be leaving. The lad's eyes widened in fear as he stumbled back from Gage, who now blocked his path.

Gage quickly looked to see Clara in her cell, appearing to still be secure. Appearances, as he was well aware, could be deceiving. His eyes narrowed dangerously as he glared down at Peter, who stared back with wide, wary eyes, hands white-knuckling the bowl he was holding.

"I don't recall giving you permission to visit the prisoner, Peter," Gage said, voice deceptively calm.

"I just thought she might—"

"I'll deal with you later," Gage cut him off ominously, nodding his head to indicate he get moving.

Peter obeyed the words for the order they were immediately, quickly and carefully sidling past his captain who snatched the bowl from his hands before he slipped out the door.

"Now what were you two little birds chatting about?" Gage asked her with an empty smile as the brig door closed behind him.

"The bees, kids old enough to know now," Clara answered sarcastically as he slowly entered her cell, dropping the bowl on the small table as he did.

"Look at you, making jokes at last."

"Passes the time," she said in her usual deadpan.

"What were you two talking about, Fox?" he asked, voice hard as he came to stand in front of her.

Clara looked like she'd been running, still a touch out of breath with flushed cheeks and hair damp with sweat. What had she been doing?

"He was trying to convince me the slop he brought wasn't poison," she told him disgustedly, drawing him away from his observations. "I think he still wants to be my friend; might want to set him straight on that matter when you get to scolding him."

Clara tried to sound tired, not wanting to oversell it. Gage's eyes were practically digging into her, trying to detect even the slightest hint of a lie in her words. She let her expression show how much she wanted to beat him to death; he'd know she was lying if she tried to hide behind a blank, emotionless mask.

"Suddenly not so fond of Peter, are we?" he asked with a raised eyebrow.

"So you can use that fondness against me later? Feel free to try; he's under your flag."

Gage sighed as he shook his head. "I've no need to use anything against you, Fox." He reached out and started to pat her down.

"Get your hands off me!" she snapped, futilely trying to pull away.

"Peter would be putty in your adept hands, love; you expect me to believe you didn't convince him to slip you some help?" he asked, patting her legs down quickly.

"What was it? A blade?" he demanded, hand skimming professionally for anything hidden on her person.

"Did he loosen the ropes?" he demanded reaching up to check. Gage froze when he saw her wrists, pink-chaffed flesh looking painfully inflamed. He had tied the ropes tightly, but he'd been sure not to tie them *that* damn tight. She'd been struggling, vigorously apparently, perhaps the reason she looked so out of breath as well.

"Bloody hell, Clara," he spat, touching the rawness on her wrists gently and making her flinch. He pulled a scarf from his belt and pressed the cool silk against the exposed skin of her wrist to ease her discomfort. He probably should have lined her wrists with cloth before tying them.

"Save your strength for something productive," he advised her.

Clara yanked her wrist so hard she dislodged his hand and the scarf, rubbing the ropes mercilessly into her skin instead.

"I've always got energy to burn," she replied, giving another hard yank on her restraints.

"Regardless it's not going to get you free," he told her coolly, clenching his gloved hand almost absently.

"What do you care then?" Clara gave another violent tug, taking off another layer of skin.

Gage felt anger stir in him that she would pointlessly continue to injure herself.

"I have a reputation of delivering goods whole; the Scarlet Queen will hold me to that."

Outrage filled her eyes; the Scarlet Queen was the one who had hired him to *deliver* her? Like she was a fucking package? Clara thought her teeth might crack, she clenched them so hard; of all the people he could have sold her out to, he'd picked a royal. Not just any royal either, but the one most well known for her power-thirsty, war-mongering, and magic-abusing ways.

"I'm not a package. You can't keep me here."

"I'm captain of this vessel, Fox; I can do as I please." To his surprise, she actually laughed at him.

"I'm sorry, you misunderstand me—I mean, you *literally* can't keep me here. You don't have what it takes to lock me down."

"I think you're overestimating yourself a touch, darling."

"Guess we'll both find out soon enough, won't we?" Clara yanked her wrist down again, keeping deliberate eye contact with his as she did it. Gage grabbed her forearm tightly.

"I said stop it!" he growled.

"Fuck you!" she spat back.

It made him angry, so unbelievably angry that this willful creature was the biggest obstacle in his quest for revenge on more than just one level now, with his curse threatening to run its course unchecked and unfettered because he'd yet to do what had to be done.

Her green eyes seethed defiant rage, spitefully vowing to be free and negating all his work to get this far. At that moment, his pragmatism reared its shadowy head and told him to do what had to be done to secure the certainty of what he wanted.

It all happened so fast that it should have been impossible for Gage and Clara to perfectly understand what was going through the other's head with no words, but they did, as they'd done before.

He pulled at the collar of her shirt to expose that skin above her breasts, Clara watching him raise his gloved hand, noticing how the silver gauge burned so brightly on it that it actually began throwing sparks.

Strangely, it didn't even cross her mind that he would turn that destructive touch on her, didn't fit what he wanted. Instead her thoughts turned to the Scarlet Queen; she wasn't sure why but she felt something, something that just made it so *clear* that he had a spell of hers on his glove—and she knew exactly what it would be for too.

Clara knew all of this in an instant, and strangely the only thing she had time to actually think was, *Oh gods.*

Gage saw all of this blaze across her face, knew that she knew. The flash of horror in her eyes ripped at something in him, stopping him cold, black leather-gloved hand resting lightly on her chest. His entire arm shook, her wide eyes locked on him as the unpleasant tingling of magic pulsed against skin that had turned translucent under his touch, a window to the racing heart beating inside her that looked to house a spark of something like fire. The warmth of his hand and her chest heated the thin slip of the glove between them as they were both caught in the stillness before whatever might happen next.

He should do it, no, he *had* to do it; she'd all but said it herself she wasn't going to stop, and he couldn't afford to be thwarted now, not being this close, not with the threat of this spell sending his power-lock awry.

But it didn't matter, because looking into those wide, now sea-green eyes that were suddenly filled with fear shook the hell out of him. Gage could admit that he was a bastard, but he'd never been a fucking bastard before.

He couldn't do it; he wasn't sure if he'd ever been able to do it. Before Clara could read anything on his face, he practically tore himself from her presence, retreating like a violent storm without a word.

She watched, completely stunned, as he almost ripped the door off its hinges and slammed it so hard behind him she was surprised it didn't shatter. Clara let out a breath she hadn't realized she'd been holding now that she was alone, her skin returning to normal.

"Holy shit," she sighed to the empty room. Clara stared at the door Gage had just stormed through, wondering why her life was still her own.

Gage grabbed the pirate sitting outside the door by the front of his shirt and hauled him to his feet roughly.

"You guard this door from the inside to keep an eye on her. Don't approach her, don't let visitors in, and don't chat with her—are we clear?"

The man nodded his head furiously as his eyes almost budged out of his head. Gage let the fistful of his shirt go so quickly the man fell back into his chair and almost slipped right off it. He turned on his heel and walked away.

This isn't working, he thought heading for his quarters; he needed to figure out his course of action, because if Gage couldn't quell this conflict inside him, his house of cards was sure to come crashing down around his ears.

Clara had apparently earned herself a friend to wait with now, and by "friend," of course, she meant "pirate babysitter." He watched her like his life depended on it (now that she thought about it, that might actually be the case), alternating between cleaning under his nails with a small knife and staring at her. He'd also locked the cell door between them.

Tap, tap, tap—

He tapped his foot like it was a tic of his, and it was driving her crazy. She bet if he was standing he'd cut it out.

"You know, I wouldn't hate a chair. How about some of that gentlemanly hospitality your captain is so fond of?"

He grunted but said nothing intelligible and continued tapping his damned foot.

"Good talk," Clara sighed sarcastically.

Tap, tap, tap—

She didn't struggle as hard in her bonds now. Clara had a feeling if she started that up her babysitter would send word up to his captain, and she'd be dealing with him again. The next time she saw Gage, she wanted it to be on her terms.

Tap, tap, tap—

Clara rolled her neck to ease some stiffness in the muscles, letting her head hang to look at the floor. She now twisted her wrists more subtly, working away her own skin. She'd kept the pain off her face by biting her tongue and occasionally being a smart-ass to her watcher thus far; he'd yet to notice what she was doing.

Tap, tap, tap—

He hadn't taken it. That was the one thought she kept coming back to as the next few hours passed; he hadn't taken her soul flame. She played that moment out in her head over and over, trying to remember what had stopped him but was unable to pick out the exact moment he'd decided not to.

Gage was dead set on his revenge for the wife he'd watched be murdered before his eyes; she got that. It didn't excuse his betrayal or what he had done, but Clara got it. Holding her very essence hostage pretty much guaranteed she wouldn't escape, and since he'd all but said that she was his only coin to buy revenge it only deepened her confusion.

Tap...

True, there was something there between them, but whatever it was, she'd seen it wasn't enough to derail his plans. *So why hadn't he taken it?* Clara didn't know, and as her wrists finally started to bleed, she decided she had to find out, to put this mystery to rest.

She'd been lost in thought, focused so keenly on her task and her musings Clara hadn't noticed something was off. After a minute, however, something nagged her brain into paying more attention. Clara listened for a moment before it hit her; the tapping had stopped.

She pulled her head up and to her surprise saw there was no one sitting in the chair the pirate had been occupying only moments before.

Clara leaned forwards and looked around; the man was now nowhere to be seen. She would have heard him leave; hell, she would have heard him get out of that creaky chair to stretch. Where had he gone?

That's when Clara heard a voice behind her that nearly made her jump out of her skin.

"Enjoying the downtime, La-vie?"

Nineteen

Clara tried to turn to see who the voice belonged to but was prevented by her restraints. Even straining her neck, the shadow of a man was all she could make out.

The sound of boots clacking on the wooden floor filled the silence as whoever it was walked into her line of vision. A man with short, ash-brown hair moved elegantly into the candlelight, dressed in some of the strangest fine attire she'd ever seen. He wore a coat with a high stiff collar that looked like some kind of snake skin that had been painted with a blood red lacquer, running down his lapels and over his shoulders. Long leather sleeves, brown cuffs with silver buttons, and a gold-like silk ruffle at his wrist from the undershirt. His boots were black and laced up past his knees, his black pants tucked in tightly.

The attire was unsettling in a way, even as he walked with an almost playful skip to his every step. He... looked like a giddy predator.

He came to stand in front of her with a wide smile full of horrid, greenish black-stained teeth, but she was distracted from his smile by how tightly his skin stretched over his face, how patches of it appeared to be like the material of his coat—snakelike. It was almost as if he'd taken bits of snake skin and sewn it where his own pale skin hadn't stretched far enough to cover his face.

His eyes held hers unblinking; it was almost as if he didn't *have* eyelids, his irises looking like spindles of black and green twine all twisted together.

"I hope so; you're going to be awfully busy later," he said, smile widening even more. Clara just stared at him, taking in his whole terrifying visage. She'd met a few monstrous creatures, she'd fought and run from a hell of a lot more—but none compared to... this.

"What the hell are you?" she asked, trying not to sound as breathless as she felt.

"Bit rude, La-vie. I believe you meant 'who'," he corrected her as he reached up and tapped the end of her nose before she could blink, like he was somehow playfully chastising her.

Clara couldn't speak for a moment, not sure if she should bother rephrasing the question. It wasn't how he looked that put her on edge, it was the feeling his presence inspired in her. It had just been a long time since she'd met someone who scared her without even doing anything of a remotely threatening nature.

"What did you do to my babysitter?" she asked as she glanced back to the empty chair where the pirate had been sitting.

He tilted his head to the side as if he found this new line of questioning amusing.

"Were you terribly fond of him?"

"Not especially."

"Oh good, that had potential to be awkward—he's no longer with us."

"I can see that. What did—" Clara stopped as she digested his answer. "Oh."

"Yes, well, he was a bit in the way." The stranger waved the matter aside like it was a silly thing of little import.

"But enough about him, I'm here to talk to you, La-vie."

"Sorry, *who* exactly is here to talk with me?" Clara asked warily, unconsciously trying to pull back from him a little.

He startled her with a piercing giggle, turning on his heel and taking a few steps towards the cell door.

"Ah, yes, of course," he seemed to say more to himself than her. He pivoted on the spot to face her again, like he was trying to give her a more complete view of him.

"Allow me to reintroduce myself." He gave a strange bow.

"Ryker Vidaris," he said, rolling the "R" of his name theatrically, "but the peasants simply refer to me as The Mage."

Clara's eyebrows flew up to her hairline.

"The Mage?" she repeated.

He looked up at her from his bow, holding the position and somehow making it vaguely threatening.

"He's a myth." She'd always thought he was anyways.

"Aren't we all in the end?" he asked as he straightened.

More dangerous players, Clara thought, unable to help herself from sizing him up. By the way he kept smiling at her, she could tell he didn't miss the evaluation. Clara, similarly, had caught his little bit about *reintroducing* himself, but if he was who he said he was she doubted he'd said it that way expecting her to miss it. She felt his gaze move along her as he started to circle her, as if he was appraising her value.

"Either way, I'm fairly certain we've never met," she finished, trying to keep her eye on him as he did. It was like he couldn't stay still for any length of time.

"Well, not that you can remember, La-vie," his said as he paced out of her line of sight again. "But me?"

He was suddenly in front of her, just appearing there with no warning. His hands reached up to gently cradle her face between his cool fingers, wide spindle twine eyes staring into hers.

"Well, I rarely forget a face, though it would be understandable if I did—you've grown up some since last we met..."

Clara tried not to show how startled she was by his sudden reappearance and carefully pulled her face back from his touch as he continued.

"But I *never* forget a contract." Contract? What the hell was he talking about?

"Think you've got the wrong girl," she told him with an insincere smirk.

"Fairly certain I don't," he replied, titling his head as he looked at her. *"Clara Fox."*

The way he said her name made her feel like he'd put ice in her veins.

He snickered at the surprise on her face, blissfully moving back to give her some space to breathe.

He was testing her, putting out the bait to see if she'd bite, leading her along. To what end she wasn't sure, but Clara disliked being pulled along on anyone's leash. She was getting the distinct feeling she was now in a game far out of her league of play; it wasn't a feeling she had very often.

"Yes, I know your name, what you do, who you do it with. Nice lad, that Fitz, and I enjoy that little firecracker he's courting."

Clara nearly bared her teeth at the mention of Fitz and the lover almost no one else knew about.

"You ever think it strange that your earliest memory starts at the ripe age of ten?" he asked as if he himself was puzzled by the question.

"How the hell do you know that?" she demanded, face turning hard and this time baring her teeth as she spoke.

More cackling, the sound made Clara curl her hands into fists.

"Oh, La-vie *La*." He punctuated "la" with a fluent gesture of his hand, the air hazing as if from some great heat, blurring the middle of his palm. Upon clearing, it revealed a perfectly round pebble, no bigger than her thumbnail, shades of aqua spinning inside it like turbulent clouds.

He closed his hand and leaned in close again, those unsettling eyes glinting darkly at her.

"There are so many *better* questions you could be asking."

"You know what?" Clara began, "I've had a hell of a few days and as much fun as you're having swanning in here and playing whatever little games you're playing, I'm not."

His expression didn't change as he held himself in that pose, perfectly still as she leaned in closer to *him* this time, filling the space between them with her hostility. "So allow me to cut through the bullshit and your theatrics." She nodded to the hand he closed around the pebble.

"How do you know all about me, what the hell is the pebble, and what contract?" she had to fight a wince as the ropes slipped roughly over her abused skin, growing wetter with her blood.

"Well, aren't you a spicy little thing?" he mocked playfully. "To someone who could potentially offer you aid no less."

"You're not here to help me," Clara stated firmly; it wasn't even a question.

"Always assuming the worst, aren't you, La-vie?" he said, opening his hand to pick the pebble up between his index finger and thumb. "Truth is I'm just here to wish you a happy birthday."

That certainly caught Clara off guard. Her *birthday*? She didn't even know her real birthday; she'd always marked it as the day she'd woken up in the Dark Forest—she might as well have been born that day seeing as she knew nothing but her first name and age.

"Sorry?" she asked, as if maybe she'd misheard him.

"The clock struck twelve some time ago; it's your birthday today, Miss Fox. Twenty-nine now if I'm not mistaken." He held up the pebble in front of her face as the colours churned inside its glassy confines.

"And as is customary, I come bearing gifts." Before she could react, he pressed the pebble between her eyes, and very suddenly Clara's vision flashed to white.

Clara waited on a dark path at the dead of night, the farthest she'd even been from the palace walls in her whole life. She was nervous, especially since she'd never been outside them before without guards.

To make it worse, it was really dark on this abandoned path. All of the trees' silhouettes felt like giants out here, and she'd never felt smaller. It had been easier to sneak out of the palace than she'd thought, but then she guessed no one expected a ten-year-old princess to try.

Clara held her lantern closer to her, coveting the little bit of light and heat with her cloak pulled tightly around her shoulders, waiting.

"I have to admit—"

Clara actually squeaked at the sudden intrusion of the smooth voice into the silence, whipping around to face the source of it with her lantern, held out as if it would protect her.

A lean figure stood just outside the light of the lantern, hedging on the shadows they cast instead.

"—the very last person I expected to summon me was such a young princess, La-vie," the voice finished, holding out a hand and releasing a small bird that came to perch on Clara's shoulder. "Nice to see some royals still keep a bird trained to my homing"—he held up the little bean-shaped "homing" that messenger birds were trained to track—"in case the worst should pass, gives me a warm feeling right here," he told her, putting a hand over his heart.

"M-m-mage?" she asked stuttered hesitantly.

The figure stepped into the light with a wide smile that bared uneven ugly teeth and snake patched skin that made her eyes almost bug out of her small head. She swallowed convulsively and the imps grin widened. He gave a bow.

"At your service, but please—call me Ryker." He straightened, taking a step closer as he did, into the light where she could better see him.

This was no comfort to Clara; she wanted to take a step back, but she made herself hold her ground.

"I was under the impression I was not welcome by the royal house of Ethona, prided as one of the very few royal houses not in some debt to me in some circles even. If your parents could, they'd banish me from their lands." He said it as if he'd love to see them try.

"But now," he continued, "here before me stands their young heir." He smiled wider at her as she looked up at him; the way he towered over her made her want to run away from him and never look back.

"Here to propose a contract in secret, past her bedtime no less." He waved a finger at her as if she'd been naughty. "Mommy and Daddy are going to be very cross with you, La-vie," he tittered.

"Who says I'll make a contract with you at all?" she tried, working very, very hard to keep the tremor from her voice.

"Don't be coy, little princess; no one calls me in a flight of fancy, not until desperation has set in do people throw caution to the wind and send for me, never without some pact in mind."

There was a heavy silence that Ryker showed no signs of breaking, waiting for her to speak.

"We're about to go to war," Clara told him, trying to get this over with before she lost her nerve.

"Ah, yes, the Scarlet Queen marches on your little kingdom," Ryker said with a nod, like this did not surprise him in the least. "Her forces fill the forest as we speak if I'm not mistaken, along with some of her allied troops—through no favour but mine," he muttered bitterly.

Clara missed the jab entirely as she focused on getting the courage up to speak.

"We won't win," Clara said bluntly.

"Oh, I know," he agreed, crouching down to her height so he could look her more fully in the eyes, seeming intrigued by her in a way he hadn't been moments ago. "Very perceptive of you to know it as well."

"Can you stop it?" Clara asked, trying not to sound hopeful.

"If you mean, can I kill Airalyn for you, the answer is no," he said, lacing his fingers together, remaining crouched in front of her.

She took a deep breath and did her best imitation of her mother, trying to be as strong as she was. "If I wanted that I would have asked for that; I want to know if you can stop the war," Clara repeated as firmly as she could.

He giggled again. "Feisty little thing aren't you?"

Clara didn't respond, trying to show how little he scared her. He scared her a lot, but she was hoping it didn't show.

He reached forwards very suddenly, and his touch on her cheek froze her, literally immobilized her; she couldn't even shiver or widen her eyes. For a few seconds, nothing happened, just him lightly touching her check, brow pursed as if he was searching for something in her eyes. Then there was a shock, not painful but definitely jarring, where his skin touched hers.

He pulled back, cackling as Clara unfroze and stumbled back from him, gasping for air as the bird perched on her shoulder took flight into the night.

"Interesting," he said to himself, making no move to follow her.

"What did you do?!" she demanded, too afraid to look away from him.

"Calm yourself, Princess. Just testing the waters. To answer your question, there might be something I can do."

He disappeared, sending Clara's eyes scattering about her for him again. She heard his voice but he remained out of sight. "I could cast an enchantment on the forest the queen's forces pass through to attack your kingdom, make it impassable as it were."

She felt a presence behind her and turned to find Ryker there, perched in midair like he'd found himself an invisible floating seat.

He leaned forwards, the yellow light catching on his every sharp feature to cast disturbing shadows over the tight scaly patched skin of his face, exposing those eerie eyes of his. Clara didn't know how she did it, but she didn't run.

"For a cost, of course. What can you give me for my services, Princess?" he asked, tilting his head.

"Is it true you take... children?" she asked hesitantly.

His grin darkened considerably.

"Well, aren't you an adorable little martyr?" He soundlessly dropped his feet back to the ground and began to pace around her, moving out of the lights reach once more.

His refusal to stay put was starting to make her dizzy as she followed his progress with the lantern to keep him in sight.

"Tempting as the offer is, I want something a bit more... precious." He didn't look at her when he said it.

Clara's little heart was beating in her throat almost painfully. Dealing with Ryker was exhausting her with fear at this point, and she just wanted to go home.

"What?" she asked when he made it clear he wasn't going to continue unless she asked.

"First things first," he said after a moment's hesitation. "This enchantment wouldn't be easy, La-vie. It'll need someone like... you," he said, pointing at her, "to stay and hold it in the forest for... nineteen years at the very least. Every year, it will become more dangerous for you there as it needs you less and less until"—he made another theatrical gesture with

his arms—"you can root the magic down from a distance! You'll be free to leave the forest without the magic waning. Would you be willing to do that?" he asked, sliding his eyes to look at her.

Clara stood straighter and held her head high.

"Yes."

"Excellent," he said, voice almost sounding like it slithered through the air.

"So we have a deal?" Clara asked, bringing her lantern up more to see his face.

"Not quite yet," he said, sounding amused.

"But you just said—"

"What you must be willing to do, not the price of my services."

"What do you want?" she asked again, voice wavering slightly.

"How about..." He faced her again before pointing one long scaly finger at her. "Your memories."

Clara's eyes widened in her tiny face. "All of them?" she asked, unable to hide the horror in her voice.

"I'd be willing to spare one or two down the road," he conceded with a shrug.

Clara stood there for a long time, thinking about it. He just watched her, not pressing her for her answer. He looked all too pleased to watch her struggle with it.

"My family will live? My people will be safe?"

He bowed his head and made another fluent rolling gesture with his hand.

"You have my word."

That was what kings and queens were supposed to do; they took care of their family and their people. If she didn't do this, she'd be letting them all down and many would die. Clara took a deep breath before she could lose her nerve all together and slowly nodded.

"You have to say you accept the contract, La-vie," he told her, cupping his ear as if to better hear her.

"I accept."

He snapped his fingers, and Clara yelped as a sharp pinching sensation nipped at her forearm. She lifted the lantern to look at it, just in time to see a small flourishing "V" magically draw itself on the inside of her forearm before fading away.

"Then let us begin, little princess."

The vision ended, and Clara came back to herself, gasping for air as her eyes flew about the dank familiar confines to assure herself she was still in the brig of Gage's ship. It was a memory, one simple memory and her whole life came together.

Clara looked above her to her forearm and watched that same letter "V" magically draw itself—as if it had always been there. Suddenly, she knew who she was; Clara knew why she'd woken in the forest that night, alone and knowing nothing. She knew why it became more difficult to navigate her forest each year, more dangerous.

Clara hadn't been abandoned to die: she'd chosen to give it all away. She had a family; Clara was a *princess*—it was a lot to take in at that moment.

Ryker watched her trying to catch her breath, staring at his mark on her arm with what was now a now familiar impish grin.

"You're not as tall as I remember, Ryker," she wheezed at last, looking back to him.

"Hazards of growing up," he replied with some amusement, reaching up and swiping his thumb quickly over the letter in her skin, wiping it away as though it never was—the contract had been fulfilled.

"Your impersonation of a snake has much improved though," she said, trying to be insolent now.

He pressed his hand over her heart, and she gasped as magic crept over her, her skin turning translucent in an unpleasantly familiar way, showing a clear path to her heart.

"My impersonation of the Scarlet Queen's favorite trick is much better, La-vie; just ask Captain Black-Gage."

For about three seconds, she forgot he was threatening to steal her vital essence as her jaw dropped.

"You're the Wielder Sinclair wants his revenge on?"

Ryker actually rolled his eyes, removing his hand and his threat with it. "It was a hundred years ago; bloke just won't move on," he said, as if it were a small annoyance he'd become accustom to dealing with.

"I suppose the queen did promise him my short sword for this little venture, me being bound to it and all."

Short sword? A hundred years? Clara wasn't sure she could show the proper amount of surprise anymore; she was being drowned in revelation after revelation. She didn't bother asking him how he knew; he had proven to have his ways.

"You don't seem very worried," Clara observed, confused.

"She's not actually going to give it to him, La-vie. The blade may be the only thing that can kill me but unbeknownst to him it's also the only thing keeping me... let's say *cooperative*."

For the first time, she saw the stirrings of anger on his face, but he smoothed them away almost as soon as they appeared.

"If you don't escape, she'll take you, kill him, and he'll be out of both our hairs. Same goes for failure, I trust."

Why did those words tighten Clara's gut?

"Speaking of the queen, she knows who you are now, La-vie; she's never gonna stop looking for you, and the forest will all but eat you alive now—all special privileges have been revoked." He watched her so expectantly then, and the implication set a fire in her.

"I wouldn't make another contract with you if my life hung in the balance," she practically snarled at him, finally managing to catch her breath.

"Feistier than ever I see. First off, it does hang in the balance. Secondly, didn't think you would." He held up another pebble, this one was white. "Hence, the second gift."

"I don't want it," she hissed.

"A princess should know it's terribly rude to refuse a gift."

Before she could protest further, he'd pressed the pebble between her eyes and Clara's brain felt like it was on fire.

Pathways, forest, monsters, a sea voyage, latitude, and longitude—

"What the hell was that?!" Clara gasped for the second time when Ryker withdrew his hand, pebble nowhere in sight.

"Directions, instructions, things you'll need," he listed to her casually. "It's the location of something I've hidden for a very rainy day; you'll need it if you want to come out victorious at last against the Scarlet Queen."

"I'm not the little martyr you once knew, Vidaris; who says I'm going up against that bitch at all?"

"Sooner or later, whether you like it or not, Miss Fox, you're going to have to finish this fight." He sounded so sure, like he knew she'd bend and do what he wanted.

"Not my fight anymore as far as I'm concerned. You kill her if you want her dead so bad; I'm not your puppet."

"I can't," he said it like the words tasted bad in his mouth. "I've seen your future, La-vie, and it's you who brings about the demise of Airalyn."

That surprised her.

"So puppet or not, you will do this."

"When all the hells freeze over," she told him sweetly.

"Best bundle up, then, La-vie; it's about to get cold."

"What are you even trying to send me after?" Clara demanded.

"I find these sorts of things are more effective if you find out yourself," he answered secretively, turning away from her. He gave a casual flick of his wrist and the locked cell door made a loud clicking noise before swinging open. "Afraid I can't help you get free, La-vie; my hands are tied if you'll excuse the phrase," he apologized as he sauntered away.

Clara made a *humph* sound. "Please."

He turned back curiously at her derisive words. She, however, glanced up at the blood soaked ropes. "If you really want something, sometimes—"

She yanked her arms down, the hardest she'd done yet. The blood had made the ropes and her wrists slippery as she had hoped. Her wrists slipped halfway out, making her bite her tongue to keep from yelping in pain.

He watched her tug once more and her arms came free, falling by her sides as she rolled her shoulders to ease the knots in them.

"—you just have to be willing to bleed a little for it," she finished.

He smiled at her, continuing through the cell door.

"So good to know. We'll be in touch, La-vie"

She thought he was going to leave then, disappear much like he had appeared. But he stopped there just past the cell's thresh hold, keeping his back to her.

"Strange thing that was, all those years ago."

There was an offhanded attitude to the comment, like she should know exactly to what he referred.

"What was?" she asked as she untied her feet, not giving him her full attention mostly out of spite.

"How you never found young Eric's body."

Clara's head snapped up so fast she almost heard her neck crack. Too late, he'd gone as silently and as abruptly as he'd come, leaving her more alone than before.

His words hung in the air though, echoing in her mind as a lump stuck in her throat.

Gage closed the door to his quarters behind him after a routine check to be sure everyone was remaining vigilant in their duties, going back to sit as his desk by the crackling fire He had found the way to quell his conflict at last, only time would tell if such a plan could work. If *she* would agree. A pair of manacles lay before him, the ones Clara would be wearing when he escorted her from the ship.

His hand searched for the screwdriver he'd been using to tamper around with them but when he reached for where he'd left them, his hand came up empty. He had time to be confused for maybe a full three seconds before he felt the point of it press into the side of his neck. Gage froze in place.

"Ah, you always go for the throat, don't you, Fox?" Gage observed cautiously after a moment.

"Still think I overestimate myself?" Clara asked.

"At the risk of having my throat opened, I'd say you're not off the ship yet, love," he replied, a small, hard smirk fixing on his face. He felt her hand reach down and relieve him of his sword as she spoke.

"Can't leave my bag of tricks behind now, can I? Take off the glove, slowly."

He obliged her, speaking carefully as the point of the screwdriver pressed threateningly against his pulse. "By all means, I seem to be missing its mate anyways," he told her good naturedly, holding it up for her to take.

She snatched it out of his hand, and he felt her hot breath hissing in his ear, pressing the point in a little harder.

"I wouldn't get cute with me right now if I were you, Captain."

The pressure at his neck disappeared and instead the point of his own sword pushed against his chest as Clara quickly moved into view. Her wrists were bloody and that fire-blond hair tussled about her face, already wearing the black cord with her confiscated pearl around her neck. She threw the glove and the screwdriver to the opposite side of the room, far out of reach.

"Where are my things?" Clara demanded.

"That looks painful," Gage said, looking to her wrists.

"Yeah, well, it's pretty far from my heart." Her eyes narrowed with the vailed reminder.

Gage opened his mouth to speak, but Clara cut him off. "If you say another word, I will run you through with your own sword and toss this cabin to find it all myself. Point them out."

Gage's mouth drew into a tight line as he pointed over to a wooden wardrobe.

"Get them," she ordered, flicking the sword in that direction.

He slowly rose to his feet and did as she asked, watching her carefully as he did. As he opened the wardrobe and pulled out Clara's pack, he saw her look at the manacles on his desk. He used the small distraction to slip something into her pack unnoticed.

"Breaking out the irons for me?" Clara asked. "I'm flattered."

Then he saw a wrinkle of confusion on her brow, as she seemed to notice something else.

"What have you done to them?" she asked.

He waved his hand as if inviting her to examine them. She backed away from him slowly, sword still trained on him as she picked the manacles up from the desk and gave them a once-over. It didn't take her long to figure out what was wrong with them; they closed, but they didn't lock.

"You've tampered with them," she said, letting the confusion show on her face. "Why?" Gage tossed the bag at her feet.

"Leave to speak without being stabbed?" he asked sarcastically. Clara glared silently, that was all the permission he needed.

"My job is to deliver you to the Scarlet Queen, love; I do that, and I receive my payment." Gage shrugged. "If you were to escape after you left my custody, what business or fault of that is mine?"

Clara just stared at him. "Are you seriously going to try to sell me on going into cahoots with you?" she asked dryly, snagging the strap of her pack with her foot and dragging it closer.

That had been his solution, yes.

"I've seen you work, Fox; you're good. All you need is an opening, and I *can* provide one; we can all get what we want. Except the queen of course, but I'm sure we'll find a way to travail over our guilt on that matter."

Clara stood and looked at the manacles in her hand, keeping him in her peripheral. He made extra sure not to make any sudden movements as he watched her think. She put the manacles down on the desk and didn't look at him. Trying to have it all—a pirate to the bone.

"It won't work," she said quietly.

"It *could*—"

Once again, Clara was cutting him off with a very firm tone, crouching down and pulling the knife she wore on her wrist out from her pack as she spoke.

"It won't work because Airalyn has no intention of giving you the short sword. She's going to kill you as soon as you hand me over."

Gage hadn't been moving, but Clara felt how the stillness about him changed when she said those words. He went from cautiously still to suddenly rigid.

"How do you know about the short sword?" he demanded, those bright cold ocean eyes fixing on her as she stood once more. He'd taken a step forwards, ignoring how his cutlass was still trained on him; Clara lifted it higher to remind him.

"I know a great deal more than you could fathom, Captain," she dismissed harshly. "So take my word for it, that short sword has more value to her than you do—you're just the man doing the dirty work."

He quietly watched her face as she said all this at first, trying to find the lie. "Why are you telling me this?" he asked when he didn't, suspicion and curiosity alight in his gaze.

"Why didn't you rip my soul flame out when you had the chance?" Clara countered.

Once again, they were left staring at each other with only silence between them.

"That wasn't a rhetorical question," Clara said when it became clear he wasn't going to answer her.

"You know why," Gage said simply.

"No, I don't," Clara hissed back, taking a step closer so the point of the sword scrapped dangerously over his chest.

"Yes. You. Do," he said, enunciating each word through clenched teeth. Clara felt lost for words for a very long and yet very short moment before she could answer that.

"Well, I'm just crossing off all my IOUs; you know how I hate owing anyone." Her words were almost colder than before. "You basically spared my life; I've spared you being stabbed in the back, literally and figuratively. While I'm at it, here's another one I'm crossing off."

Clara dropped his cutlass, and before he could react, she was slamming him against the cabin wall holding her knife to his throat.

When she spoke, it was in a whisper. “I want you to know that I could have helped you, to take out the queen with a little something I’ve got up my sleeve, probably get you that all-important short blade for your revenge in one fell swoop.”

Gage’s face was a mask of stone at first with the knife to his throat. His eyes locked with hers, and when he saw she believed every word, his face softened.

“Could have. Won’t.”

“Clara—” he tried, hoping to reason with her but she shook her head and spoke over him.

“I told you the very first day we met if you crossed me you’d regret it.” She said it without any anger or spite. Clara said it as if somehow he’d managed to make some small part of her regret it too. “Now you will. Square on all accounts.”

The knife pushed into his throat a little harder, making Gage press the back of his head to the wall to avoid being cut.

“I better not ever see you again, Sinclair, or I’ll kill you.”

He was surprised; it was the first time she’d said his name since his betrayal; he found, even though it was in a threat, he’d missed it.

“But hey, here’s something to remember me by.”

She pulled the blade back as if to get a better angle on her strike. He thought for a split second she was going to run him through, give him a nonfatal wound that would forever remind him of this mistake.

At the last second, she changed direction with the blade and drove it into the sleeve of his shirt, pinning his good hand to the wall.

The fingers of her other hand tangled in his hair as she brought her face to his and kissed him. Her mouth was hot and hungry against his, and despite his surprise, he found himself returning the passionate kiss in full force, catching her lips between his. For one precious second, the world slipped away, and everything went with it. There was just him and her—how she smelt like trees and tasted like silk, how he smelt like the sea with the numbing tang of rum on his lips. That fire, so often in their eyes, set them both ablaze and sent their pulses racing. It was heaven, it was hell; and it was far more devastating than any blow inflicted by cold steel.

Clara tore herself abruptly away from the kiss and the suddenness jarred them both back to the cold reality. Before Gage could react, her fist was colliding with his face, leaving him seeing stars.

She let go of his head, and his knees hit the ground, stunned by the blow.

She was picking up his cutlass and slipping her pack onto her shoulders before he could collect himself, turning her back on him and making for the door. Clara didn't look back once.

"Clara!"

It was harder than she thought it would be for a moment, and made easier only by her rage the next. She ripped the pearl from the cord around her neck and clutched it tightly in her hand, wrenching open the door, passing through it and striding into full view of the pirates on deck.

It didn't take long for everyone to notice the fierce blonde standing tall and brandishing a sword. The wind lashed her hair out behind her like the snap of whips, blood drying on her injured wrists with fire behind those vivid green eyes, burning for a fight.

"Evening, boys."

Twenty

Gage's face throbbed as his knees hit the floor, a sharp pain jolting up through his legs as his head spun. Clara had hit him right on the chin, the only thing keeping Gage upright at that moment was the arm pinned to the wall by her knife. He heard her heading for the door, and all he could think was, *Stop her!*

"Clara!" he yelled, trying to clear his eyes of stars. He saw the flash of her reddish-blond hair, her purposeful stride, and the door slamming shut behind her.

"Sonuvabitch," he cursed, trying to yank his hand free, hoping to tear the sleeve keeping him trapped but having little success. He clenched his teeth, getting to his feet and using the opposite forearm with his damaged hand to hit the hilt of the blade, trying to rip it out of the wall.

On the fourth try, he heard all hell starting to break loose out on deck. He hit the blade so hard he was sure he bruised his forearm, managing to knock it free of the wall and to the floor with a loud clatter.

Gage ran for the door, only stopping to pick up his glove as he tore after her onto the deck. What he saw upon catching up to her was enough to make him hesitate a moment.

She moved like the crack of a whip, even in the thick of his crew trying to get at her, fluid yet somehow impossibly sharp. Clara surged into any opening, out from the path of any blow, making it seem like she were some insubstantial ghost one could never hope to touch before striking back like a cobra. When there was no space to move she *made* a space, and she attacked the same way she evaded, without pause. But even armed with his sword, no one drew blade nor pistol on her, knowing she was wanted alive.

Clara held his sword so the blade was pointed to the ground, using the hilt to make her punches that much harder.

It seemed she didn't like killing those who weren't trying to kill her. That said, Clara mercilessly dealt with all on-comers with the force of a violent storm.

There were already a few injured men being pulled from the fray by William, Jared, and Squint. His first mate and the other two knew better than to try to test their metal against Clara.

Someone screamed, drawing his attention back to the fight to see one of the pirates had *his* sword speared through his thigh, dropping a knife to grasp the bleeding limb before falling.

A man took a wide swing at her, but Clara sidestepped, easily evading him. She gripped his elbow as she did, using his own momentum to drive that fist into the face of the man attacking from behind.

A third man advanced on her left, preparing to lunge. Still gripping the first man's elbow, she ducked beneath his arm, twisting it violently so a sharp crack pierced the air with his scream before she kicked her leg out.

Her foot caught her third assailant full in the chest, successfully knocking the now winded man back a few steps to give her enough space to better visit her violence upon them. Clara let the man's broken arm go so he crumbled to the ground in a useless heap and drove her clenched fist into the winded pirate's throat, dropping him like a stone. All before he could blink.

The forest had imposed a deadly craft on her, and she had learned it well.

Seeing the damage she'd dealt in so little time would give most men pause, but failure in this matter was not permissible from their captain and they all knew it. A fourth man entered the fray, meaty hands grabbing Clara by her backpack and pushing her with the intention of slamming her into the mast.

She didn't fight him or dig her heels in; as before, she used the momentum to her advantage.

Clara just kept running, right up the vertical length of the mast before landing behind the bigger brute of a man who hesitated a moment, confused as to where she'd gone.

Clara reached to his belt and relieved him of the two knives sheathed at his sides. She swept her leg out behind her to catch a man in the jaw trying to take advantage of her turned back while slamming the brutes head into the unyielding wood.

Then she was climbing, using those blades to stab into the wood of the mast and heave herself towards the crow's nest.

Gage watched her scrambling beyond the reach of his men and narrowed his eyes. Too much woman for his crew to handle apparently. He slipped his glove on and strode over to the crew member with his sword stuck in his leg, Peter just tying the tourniquet.

"Tied off?" he asked simply. Peter pulled the bandage above the wound tightly before answering with a nod.

"Good." Gage reached down, grabbed the hilt of his sword, and pulled it out of his crewmember's leg, the man crying out in pain as he walked away.

The sea had imposed a deadly craft upon him as well. It appeared, if he wished to stop her, he would have to see who had been the better pupil.

"Mr. William," Gage snapped, walking over to a rope tied down by the railing.

William moved to his side almost immediately as Gage sheathed his still bloody sword to free his hand.

"Yes, Captain?" he asked as Gage took hold of the taunt rope tightly.

"Kindly send me up."

William's eyes widened in surprise as he looked from the rope to his captain.

Just then, there was a scream as the man on lookout duty fell through the air. He shrieked the whole long way down before crashing into a bunch of supply barrels, sending broken chunks and splinters of wood in all directions.

"Preferably before she tears my ship apart, if you please," Gage growled.

Clara stood holding onto the edge of the crow's nest, breathing hard, running hot on adrenaline after throwing the lookout who'd tried to shoot her from the nest.

She turned her attention to the sky, starting to blue in preparation of the coming sunrise, before throwing the pistol to the waters. If she wasn't off this boat before then, she wasn't getting off; she'd be too worn out to keep fighting them.

Clara opened her hand and saw the siren's pearl nestled against the hilt of the blade she'd also just relieved from the lookout. It was the only way off this boat now, unless she was planning on killing everyone on the ship and somehow sailing it back to shore on her own.

Clara was good, but she wasn't that good, and sadly she was not that ruthless. She'd have just killed Gage if she were, Clara thought as she watched a couple pirates beginning the climb after her.

You'd think they'd learn.

It was now or never. She popped the pearl into her mouth and cracked it between her teeth. The pain sunk all the way into her gums as she opened her mouth to say something along the lines of a curse.

However, some unseen force inside the pearl had seized Clara's vocal cords and was forcing them to do something that felt like screaming. It didn't sound like her voice as it came out, ringing impossibly loud through the air.

Clara felt the wood vibrating under her hands as a shrill almost mournful musical note filled the coming dawn, sounding like it was cutting into even the deepest, darkest depth of the ocean. Then it just stopped, leaving only the memory of an echo whilst Clara's throat was left feeling raw.

She swallowed the pearl and hoped Fitz was right about it summoning help, she was going to need it soon.

Clara glance below her to see how soon she was going to have company when a blue cap caught her attention on deck. She squinted as she realized it was William, accompanied by Gage who appeared to be holding onto something...

William drew his sword and cut the rope just under Gage's hand.

He was suddenly shooting towards her as a weight dropped on the other end of the rope, his coat flapping in the wind as he held on for the ride up to the crow's nest.

Clara backed out away from the crow's nest and out onto the narrowing plank that spread the ship's sail wide. He made it to the top, reaching out with his last good fingers of his bad hand to latch onto the edge of the nest, letting the rope go and steadying himself, sail dropping as he did.

"Brace yourself, love!"

Clara eyes widened as she quickly dropped to her stomach, hands gripping the rigging a heartbeat before the wind caught the open sail, rocking the ship with a suddeness that would have thrown her from the mast and to her possible death. She almost lost hold of the knives, just managing to keep her grip on them.

She forced herself back to her feet the moment she felt she could, tryingto keep her balance as she watched Gage joining her on the narrow riggings, drawing his sword.

"Neat trick," Clara spat. "You should try the circus."

"I aim to entertain all my guests," he told her, shifting one foot in front of the other to accommodate the narrow ground on which they'd be fighting. "Though I must say, you're a terribly unruly one."

"I was rambunctious as a child too," she said, readying her blades and mirroring his stance. Clara had never been in a sword fight before. Sure, she was used to fighting with knives, but that was for extremely close combat. This, she knew already, was much different.

"With apparently one hell of a pair of lungs," he added, watching her seriously. "What have you done, Clara?"

She didn't answer him, not even with a smart-ass remark. Clara readied herself and Gage's eyes narrowed, the arctic blue of his gaze noting the pair of knives she held before going back to her face.

"Good form as always—but it won't be good enough I'm afraid," he told her.

This was unfortunately very true; he had every advantage from his knowledge of sword play, the fact she only had the knives, even the place they fought was a field all his. But when had odds ever stopped her from trying?

"Let's find out." Clara lunged at him. She tried to lock his blade between hers, hoping to tear it out of his hands, but he twisted his cutlass expertly, knocking one blade from her hand with the violent motion.

He moved almost faster than she remembered when he struck out at her other hand. For a split second she thought he was going to sever the hand from her wrist. Instead he used the flat of the blade to hit her, right on the raw skin on her wrist. Her hand jerked back reflexively, causing her to drop her last weapon.

Disarmed, Clara tried to back away but was unused to the movement of the ship under her feet or the narrow grounds, her footing slipped. She instinctively reached out to grab something, anything to stop her from taking the long tumble down.

Warm leather bunched under her hand, a steady weight keeping her from falling to the deck below. Gage's blue eyes stared back at her as she gripped his forearm, leaning back a little to compensate for her weight, the point of his sword pressed over her heart. Round Three went to him in no uncertain terms.

Clara looked over her shoulder as she gasped for air, seeing at the long way she had left to fall, grip on his forearm tightening.

"Are you quite finished?" he asked steadily, making no move to pull her to a more solid footing.

Clara slid her eyes down to look at the point of his sword pressed as a warning to her chest. She cast one last look over her shoulder as her heart thudded loudly in her chest. There he was again, thinking he had her in a corner. Clara wasn't afraid to fall.

When she met his gaze again, she smiled, those eyes that defied the light as unwavering as he'd ever seen them, definitely not the reaction he'd been expecting.

He looked warily back; there was no way she was that crazy.

Time to roll the dice, Clara thought. She swore from Gage's expression he'd heard the thought.

"Clara," he said carefully. She said nothing as her grip slackened and his tightened to keep a hold of her, eyes widening when she uncurled her fingers completely.

His damaged hands hold on her was not strong enough; she was sliding from his grip.

"Clara!" he almost shouted, his alarm instead hissed through gritted teeth. She'd die! Did she not see that?

"Same cloth, remember?" she replied

Before he could answer her, he lost his hold. She slipped through his fingers and fell.

Twenty-One

Her hands flailed as she fell, trying to grab hold of anything blurring past her vision to slow her plummet to the deck below. Clara's fingers scrapped the sail, netted ropes burnt her hands when she tried to grab them; her shoulders ached painfully at each unsuccessful attempt to grab something, trying to hold on and failing.

The ropes and sail were torn from her grasp, only halting the fall for brief moments before her own weight tore her grip from the ropes. She turned one big fall into a multiple of smaller painful ones, ass over teakettle the whole way down. It was the only reason she didn't break any bones when she threw her arms out and landed face down on the deck with a solid *thud*.

Her whole body hurt, the breath left in her lungs so scant she couldn't even groan. Still alive. She'd have to find a way to celebrate later.

Clara staggered to her feet even though all she wanted to do was lie there until at least some of the pain faded away, every part of her body still thrumming with that distinct ache only a hard impact could inflict. She wiped away the stream of blood trickling from her nose—she didn't have the luxury of resting.

Stumbling to the rail of the ship, her hand grasped the solid wood just to keep herself upright while her head continued to spin from the fall. Surrounded once more, the pirates warily closing in more thickly now. Seemed the others had woken after all the commotion and come to investigate. They didn't attack immediately; most were now more cautious after facing off with her the first time.

Clara may have taken Round Four (out of pure spite really), but she wasn't sure she had much more fight to give at this point, even while she tried to square off against her new attackers.

As Clara hazily surveyed the prospects of who she thought she had the best chance against among the pirates, she felt it.

A strange pull took hold of her, as if the whole ocean was suddenly calling to her. It was so strong she actually looked away from her soon to be attackers just to see the water, almost expecting to see someone.

Guess that was her cue. She hopped up on the rail, pirates behind her and nothing but dark water in front of her.

"Don't!"

Clara looked back at the sound of a young voice to see Peter's hand outstretched, as if he could pull her back through sheer force of will from ten feet away.

"You'll drown!" he yelled, sounding panicked, his wide eyes fixed on her.

How did such a good kid end up joining with the likes of pirates? Clara wondered absently as she teetered on the edge.

"Listen to him, Fox."

She glanced up to the sound of Gage's voice, seeing him climbing down the netting of rope, sword safely in its sheath; still the nimble climber she saw. He looked properly angry now as he faced her.

"You could have been killed, you damn fool," he hissed.

"Sounds like my usual brand of gambling," Clara managed to wheeze back.

Gage's feet hit the deck, and his men parted out of his way as he approached her cautiously, his hands held up in a pacifying gesture.

"Don't be rash, love; we both know you can't swim. That's not a gamble, that's foolish." Once more, he was trying to sound reasonable and calm, coaxing even. "And you're not foolish, darling. I believe you've hit your quota of crazy stunts for one night," he said, eyes fixed steadily on her motioning for her to come back on the deck to relative safety as he continued to inch closer to her.

Clara looked down at the dark water frothing below her and back at him; she actually *really* didn't want to jump, but her entire body was screaming for her to do it now, and she didn't think she could refuse much longer.

"Oh, I don't know, I think I have one more left in me."

His eyes widened, and he lunged to grab her.

It was too late, his hand only managing to sweep through the tips of her hair as she stepped off into thin air.

She was falling again in less than five minutes. Hitting the water was a shock to her system as the cold darkness enveloped her and she started to sink. It was so damn cold for a moment she couldn't even thrash as she sank.

Finally, she kicked her feet and waved her arms, trying clumsily to propel herself back to the surface. Clara only kept sinking despite her efforts, her pack weighing her down. Her lungs were already burning with a need for air.

That's when Clara felt a scorching pain on either side of her neck, like being cut with a hot knife. She screamed but only bubbles poured out of her mouth, racing to the surface without her.

The pain was shoved from her mind when the bubbles came to an abrupt stop, and she choked on a breath she didn't have, a darkness of a different kind began to race into her from the edges of her vision. She tried not take the water in, to somehow make it to the surface for air but she couldn't, she'd sunk too far below the waves now. No time, no strength even as she clawed to make it there.

I'm going to drown.

Water rushed into lungs as her body overruled her mind in its desperate need for oxygen. And then it rushed out of her lungs. And in again. The burning need for oxygen had... gone? That sinister darkness fled her vision, confusion growing when she confirmed that, yes, she was still underwater. Clara was breathing underwater. She stopped trying to paddle to the surface from sheer surprise. *The pain...*

She touched the side of her neck and felt flaps of skin opening and closing as she drew each breath.

Gills? The pearl gave me gills?

Red-letter day if Clara had ever had one. Before she had much time to process, she was suddenly staring at a face only a few feet from hers. Clara jerked back, startled by the pale blue-skinned... face of a girl? She was only barely able to make her out with her water blurred vision, long black hair floating like a shiny curtain in the water, and if Clara was right, smiling at her.

The girl gave Clara a small wave; she hesitantly returned it somewhat awkwardly while she continued to sink. The girl looked human shaped despite the blue tint in her skin and the impression of unusually sharp teeth, right until you got to her waist, transitioning from humanoid to fish in the form of a unmistakably long and powerful, scaly tail.

Clara just stared at it; Fitz had said help would come—he hadn't told her it would be one of the merfolk.

The mermaid reached out and took a firm hold of Clara's arm to stop her from sinking any further.

"I heard your call," a musical voice murmured through her mind. *"How can I help?"*

Clara opened her mouth to speak but then remembered she was underwater. How was she supposed to tell her savior she had to get to shore?

She was surprised yet again when the mermaid nodded as if she'd heard the request out loud.

Her grip on Clara tightened, and with a powerful stroke of her tail, she began to swim them both in the direction of land.

He'd thought for sure, with that look in her eye, she was going to pull him off the edge with her and kill them both for a fraction of a second. When she simply let go and chose to fall, he'd been sure she was as good as dead.

The feel of her slipping from his grasp, watching her tumble, snagging hold of ropes and the sail before hitting the deck was possibly the worst feeling he'd had in years. A bundle of knots and terrible, freezing dread in his gut loosened when he saw her stumble back to her feet.

Then tighten again when it was clear she then planned to jump off his ship—she was mad as a fucking march hare.

Gage looked over the edge of his ship, hearing the splash of Clara hitting the water.

He waited a few seconds, eyes searching the water for her red-blond head to reemerge. When he didn't, he began to rip his coat off, intending to go after her.

"Dammit, Fox," he cursed under his breath.

"Captain, stop!" William yelled, grabbing him and pulling him roughly back from the edge.

Gage shook his first mate's grip from his shoulders and fixed William with a murderous glare. William held up his hands before pointing frantically to the water.

"Look!" he urged.

Gage followed the direction William was pointing in and saw a blue head with long, flowing black hair bobbing in the water. He'd seen only a few mermaids in his life but enough to pick one out without having to see the tail; they were not creatures to tangle with lightly. Mad men alone treaded water with mermaids. He felt a brief moment of hope, most of the merfolk took pity on lasses about to drown, or so went the tale.

The only sensation he registered after the mermaid hissed at him before diving underwater after Clara was relief. But then he wondered, what in all the hells was a mermaid—

He stopped, something nagging at the back of his mind.

The shrill supernatural cry, the necklace she'd been so distressed at having been taken from her, the convenient appearance of a mermaid. It took him a moment to pull everything together, but when he did it all made sense.

It had been a godsdamn *siren's* pearl. He'd never seen one before, but he'd heard of them, incredibly rare, only given to people who had earned a favour from the merfolk. How the bloody hell had Clara acquired a favour from *them?*

It didn't matter now; there would be no catching her. He slammed his fist against the unyielding wood of his ship in sheer frustration, causing his men to take a healthy step back from him.

This is not over, not by a bloody long shot, he thought as he stared into the waves.

Clara never thought it would feel so good to have the sand beneath her soggy boots as they finally reached the shallows and she was able to stand. As soon as her feet touched earth, she felt her gills seal close as if they'd never been there. She nearly collapsed when they did, coughing out a lungful of water, bracing her hands on her knees to stay upright.

The beautiful blue face of the mermaid was still smiling at her as she coughed and hacked for a full minute, gasping in her first breath of glorious air.

"Thank you," Clara said hoarsely at last, the taste of ocean in her mouth sending her close to retching.

The mermaid shrugged, reaching a hand up and gently placing it on Clara's stomach.

"The debt has been repaid."

There was a quick sharp pain where the mermaid touched her. When she pulled her hand back, the beautiful cracked pearl Clara had swallowed was in her hand.

A splash and a flash of scales was all Clara saw before the mermaid disappeared, swimming back into the grey waters as the sun began to rise in earnest.

Clara gazed out at the rising sun, seeing the tiny black pinpoint that was *The Grey Ghost* on the ocean. Sopping wet, standing in three feet of water, Clara made no move to go to the shore; she just stared out at the distant ship Gage sailed on.

"An interesting first try indeed," she muttered to herself.

Everything she'd learned began to move to the forefront of her mind as the heat of the fight cooled in her blood. Clara pushed it all back, not ready to deal with any of it just yet. She should get moving; after all, Clara had found a hell of a pair of enemies in the famous Captain Black-Gage and The Scarlett Queen.

Get moving? Get moving to where exactly, Clara?

For the first time in many, many years, she had no idea what she was supposed to do next.

Gage paced behind his desk, shard of looking glass clutched so tightly in his hand it threatened to cut him. The Scarlet Queen would be contacting him any moment now, intending on setting a meeting place in which they could conclude their business.

If Fox was to be believed, after he handed over the cargo part of that conclusion would be his death. Since it was cargo he no longer had, he might be headed to that same end anyways.

The question wasn't *if* Clara was lying; he'd seen she very much believed what she'd told him. However, simply because she believed it didn't necessarily make it truth. There were too many gaps on how it was possible for her to know any of it; she hadn't even known her role in holding an enchantment down in the forest she lived in. For that reason alone, he wasn't entirely sure how good the information she'd given him to "balance the scales" was.

He actually smirked bitterly at that thought, balance the scales, cross off IOUs—Clara may hate his guts but she held fast to her ideals. That she did only further served to nurture that seedling of shame in his chest. He brought his hand to his mouth, still clutching the mirror as he brushed his fingers over his lips, as if to trace the brands of anger and regret she'd seared into them with her kiss before dropping his hand. So much said without a word, an invisible scar that would never leave him. Dangerous, so much more so even than he'd first imagined. No doubt, he had made himself a superlative enemy in Clara Fox.

"Lucas."

Airalyn's voice startled him from his pensive thoughts, lifting the mirror again to find the unamused face of the Scarlet Queen, staring back at him with those unsettling pale red eyes.

"Lost in thought, are we?" she asked in her usual cool manner, a hint of suspicion underlying her tone. Conversation barely started and already a fine string of tension between them; it was like she sensed something amiss.

He had no intention of telling her he'd lost Clara, but he'd have to lull the queen into a false sense of security if his ruse was to yield fruit.

"Simply mulling over the finer details of my revenge," he told her smoothly, "since it's so close at hand."

She seemed to accept this answer easily enough, moving on to what she wished to discuss.

"How went the removal of the pretty little Guide's soul flame?" she asked, a cruel smile turning up the corners of her lips. More tests.

Now came the difficult part. Gage held his famous gloved hand up to the mirror so she could see it, schooling his face to an expression of annoyance.

"I believe you've given me a faulty spell," he drawled.

The queen's eyes took on a decidedly dark and insulted look. "I beg your pardon?"

"Nothing to be ashamed of, I'm sure," Gage said with a sympathetic shrug as if to soothe her ego. "It mustn't be easy, casting through a looking—"

"There is nothing *wrong* with my spells," she cut him off in a snarl.

Gage made it appear as if he were on the verge of rolling his eyes, he almost saw the steam shooting from her ears. "Of course not, Your Majesty. Perhaps the girl is simply immune to your charms."

She'd certainly been immune to his.

"That is impossible. You're lying—you've spared her and are lying to me now," Airalyn accused scathingly.

It was true of course; he'd inexplicably chosen to take his chances and play with fire, but he wished to convince her it wasn't.

"I'm afraid I'd have to beg to differ. I assure you I'm not the kind of man who would risk dampening the power-lock keeping my curse at bay, Your Majesty," he maintained, pretending to join her in her anger. *Only you did, didn't you?* "There must be a reason she was chosen to root the Dark Forest's enchantment as you said, it should have killed her. Perhaps she has some gifted nature," he suggested.

The queen looked angry and frustrated by this news, seeming to wrack her brain for some explanation to this new information. He watched her fume for a minute and swore he saw something like fear before she inexplicably seemed to calm.

"It's no matter," she said, almost pleasantly.

Instantly, Gage was wary.

"I've taken the liberty to secure some extra leverage, on its way now. Backup insurance if you will." Airalyn said it like she was trying to make him ask, once again wishing to show off how very clever she was. Probably more so since the "failure" of her signature spell.

"I'm not entirely certain there is leverage enough in the world to bend this woman."

The first honest words he'd spoken during this entire conversation. The Scarlet Queen smiled that ominous, falsely bright smile that belied impending unpleasantness for someone.

"I wouldn't be so sure."

Her image disappeared and was replaced with a room, a brig much like the one on his own ship. A man with a burlap sack over his head was on his knees, hands obviously tied behind his back. A boy no older than eighteen or nineteen was standing beside the man, dressed in the armor of the queen's personal guard with a sword in hand.

Gage couldn't help but find the boy's messy brown hair a little strange since most royal guard were kept impeccable, his slate coloured eyes looking hard and stubborn even for his age.

"Eric, be a good boy and remove the hood would you?" the queen's disembodied voice asked pleasantly.

For some reason, Gage felt his heart skip a beat. *Eric?*

He almost shook his head as he dismissed the thought immediately. There were a thousand lads out there with the name Eric; besides, she'd said her son was dead. The boy did as he was ordered and pulled the burlap sack off his captive's head to reveal his identity.

Quite suddenly, Gage was looking into the face of Clara's contact and only friend, Fitz. He'd been gagged, eyes glazed over in a way that suggested he was drugged as they tried to adjust to the light, the Scarlet Queen narrating the scene for him.

"I had him collected the day after you and the Guide went into the forest," she told him.

Fitz had turned his head and was looking at the boy called Eric. Gage couldn't help but notice how his face paled, recognition flaring in those hazy eyes, as if he was looking at a ghost. He was trying to speak to the boy, but his words were rendered into muffled gibberish by the gag.

The boy glanced at him curiously but looked away with no signs of the same recognition. *Was it possible...?*

"With your help, he was far easier to find than the elusive Guide, I must say, but then again being the contact I suppose that was the point."

The image disappeared, and he was once again looking at the all-too-pleased, smiling face of the queen.

"I trust this will be all the leverage I'll ever need over her," she assured him smugly.

He forced a smile and nodded his head as if to commend her.

"Hats off to you, Your Majesty." She preened at his praise, like she was above it but enjoying it nonetheless.

"Just one question," he began while she still basked in the glow of her own narcissistic love.

"What would that be?" she asked with no real interest.

"How is it you plan to keep the Mage under your thumb when you've given me the weapon that has kept him so pliable to your whims?"

Airalyn's entire body froze, face showing open shock at the unexpected knowledge and a touch of fear at being found out. That split second of honest surprise was her undoing, not a hint of confusion. It was how her face closed down after that honest surprise that revealed exactly how she had intended to deal with that problem. Clara had told him the truth; she'd never planned to give him the weapon.

"You backstabbing sow," Gage growled, suddenly overcome with rage at the unearthing of her deception.

Her face twisted into an ugly snarl.

"Shame to kill such a pretty toy so soon."

Airalyn pulled her hand back as a roiling ball of flame was conjured into her palm.

Gage's eyes widened. His gloved hand flashed to the glass of his window, the pane melting away to ash and threw the mirror through, just as a jet of flame that would have burnt him to a crisp spewed from the mirror's glassy surface.

He heard it hit the water, still jettisoning fire that boiled the water as it sank. Gage kicked the chair at his desk cross the room and roared in anger.

The Scarlet Queen liked fire, did she? See how she liked it when he burnt her empire to the ground and danced through the ashes of what she treasured. That was her coming fate, for being in league with Ryker Vidaris and trying to use him as a disposable puppet, tempting him with his own revenge.

He would be a wanted man in both kingdoms now—his once ally now turned powerful enemy still holding the one thing he needed most for his revenge. As much as he hated admitting it, he needed help now.

I want you to know that I could have helped you...

And he needed it from someone who now considered him a foe for his betrayal, one who had threatened to kill him if she ever saw his face again. But the queen had given him an unintentional gift by flaunting her moves so carelessly, possibly exposing far more than that of just her schemes. A plan was already taking shape in his mind.

If he was to get Clara back on his side, he would need what the Scarlet Queen was so very fond of—leverage. He preferred peace offerings of course but he had to be practical if he wished to succeed. He might have to make himself her only option if there was any chance of "making nice," as it were.

William burst through his cabin door without knocking, still on high alert.

"Captain, are you all right?" he asked, eyes sweeping for the reason behind the commotion that had drawn him.

Gage ignored his question, already giving his new orders.

"Mr. William, turn this ship around."

47709568R00146

Made in the USA
Lexington, KY
12 December 2015